The Last Days of Fairhaven

The Last Days of Fairhaven

Doug Bedwell

Space Bear Press
Cloverdale, Indiana

And *please*, no spoilers!

For information, please contact:
Space Bear Press
P.O. Box 182
Cloverdale, IN   46120

On the web at: spacebearpress.com
Our online store: https://space-bear-press.square.site/
On Facebook at: Facebook.com/spacebearpress

Bedwell, Doug
      [Dystopian; Science Fiction; Adventure]
      The Last Days of Fairhaven
      First Edition: August 1, 2022
      ISBN-13: 978-1-943219-16-2 (Paperback)
      ISBN-13: 978-1-943219-17-9 (Hardcover)
      ISBN-13: 978-1-943219-18-6 (Ebook)

Original Cover Artwork © Amy Nagi – www.amynagi.com
Cover and Interior Layout and Design by Doug Bedwell

"Look at that, you son of a bitch."

– Edgar Mitchell

The Genesis of Fairhaven

Sometime near the end of the 21st century – it's hard to say precisely when, because unlike other centuries, the 21st did not end according to schedule – world civilization was hovering at the brink of total collapse.

A coalition of scientists and engineers unveiled a proposal for a massive construction project, designed to save the human species from extinction.

The project – romantically dubbed *Fairhaven* – called for the construction of an enormous suburban complex, fully isolated from the Earth's critically damaged ecosphere by an impenetrable dome.

In its completed form, the city became a sort of time capsule, meant to preserve the human species at the very height of its evolutionary success, until the rest of the planet became safely habitable once more.

That was the plan, and it worked out well at first.

But that was a very long time ago.

Book One:
Chapter 1:
Sunrise

"Sunrise, Fairhaven."

Gloria spoke, and the world began to fill, ever so slowly, with light. Her voice was quiet and gentle, and yet it could be heard everywhere – along every deserted footpath and avenue, inside every empty house, and in every dustless corner of every long-abandoned room.

That flawless voice could be heard in the shadowed depths of the forbidden Central Forest, and all across the gently rolling lawns of the city's Middle Ring. It could be heard among the blooming trees and the flowers of the endless Circle Park, and up and down along the full expanse of the Great Promenade.

It could even be heard beyond the river, inside the ragged enclaves that stood along The Periphery – that barren stretch of empty pavement which lay between the water and the wall. The voice was everywhere, and everywhere it was precisely the same, and exactly as it had always been.

Here and there throughout the Middle Ring, and indeed everywhere inside the encircling arc of the river, worker bees – the small, semi-autonomous robots that maintained the great city – continued with their various tasks. The coming dawn was, for them, a matter of little concern, and the sound of the voice was hardly noticed. They had their chores to attend to, and there was always more to be done – trimming the grass and pruning the trees, making their deliveries, and tirelessly cleaning the empty rooms of the immaculate houses where people no longer lived.

Though the start of each new day was announced as *sunrise*, there was in fact no sun in the sky, just as at night there had been no moon. Inside the great enclosed dome, there was only the gently rising daylight, which filtered softly across the rolling landscape, far beneath the pristine blue of the city's vast and artificial sky.

The animated clouds which would sometimes appear, drifting slowly overhead, were never a cause for concern. In Fairhaven, it did not rain. When night returned, those clouds would vanish, and the paneled sky would once again be filled with the familiar scattering of tiny white dots... a flickering illusion of stars.

It was a beautiful sky, and a beautiful place, and in almost every way an almost perfect imitation of an almost perfect world.

Chapter 2:
The Battery Run

The ferry raft bumped lightly against the high concrete curb that ran along the inner bank of the river, and one by one the harvesters climbed over the side railing and onto the damp, spongy grass of the Circle Park. Once the passengers had fully debarked, the boatman pushed away from the curb again with his oar, and quietly began to row the empty raft back across the slow-moving water, toward the enclave known as River Towne. There, all along that outer bank of the river, many more harvesters were already gathered, each of them awaiting their turn to make the morning crossing.

With her feet once again on solid ground, Barbara stretched her legs and adjusted her empty backpack, waiting patiently while the young girl following her sat down on the smooth stone surface of the path to secure an errant shoelace. The other harvesters set out immediately, some of them turning to their right to venture riverwise along the Promenade, others heading counter-river; all of them on their way to search the houses further in from the water, and further around the city's Middle Ring. Under ordinary circumstances, Barbara would have done much the same, but today she had a different task to attend to.

At nineteen years of age, Barbara had been the oldest passenger aboard the raft (aside from the boatman), and her companion – who was only ten – had been the youngest. The younger girl's name was Alison, and she was still very much a novice in training. This was, in fact, her first official excursion as a harvester, and Barbara – assigned as her mentor for the day – would be shepherding her on a *battery run*. It was a simple task, but it made for a useful training exercise. Depleted batteries had been left at a nearby house to charge overnight, and this morning Alison was being sent to collect them again, under Barbara's watchful supervision.

"All set?" Barbara asked.

"Uh-huh," Alison said, bouncing to her feet again. "Sorry!"

"That's OK," the older girl replied. She was in no hurry. They didn't have far to go, and Barbara was glad to see that her young charge was paying attention to important details like shoelaces. Even on a battery run, they could not afford to be careless. "We don't want any accidents," she added. "You never know when we might have to start running."

"Are there gonna be fells?" Alison asked. Her voice was shaking a little, somewhere between excitement and fear.

"Probably not," Barbara admitted. "The Training Grounds are usually pretty safe, but you never can tell. We'll have to keep a careful lookout."

"I'm a good lookout," Alison declared bravely. "I've been on this side of the river lots of times, but just in the park. They'd bring us over here sometimes for lessons."

With Alison's shoes now securely tied, the two girls set off together, following one of the many footpaths that gently wound its way among the neatly manicured lawns further in. They chatted quietly as they walked, always keeping an eye to the landscape for any sign of movement, or anything out of the ordinary. Alison had questions about almost everything she saw – a rosebush; a garden sprinkler; a worker bee that was planting flowers – and Barbara was generally willing to indulge her curiosity. However, she also tried to keep her young pupil's attention on the specific task at hand. After they'd been walking for several minutes, Barbara stopped and gestured back along the trail.

"Look back the way we came," she said. "We can't see the river any more; do you remember how we got here?"

"Uh-huh," Alison replied, pointing toward some of the landmarks behind them. "There were all those big trees, and the house with the yellow flowers. The path splits and goes three different ways, but the trail *we're* on went by a blue house. Then right past that, there's a little hill where you can see the river if you stretch up real tall and look."

"That's very good," said Barbara, genuinely surprised. "You remembered a lot."

"I have a great sense of direction," Alison replied proudly. "I'm the best at maze tag; I can catch anybody! Well, almost anybody... But nobody ever catches *me*."

"Never?" Barbara asked, skeptically. "Are you sure?... not even once?"

"Nuh-uh," Alison said, scrunching her face into the sort of fiercely serious scowl that only a determined 10-year-old can make. "That's 'cause I'm sneaky... And I'm super-fast."

"Well, that's pretty impressive," Barbara replied, playfully tussling her young companion's hair. "And I bet you'll even be faster when your legs get a little longer."

Alison giggled, and swatted her mentor's hand away. Barbara turned and continued down the path, but her pupil still had more questions.

"Can *you* run fast?" she asked, catching up with the older girl and walking beside her.

"I can," Barbara replied. "And I was good at maze tag too, when I was your age. I bet you'll be a good harvester."

"Uh-huh," said Alison, as if the compliment was to be expected. "And when I get old enough, I'm gonna be on the Privy Council."

"Maybe you will," the older girl replied, though the smile on her face was bittersweet.

Not so very long ago, Barbara had been a starry-eyed novice herself; but now things were quite different. She was getting older, and though she still clung to the faint hope that she might one day be selected to continue, she knew that the chances of that were terribly slim. There were only so many spots on the Lesser Council to be had, and harvesters younger than her had already been promoted, while she was left behind. Of those that could not earn a place, few would ever see their 20th birthday. Barbara knew these things all too well, and already so many of the friends she had grown up with had never come home.

But it was easy not to dwell on such things on a brightly lit morning, with a job to be done and a cheerful novice beside her for company. Barbara set her darker thoughts aside, as the two girls continued along the winding path.

Alison was amazed at the size of the houses. Some were near to the trail, while others lay further off, but every time she spotted another one she would point to it, and express her astonishment. It was almost inconceivable to her that people had once lived in such places. She wondered aloud what their lives must have been like.

The young pair had been walking for some time, when at last they reached a little grove of birch trees, where several large grey boulders lay scattered across a circular patch of lawn. It was a decorative landscaping feature and a distinctive landmark, one that was difficult to miss. Barbara stopped there and slipped cautiously off the path to one side.

"We're getting close now," she said quietly. "We can go this way, across the yards from here."

"OK..." said Alison. "We aren't gonna take the road?"

"*Avoid patterns*, remember?" Barbara said. "We don't want to take the road every time. Aaaand..." she added, with a hint of a smile, "it's more fun this way... come on."

Alison bounced off the trail after her mentor, and the two of them cut across the gently rolling terrain, past a tidy little patch of brightly-colored tulips, and then on through a stand of flowering ornamental trees. Beyond that, they came to a wide stretch of lawn, which ended at a dense and neatly-trimmed hedge of leafy green bushes.

"There it is," Barbara said, pointing over the top of the hedge toward the large two-story house that stood in the next lot. "There's a gate over this way, down at the far end."

Barbara knew this little section of the Middle Ring very well, and had visited this particular house many times before. In fact, at one time or another she'd been inside almost all of the buildings that could be found in the Training Grounds.

"We can go under!" Alison suggested, dropping to her hands and knees and peeking through a narrow gap in the bottom part of the hedge.

"You can go under, if you want to," Barbara replied, indulging the younger girl's enthusiasm, "but I'm too big for that."

It wasn't entirely true. Barbara could certainly have crawled under the hedge if she'd wanted, but she didn't feel inclined to start her morning off by getting needlessly scratched up and dirty.

Delighted as if she'd just been given permission to raid the enclave's candy vault, Alison squeezed herself through a narrow gap in the lower branches, scrambled to her feet again on the other side, then raced along the hedge to meet Barbara as she came through the swinging wooden gate.

"I win!" Alison squealed.

"Shh..." Barbara cautioned her, sternly. "No shouting; remember where we are."

Alison was instantly chastened.

"... sorry..." she mumbled, remorsefully.

Barbara bent down, and helped the younger girl dust herself off. Then she smiled, and gave her companion a quick and reassuring hug.

They slipped quietly into the house through the back door. It wasn't locked. None of the houses of the Middle Ring were ever locked, as no locks had ever been installed. The people who had once lived here had not worried about burglaries, or any other sort of crime. Aside from history lessons, crime was almost unknown in Fairhaven. From its inception, it had always been – or rather, had been intended to be – a secure and peaceful place.

It took well over an hour for the two girls to thoroughly search the house. Not all of the batteries were easy to find, as the harvesters from the day before had deliberately hidden some of them in out-of-the-way places, to add an extra measure of challenge for whoever might be assigned to collect them again in the morning. Barbara could have finished the job in much less time, had she been by herself; but the whole point of the exercise was to help her companion develop the harvesting skills she would need as she got older. And so while Alison carefully searched the house's spotless interior, Barbara dawdled, closely watching her progress and offering occasional bits of advice.

8

Once all of the batteries had been found and safely tucked away into one or the other of their backpacks, the two girls took some time to attend to other necessary matters. The bathrooms of the Middle Ring were much, much nicer than the old latrines back at River Towne, so Barbara gave Alison a quick tutorial. They used the toilet, washed their hands and their faces in the sink, and then spent a few minutes making funny faces at each other, in the mirror above the vanity.

After that, they went back downstairs to have a look in the icebox and the kitchen cupboards. They were hoping that there might be some food packets hidden away somewhere, but they found nothing other than empty shelves. They were disappointed, though not at all surprised, since the harvesters who had brought the batteries would almost certainly have searched those cabinets just the afternoon before.

Lastly before leaving the house, they filled their water bottles at the kitchen faucet. River water was safe enough to drink, but the water that came from the taps in the houses was always nicer. Frequent access to the functional plumbing of the Middle Ring was one of the few special perks that harvesters were able to enjoy.

With their business inside the house concluded, the two girls slipped quietly out through the front door, and set off across the open expanse of lawn, back toward the footpath. Barbara was feeling almost cheerful. There was never any telling what to expect from a novice, especially on her first assignment; but Alison was a quick learner, and attentive, and even seemed to be enjoying herself. Barbara could not have asked for a better student.

They were halfway back to the path, when Alison grabbed her mentor by the arm.

"What is that?..." she whispered.

Barbara turned to look, and gasped. Off to their left – not more than ten meters from where they were standing, and partially hidden amidst a small cluster of flowering bushes – was a large, darkly metallic object. It was egg-shaped, nearly a full meter tall and perhaps half again that long, sleek, and almost perfectly smooth.

Barbara knew instantly what it was, and for that matter so did Alison, even though she had never seen one before.

"Oh, Gloria..." Barbara muttered. *"It's a fell."*

They both stood motionless, not even daring to breathe. Unlike Alison, Barbara *had* seen fells, many times over the years. But she had never been so close to one as this. In the bright daylight its metallic carapace glistened softly like satin, and a fine tracery of seams could be clearly seen, where the otherwise featureless shell would crack apart if the mechanical monster awoke. Barbara found herself absolutely captivated by the sight of it. She had never realized before what an elegant and beautiful thing it was: perfect, and placid, at rest.

"Is it gonna kill us?"

Alison's whispered question brought the older girl back to her senses.

"It's asleep," she whispered in reply.

Barbara slipped off one of the straps of her backpack, to carry it free on one shoulder, and signaled to Alison that she should do the same. Looking down at the younger girl, she pointed cautiously, out toward the footpath.

"Very quietly..." She mouthed the words without a sound, and the two girls crept the rest of the way across the lawn, as quickly and silently as they could.

A sleeping fell was not immediately dangerous, not unless it woke up, and there was no telling when that might happen. Fells had been known to sleep for days at a time, seemingly oblivious to everything around them, only to wake up suddenly, for no apparent reason. In that regard, they were notoriously unpredictable.

This particular fell appeared to be fully dormant; its inert form did not reveal any outward sign of activity or awareness. All that Barbara and Alison could do was to try and put some distance between it and themselves, and hope that their luck would hold.

But it would not.

They had almost reached the path, when they heard behind them a strange and quiet sound, like a puff of air blowing out a candle.

Barbara looked back, and her worst fears were realized. The cocoon was slowly cracking open. The fell was waking up.

"Run!" she said sharply, pushing Alison forward along the path. "Drop your pack! Straight to the river! Don't stop! Don't look back!"

Alison instantly dropped her pack and ran, as fast as she could, along the path. Barbara shrugged off her own pack and let it fall to the side, looking back toward the fell with horrified fascination.

The dark metallic shell split neatly apart, and the mechanical predator inside slowly unfolded itself until it was standing, crouched low to the ground on its four metal legs. Its movements were smoothly elegant, but incremental, coming in short, precise adjustments. Even at this distance, Barbara could hear the low hum of electric servos, and the occasional hiss of air from tiny hydraulic pistons, expanding and releasing.

The creature's head swiveled briefly from side to side, scanning the terrain, trying to pick out any human forms from amid the visual clutter of the trees and the houses and the rest of the rolling landscape. Then suddenly that metallic head snapped into a fixed position, as its twin camera eyes, glowing with a faintly amber light, locked in on its prey.

Barbara turned and ran, and the monster raced after her in pursuit.

Fells could run faster than a human over clear and level terrain, but not much faster, and they were slower over broken ground. They could also become confused in complex environments, like the interior of a building, or a grove of trees. But unlike a human, a fell would never get tired. It could run forever, or at least until its batteries wore down.

Barbara knew that her best hope was to lose the thing quickly, by going through one of the houses, or climbing over fences and dodging in among the trees. But if she did manage to lose it, what then?

Fells always hunted the oldest; that meant that *she* was the one the monster was after. But if she lost it, if it could not find her, would it go after Alison instead? Alison was so young... but then, if the thing had no other targets...

All of these thoughts and more flashed through Barbara's mind, though they came to her as images, too quick and too fleeting for words.

The fell was still some distance behind her, but it was slowly gaining ground. Having had a significant head start, Alison was out ahead on the path, but already Barbara had nearly caught up to her. She was faster, much faster than the younger girl, and in a few seconds more she would be beyond her.

Barbara's heart and her lungs were pounding, as if she could feel the unfairness of everything collapsing in on her.

Why am I running?

The thought had just popped into her head... *Why am I running?* It was a question for which she had no answer.

And then suddenly she was done. She stopped, and turned around.

The fell was there, only a few meters behind her. It pulled up short, and hesitated for a moment, gazing at the young woman who was no longer trying to escape, but rather simply standing there on the path ahead. The circuitry of its electronic brain – puzzled perhaps by this unanticipated turn of events – paused, as it worked its way through a short series of contingent recalculations.

Then it sprang forward.

Barbara did not flinch, nor try to flee. She was done with fleeing, and all the rest of it. All of her choices had been made.

Half a moment later the fell was upon her, and it tore her to pieces.

Chapter 3
River Towne

To all appearances, the enclave known as *River Towne* was nothing more than a precarious assemblage of tents and shanties, each of them thrown together out of whatever materials could be safely transported across the river. But despite this makeshift appearance, River Towne was a permanent settlement. It had first been established long ago during the time of the exodus, and it had remained there, nearly unchanged, ever since.

River Towne stood on *The Periphery* – the narrow stretch of empty concrete that lay beyond Fairhaven's encircling river, in between the water and the wall. The flat, continuous expanse of the Periphery was interrupted only by the massive pumping stations, which filtered, processed, and propelled the slowly moving river on its endless circular course. There were five pumping stations in all, positioned at regular intervals, and it was in the desolate, unused gaps between those stations that the five enclaves had long ago been hastily assembled.

Fairhaven's original designers had never intended, nor even imagined that people might one day try to live in those inhospitable spaces beyond the river. There were no amenities there, no proper buildings or electrical outlets, nor even running water, aside from the river itself. There were no trees, nor grass, nor gardens. The only plants to be found were a few potted flowers, which had been scavenged, like everything else, from the abandoned houses of the Middle Ring. The worker bees never came to River Towne, because there was nothing there – or should have been nothing there – for them to do.

With a smile on her face, and a heavy backpack on her shoulder, Kady stepped lightly off of the ferry raft and back onto the familiar concrete surface of home. It was only a few minutes past noon, but even though there were still many hours before sunset, she was already returning from her harvesting run. She was in high spirits, feeling energized and self-confident.

Never return early unless you've found something. That was one of the Glorious Laws which every harvester was expected to follow, and in that regard, Kady was no exception. But it was also understood that if you *did* find something – that is, anything worth finding – you grabbed as much of it as you could carry, and hurried home as quickly as possible. There was no point in continuing to search, not once the backpack was full.

Kady's pack was very full indeed. In the first house she'd searched that morning, she'd been lucky enough to come upon a large stash of clothing, freshly delivered by the bees. Clothing for adults wasn't valuable; it was plentiful, and could be found almost anywhere. But children's clothing was another matter. Kids were notoriously hard on their outfits, and any apparel in smaller sizes was almost always in short supply.

The one piece of new adult clothing Kady *had* brought back with her was the heavy cotton t-shirt she was now wearing. It was a bright undersea blue, and for no particular reason she'd fallen in love with it that first moment she saw it. It was a little too big for her, but it was sturdy and comfortable, and just pulling it on had made her happy. She'd worn the shirt back to save space in her pack for more valuable items, but she would still have to report it, of course.

Harvesters were not, as a rule, allowed to keep the items that they found. Perhaps the most rigidly enforced of all the Glorious Laws was *Everything first belongs to the enclave.* Whatever a harvester might discover had to be deposited into the Warehouse, where an underkeeper would catalogue it, then award the harvester with a portion of the item's value in food credits. *Good work is fairly compensated* was yet another law of harvesting.

Kady bounced eagerly into the main tent of the Warehouse Exchange, and since there was no one else returning to the enclave at this early hour, she was able to step directly to one of the counting stations, without even having to wait in line. Seated on the opposite side of the table was a tall young man, who was absently fiddling with an electronic registry device.

"Well well..." he said, looking up as Kady approached, "someone's back early... Full backpack? Anything good?"

The underkeeper's name was Peter, and he'd only recently been elevated to the Lesser Council. This put him at the very bottom of the enclave's adult pecking order, but by the same token he now outranked Kady and all of the other harvesters, even though they had been his peers only a few months before. He was almost two years older than Kady, so she didn't know him all that well. But she did know him well enough to remember that she didn't particularly like him. She unslung her pack, and dropped it on the table.

"What's the going rate for clothes?" she asked.

Peter scowled. "Unless we're talking about shoes, not very good. We've got more of that sort of thing lying around than we know what to do with."

"I mean for kids," Kady said, unzipping her backpack to reveal a large, not-so-neatly folded pile of socks, shirts, and underwear.

"Ah..." said the underkeeper, who was now slightly more interested. "That's a different matter."

"I want to keep this one, though" Kady added, hastily straightening the t-shirt she was already wearing. "Adult t-shirt, blue, extra large. But everything in the pack is children's stuff, so if you can just take this one out of my total? Thanks."

"I see," the young man replied, eye-balling the shirt with a frown. "Give me a few minutes to tally this up."

Kady bit her lip, and waited nervously as the underkeeper added each new item to the database. He'd seemed unhappy about her shirt, but she couldn't imagine why. It wasn't like she was trying to sneak it past him. She knew she'd have to pay a repurchase fee to keep it, but that shouldn't amount to anything. The clothes she was checking in were so much more valuable than the shirt, she was almost hoping that he'd let the matter slide as a sort of informal bonus.

Kady was never one to break the rules, even though she knew full well that some of the other harvesters would sneak things past the underkeepers on a fairly regular basis. The unfairness of that bothered her sometimes, but she was confident that when the time came, her honesty and hard work would be fairly rewarded.

"Two point one eight," Peter said eventually, looking up from his tablet.

"That's all?" Kady asked. She was crestfallen. She'd been expecting at least four, and was more than half-hoping for closer to five or even six.

"I don't set the rates," he replied. "Food stocks are down, so all the prices have changed. But I also had to dock you two credits for sneaking the shirt," he added, pointing a finger for emphasis, "don't think I didn't notice."

Kady was almost in shock. "I didn't sneak it!" she blurted out, defensively. "I showed it to you. I only wore it back to save space in my pack, and my old one was falling apart."

"*Everything first belongs to the enclave*," he reminded her. "You'd already put the shirt on. You didn't check it in first. That's a violation. Now, if you don't really want the shirt any longer, you can always take it off and leave it here, but I'll still have to fine you for trying to sneak it by me in the first place."

The young man looked up at Kady with a smug expression on his face, openly daring her to strip the shirt off in front of him, then walk all the way back to her clade half-naked.

"I'll keep it," she said, bitterly. "I left my old one there."

"Well, that's your decision, but I wouldn't worry about it too much," he replied, looking back down at his electronic registry. "The day's still not over yet, and if you're inclined to pick up a little extra, there's a special job that needs seen to. You could earn back the fine and then some. It shouldn't take you long."

"What sort of job?" Kady asked. She was more than suspicious about what this obnoxious young man might have in mind.

"One of the mentors didn't make it back this morning," he said. "Took a novice on a battery run and they stumbled onto a fell. Bad luck, though the younger girl got away, or so I gather. But the mentor... well, you can probably guess how that turned out. I don't have all the details."

"Who was it?" Kady asked.

"I can never remember names," the underkeeper replied. He looked up from his electronic registry and shouted to a visibly-pregnant woman who was standing on the opposite side of the large open tent.

"Margaret?... Sorry to bother you, but who was that harvester?... The girl the fell got this morning, what was her name?"

"Barbara," the woman answered him, without apparent interest.

"That's right," Peter muttered to himself, before looking up at Kady again. "Barbara. Older girl... older than you, I think; not much of an achiever, evidently enough. Someone you knew?"

"Not well," said Kady, who wasn't sure if she felt sad or relieved. She *had* known Barbara, at least by sight, though she'd hardly ever spoken with her that she could recall. Still, it bothered her to know that a harvester wasn't coming back, even if they hadn't been one of her closer friends. She tried to set such thoughts aside.

"So what did you want me to do?" she asked.

"Ah, yes..." the underkeeper replied. "Well, the batteries they were supposed to fetch are still out there. The mentor got herself killed, of course, and the novice apparently dropped her pack while she was running. So you'll probably need someone to help, otherwise you'd have to carry both the packs yourself, and batteries are heavy. But I can give you five credits, assuming you bring them all back. You'd get two and a half credits each that way. That's not a bad return for an easy afternoon's bonus – that is, if you can find someone else who's willing, and if you're so inclined."

He looked up again with a transparently insincere smile, as he unconsciously scratched at his cheek with a fingernail. Kady couldn't help noticing that he was not really looking her in the eye. His gaze was lower, and his mind was clearly elsewhere.

"All right," she replied, crossing her arms defiantly, "where do we have to go?"

Chapter 4:
Raft and Retrieval

Kady had not intended to make a second crossing into the Middle Ring today, and yet, here she was, sitting on a perch aboard the ferry raft, and lightly clutching the side rail for balance. Seated across from her was her friend Eloise, who had agreed to help retrieve the abandoned batteries. For her part, Eloise had not intended to make a harvesting run at all today. She had plenty of warehouse credit saved up on account, and could afford to take a day off now and then. But Kady needed her help, and Eloise was available, and more than willing.

Though the two girls had much to talk about, they sat in silence and waited patiently as the boatman rowed them back across the river. There would be ample time for a more private conversation once they were safely ashore.

The ferry raft was a long, narrow contraption, more akin to a punt or a canoe than a rectangular barge. It had been cobbled together many years before, from empty plastic bottles, and water jugs, and random sections of hardfoam paneling, all mounted onto a rigid framework of polymer tubing. The raft often required new floats or other minor repairs, but as it had been constructed almost entirely from materials which did not readily degrade, it had otherwise persisted from generation to generation, largely unchanged.

Unimpressive as the raft might be, it could easily traverse the river, though it hardly provided a stable platform. It would toss and bob unsteadily atop the surface of the slowly moving water, and could sometimes send even an experienced passenger tumbling into the river if they were insufficiently cautious, particularly while boarding or debarking.

This instability was actually a deliberate feature of the raft's design, and not – as it might have appeared at first blush – a flaw. The reason for this, curiously enough, was *safety*. Every harvester was taught to swim from an early age, and if one or another of them clumsily spilled into the river now and again, no serious harm was likely to come of it.

18

The river's current – aside from the whitewater rapids near the pumping stations – was fairly gentle, and it was easy enough for a competent swimmer to tread water while waiting for a safety rope to be thrown their way. The net result of someone going overboard would typically be nothing worse than a damp reminder of the ever-present need for caution.

But while the harvesters could swim, the fells on the other hand could not. Or rather, they could not so far as anyone knew. Though they might prowl everywhere else in the city, in all the years since the exodus the fells had never once crossed over the water to reach River Towne, and the deliberately slapdash construction of the raft was partly intended to ensure that they never could. If a fell ever did try to leap aboard – none ever *had*, but the fear of that possibility remained – the raft's makeshift structure would break apart into pieces and send the monster tumbling into the river, shorting out its electronic brain in the process, and effectively destroying it.

That was the hope, or at least the general idea.

Flimsy as its construction might have been, the raft could safely transport six to eight passengers at a time (provided they were light of stature), plus the solitary oarsman who – being an adult and a member of the Lesser Council – would never willingly set foot onto the soft grass of the Middle Ring. As soon as his human cargo had debarked (or boarded), he would return the raft to the opposite side, endlessly rowing back and forth, every day from sunrise to dusk.

After safely stepping ashore, the two girls headed in across the Circle Park. Once they were confident that the oarsman was well out of earshot, they resumed the conversation they had begun back at the clade.

"I still can't believe he fined me for it," Kady grumbled.

"You'll never get away with a shirt," Eloise remarked.

"I wasn't trying to get away with anything! I told him up front that I wanted to pay for it. I swapped it for my old one so I could carry more stuff back. If I'd kept it in my pack with the other clothes, I would have had to leave something else behind. He still wouldn't have given me zero point zero one for it, but he docked me two full credits anyway."

"He fined you because he *could*. He didn't need a better reason than that. The shirt was just a convenient excuse; it gave him an opening. Underkeepers get full of themselves, and then they take it out on us. You getting upset over it probably just made him enjoy it more."

"It isn't fair. Bridget gets away with way worse than that all the time."

"Bridget is Bridget. Was that the first time you've ever been fined for something? It probably was, wasn't it?"

"No..." said Kady, but her denial wasn't very convincing, and her companion obviously wasn't convinced.

"I'm always careful about clothes," Eloise said with a shrug. "They're not that important, and it's just not worth it doing anything else. Sneak *food*, if you're sneaking anything... they can't get you for that."

"Yes they *can*."

"Not if you eat it here," Eloise said. "Seriously, don't be in such a hurry to get home, especially if you've found more than you can carry. Every house has a kitchen, and anything you eat on this side of the river is a free meal. Just leave the empties behind for the bees to collect, and who's going to know? I do it all the time."

Kady was shocked.

"You don't do that... Not really, do you? You'll never make the Lesser Council if they ever found out about it."

"As if I'm ever going to make the Council anyway."

Kady frowned, but decided not to push the matter further. She stopped walking and took a critical look at the surrounding landscape.

"We should get off the path," she suggested. "Maybe come at the house from the other side? That fell might still be around there somewhere."

"It probably went back to sleep, if it is," Eloise replied, "but you can never tell. It seems like the fells have been everywhere lately. I'm more worried about whether we can find the backpacks, or if they'll even still be there."

"The novice dropped hers on the path, or at least that's what the underkeepers told me. If it's just lying there, then the bees probably wouldn't bother with it, not unless it got left there overnight. I don't know what happened to Barbara's though. It could be anywhere."

"If she was still wearing it when the fell caught her, we might never find it."

"I don't think we'd want to," Kady noted grimly.

The two girls turned off the path to the counter-river side, and cut across the lawns and the other open terrain between the distantly-spaced houses. They'd been walking for several minutes when they came upon a shallow stream. The false stone creekbed was covered with smoothly rounded gravel, and the clear, ice-cold water was flowing away from the Circle Park, and inward in the general direction of the Central Forest.

Eloise was startled, and looked at the little stream with surprise. "I didn't know *this* was here," she said.

"Don't you ever come this way?" Kady asked. "It's always been like this. There's another one almost like it, riverwise from here, maybe a kilometer or two off."

"I know *that* one; that's what I thought this was at first, but then I realized we were going the opposite way."

"It's always been here; I'm surprised you don't remember it."

"I don't spend much time in the Training Grounds anymore," Eloise said with a shrug. "I almost never get assigned as a mentor. I don't think the Privy Council wants me anywhere near the novices; not if they can help it."

"That doesn't make any sense to me," Kady replied. "I think a novice could learn a lot more from you than they probably would from me."

"I don't doubt that's what has the Council worried." Eloise added.

Kady crouched down beside the little stream and dipped her fingers into the water.

"Why do you say you won't make the Council?" Kady asked. "You're the best harvester I know; I'd think you'd be at the top of the list. How many credits do you have in reserve now? One hundred? Two hundred?"

"Something like that," Eloise replied, easing herself down onto the grass. "I haven't checked."

"I've had such a string of bad luck, I've almost run my account dry," Kady continued. "I thought this morning I was finally breaking out of it, but then he fines me over a bogus violation and a crummy t-shirt. It's my own stupid fault."

"It's a great color," Eloise said, "but it's really too big for you."

"I like it like this," Kady replied, tugging at the loose, baggy shirt demonstratively. "And anyway it'll draw up a little, after it's been washed a few times."

The two girls dallied there beside the creek for several minutes more, dipping their hands into the cold water, and sometimes playfully splashing each other with it. Then they turned inward again toward the Central Forest, and followed the stream until it came abruptly to an end. The water flowed over a series of low stone terraces in a gentle cascade, before emptying into a broad shallow pool, then draining through a hefty metal grate and vanishing again beneath the ground.

"All good things..." Eloise said with a sigh. "But now I'm half lost. Which way from here?"

"Across and then back," Kady said. We're already past the house we want, but we'll come at it from the opposite side. The footpath is right over here."

Sure enough, the path was exactly where Kady had said it would be, and as the two girls turned back along it the house they were looking for soon came into view.

The pair fell silent again, carefully scanning the landscape as they walked. There was no telling if the fell might still be somewhere nearby, and this was neither the time nor the place to be careless.

Eloise suddenly held out an arm to stop her friend, and pointed to a spot up ahead. There, just off to the side of the paved trail, was one of the backpacks, lying in the grass. Kady nodded, silently confirming that she had seen it too. They moved toward it together, still keeping a careful watch to either side, more than half-expecting that at any moment the fell might leap out at them from hiding.

But that did not happen. The fell had apparently gone elsewhere, and all around them was nothing other than the trees and the flowers and the perfectly manicured lawns. They reached the discarded backpack without incident, and soon spotted the second one only a few meters further up the path. Neither of the packs had been damaged, and the hydrogen batteries inside were still intact and apparently unharmed.

"This pack must have been Barbara's," Kady muttered quietly, indicating the larger of the two.

"They probably dropped them as soon as they saw the fell," Eloise guessed. "I wonder where it was hiding."

"From where her pack was, I'd guess she took off running straight up the path," Kady said. "The novice I mean; but it wouldn't have been chasing *her*. I wonder what direction Barbara went."

"Depending on where the fell was, she might have headed for that patch of trees," Eloise suggested. "That, or back to the house. I don't see any better cover."

"Or maybe she would have made for the hedge," Kady added, "if the fell came at them from the other way."

"I wonder how far she managed to run..." Eloise pondered sadly. "We'll probably never know."

Kady nodded unhappily in agreement.

Now that they had found the batteries, there was nothing left to do but return them to the enclave. The two girls slung the abandoned packs across their shoulders and started up the trail again, back toward the Circle Park and the river.

But they did not get very far. Less than a hundred meters from where they'd found the backpacks, they came upon a worker bee which was oddly flitting about, back and forth above the path ahead of them.

As they drew closer, it became apparent what the little robot was doing. There was a broad wash of drying blood, which lay across the full width of the path and on into the grass to either side. The bee was methodically spraying the ground with a chemical solution, to dissolve the blood and remove the stains.

Kady froze, and her breath caught in her throat. Eloise grabbed her friend by the arm and pulled her roughly out onto the grass, far around the fluttering bee, then back onto the path again on the opposite side.

The two young women looked at each other, miserably, then turned back toward the river again and continued walking in silence.

Chapter 5:
The Warehouse Exchange

Safely back at River Towne, Kady and Eloise returned to the Warehouse Exchange. It was now late afternoon, and the tent was much busier than when Kady had been there earlier in the day. Scores of harvesters were standing in multiple lines, each of them awaiting their turn to meet with one of the underkeepers, and to receive their compensation for whatever items they'd managed to scavenge over the course of the day.

"Just our luck..." Eloise said, looking at the seemingly endless lines. Kady sighed, and nodded. They both were feeling deflated, and wanted nothing more than to put their increasingly depressing assignment behind them. But given the crowds, that did not seem likely. They dejectedly moved to the end of what appeared to be the shortest queue, and settled in for a long and tedious wait.

However, only a few moments later (and much to their surprise) they were approached by one of the underkeepers – a middle-aged man with thinning hair and a sizable bald patch – who pulled them out of the line, and off to one side.

"You're Kady, is that correct?..." the man asked.

Kady nodded, somewhat hesitantly.

"Did you find them?" he asked, pointing to the backpacks she and Eloise were carrying. "The batteries, I mean. Are those the ones from this morning?"

"Yes."

"Follow me, please."

Kady and Eloise followed the man through a closed flap at the back of the tent, and into a smaller, more private compartment. There, a much older woman was seated behind a large, empty table. She set her electronic registry down, and looked the two girls over critically, from head to toe.

The woman did not ask for names, and did not bother to introduce herself. There was no need. Kady and Eloise both knew very well who she was, though neither of them had ever spoken with her before. The older woman's name was Helen, and she was not an underkeeper. She was *the* keeper, the ranking official in charge of the enclave's entire warehouse operation, and a member of the Privy Council. This made her an enormously important and powerful woman.

"Thank you, Charles," she said to the balding man. He nodded once, and quickly shuffled himself out of the room.

Kady and Eloise had no idea why they would have been called in for a private meeting with such a prominent and imposing authority figure. They were puzzled – not to mention terrified – but the old woman was all business.

"On the table, please," she said, patting the surface gently with her right hand.

Kady and Eloise carefully set the two backpacks down on the counting table, then waited in silence while the older woman inspected each of the batteries and confirmed them one by one in the registry. When that task was finally complete, she set her tablet down on the table and looked up again at the two young harvesters.

"Did you..."

The old woman hesitated. She looked down for a moment and adjusted her eyeglasses, then turned to look squarely at Kady.

"Did you find any evidence of what happened to the older girl?"

Kady stole a glance over at Eloise, half-hoping that she would take the initiative. But the keeper had clearly addressed the question to Kady; Eloise was only biting her lip and staring at the floor. Kady took a shallow breath to steady her nerves.

"Yes," she answered quietly. "There was some blood there, on the path... quite a lot of it. That was all we saw."

Kady did her best to sound confident and composed, but she found it almost impossible to look the warehouse keeper directly in the eye. The old woman said nothing more for a long while, but she stared at Kady with such detachment that neither girl could make a guess at what the old woman might be thinking. They tried not to move, unsure if they were about to be rewarded, or instead punished for some dire offense that they weren't even aware of committing. The silence in the room seemed to drag on for a merciless eternity.

"Everything appears to be in order," the keeper said eventually, to the great relief of the two young harvesters. "You will each be awarded two point five credits, and the smaller pack will be returned to the girl that lost it."

"Thank you," Eloise and Kady replied, almost in unison. They both felt as if an enormous weight had suddenly been lifted from their shoulders. But still they did not move. They had not yet been given leave to go.

Helen looked down at the counting table again for a long moment, long enough that Kady and Eloise began to feel decidedly uncomfortable all over again. Then, quite to the surprise of both girls, she lifted the other empty backpack and held it out to Kady, as if she were expecting her to take it.

"You may go," she said, somewhat abruptly. "Thank you for your service."

Kady was so startled that she didn't know what to do. A backpack was a valuable item, and she had naturally assumed that Barbara's would become property of the enclave. Had the keeper made an error? Kady didn't have her own backpack with her; she hadn't needed it for this run, since Barbara and the novice had both left their packs behind. Was the warehouse keeper mistakenly assuming that this empty pack was hers, or did she know that it had belonged to Barbara, and yet she still intended to let Kady have it?... Neither possibility seemed possible, and the old woman's face was entirely inscrutable. She gave no clear indication either way.

Kady felt a thump on the back of her calf, and realized that Eloise had given her a kick under the table, where the keeper wouldn't see. But Kady had no idea if Eloise was urging her to admit that the pack wasn't really hers, or rather to simply take the thing and run.

Afraid that she might give offense by pointing out the error – if error it was – Kady took the proffered backpack, nodded gratefully, then turned and slipped quickly out of the private little room without another word.

Eloise was right at her heels, and when she saw Kady staring at the backpack with a dumbfounded look on her face, she grabbed her friend by the arm and pulled her swiftly out of the tent, before anyone else could notice that something unexpected and very puzzling had just transpired.

Chapter 6:
The Clade

The long day was finally drawing to a close, and Gloria would soon be announcing the sunset. The vivid blue of Fairhaven's vast and artificial sky was slowly fading toward a rosy twilight glow, as here and there around the sprawling enclave of River Towne, battery-powered lanterns were being switched on, and could be seen shining faintly through the open doors and windows. Eloise and Kady, glad to be leaving the Warehouse Exchange behind them, now walked their familiar winding path through the loosely clustered tents and shanties, back to their own clade.

A *clade* was, technically speaking, a small collective of harvesters – all of the same gender and roughly the same age – who would live and sleep together in a single housing unit. In more casual usage, the term "clade" could refer either to the group of harvesters themselves, or to the housing structure in which they lived.

The unit where Kady and Eloise lived was a typical example of the many clades in River Towne. It was part tent and part hardform structure, housing six harvesters who had lived together as a group ever since they were all first promoted from the Nursery. The unit itself consisted of a large single room, with cots along the walls and a simple kitchenette and dining area tucked away into one of the rear corners. Because Fairhaven had no weather to speak of, there was no need for any sort of heating or insulation or weatherproofing. Windows were simply openings in the walls, with a hanging flap of cloth to cover them at night, or as needed for some small measure of privacy. The front door was nothing more than an open frame with a sliding hardfoam panel.

But as sparse as these accommodations may have been, for any harvester their housing unit was their home, and their clade was the closest thing they had to a family. No harvester in River Towne knew who their biological parents were. Children were raised in the Nursery until the age of ten, when a small group would be split off together as novices, to form a new clade. They would remain under the supervision of the two councils for a time, but at age twelve, or thereabouts, they would be elevated again, losing their novice designation. From that point forward each member of the clade would be expected to operate more or less independently.

By the time Eloise and Kady reached their housing unit, most of the other girls had already returned from their own harvesting runs. Everyone seemed tired, and the mood inside the tent was quietly somber. Nora was sitting alone on her cot, wrapped in a blanket and browsing half-heartedly on a digital reading tablet. Her slender arms and long legs were folded awkwardly together, as if she did not know quite what to do with them. In the fading light she looked something like a timorous spider, trying not to be seen and reluctant to fully uncurl.

On the opposite side of the room, Audrey and Gwen were huddled together in a corner, rolling dice. They both had come up empty on their harvesting runs, and were trying to put a bad day behind them with a few casual rounds of Knucklejack. Neither of the two was particularly intent on the game; they both thought they were losing.

Bridget, the youngest member of the clade by several weeks, had not yet returned from her harvesting run. It was now past sunset, and Eloise wondered what might be keeping her. It wasn't unusual for Bridget to be the last of the group returning home, but as her own day had provided a stark reminder of how hazardous harvesting could be, Eloise couldn't help worrying about her, just a little bit, in spite of herself.

Feeling tired and puzzled, and not entirely sociable, Kady paid little notice to the other girls. She retreated to her cot, hoping for some quiet time and maybe a quick nap before dinner. But soon however, she found herself staring once again at Barbara's backpack.

She had no idea what to do with it. A backpack was a valuable item, every bit as essential as a good pair of shoes, and Barbara's pack was especially nice. It was large and sturdy, and practically new; easily better than the one Kady already had.

But while Kady's old pack might have looked dull and unimpressive, it was still perfectly good, and far from worn out. And all the more importantly it was *hers*... it was comfortable to wear, and as familiar to her as if it were a part of her own body. Kady always felt a little out of balance when she didn't have it on, as if she were incomplete without it. She did not need or even want a replacement, and she wasn't the least bit excited by the prospect of carrying around a dead woman's satchel.

Had she found a pack like Barbara's, hanging in a closet somewhere in the Middle Ring, she could have turned it in at the exchange tent and gotten maybe as much as five or six credits for it. But she couldn't sell this one; the warehouse keeper herself had given it to her. If Kady were to return it to the exchange tent now, that would only call attention to the fact that she should never have ended up with it in the first place. It was all so confusing.

Not knowing what else to do, Kady stuffed the pack underneath her cot, and resolved to forget that she had ever even seen it.

Standing by herself in the clade's little kitchenette, Eloise felt strangely conflicted. She was glad to have helped Kady out, and to have picked up a few easy food credits in the bargain; but just the same, she was now more than half-wishing she hadn't agreed to go along on the extra run at all. She hadn't known Barbara any better than Kady had, but seeing exactly where and how the older girl had died had been more of a blow than she'd expected, and it had left her feeling drained and depressed.

She went to the foodwall to make herself some dinner, but her mind was elsewhere. She grabbed a meal packet from her storage box and popped it into the hotmaker, without even looking first to see what it might be. It turned out to be a basic cheese lasagna; bland, but filling. Eloise sat down at the table and picked at the bulky mound of layered pasta with her fork, hardly noticing the flavor.

Nora soon joined her, though she had not prepared a proper meal of her own. All she'd brought with her was a dessert-sized packet of yogurt, which she was eating very gingerly, taking tiny scoops with her spoon. Eloise noticed, and gave her a questioning look.

"This is all I'm having," Nora explained, in answer to Eloise's unspoken question. She seemed a little embarrassed with herself. "I've been taking more volunteer shifts at the hospital tent, so I've missed a few harvesting runs. Then I'm also trying to save up for a new pair of shoes. My old ones are coming apart at the toes."

Eloise nodded with understanding.

Nora was, even by her own admission, a terrible harvester. She was unusually tall, and reasonably bright, but she was also awkward and unathletic, as if she had never quite mastered her body again after her last growth spurt. She also tended to be overly cautious, never venturing far from the boat landing. And, apparently, she was simply unlucky. If she was ever to have any hope of making the Lesser Council, it only made sense for her to try to find some other way to make herself useful to the enclave. In that regard, apprenticing at the hospital tent seemed as likely a choice as any.

Eloise stared for a moment at Nora's little cup of yogurt, then looked down at the congealed mass of food on her own plate. A few seconds later she stood up and walked to the foodwall, then returned to the table carrying a second fork. She held it out to Nora.

"Share mine," she said.

"I'll be ok," Nora replied, trying to refuse.

"Please?..." Eloise insisted. "I don't have much of an appetite anyway. It'll probably half go to waste if you don't; I don't think I'd even want to finish it all."

The two girls looked at each other for a few seconds, until Nora nodded, appreciatively.

"Thank you," she said, as she took the fork. She cut off a bit of the lasagna from the near side of Eloise's plate, and began to eat. In response, Eloise picked up her own spoon, reached across the table, and scooped a tiny bit of yogurt out of Nora's cup.

"Just a taste," she said teasingly. Nora couldn't help smiling.

Before long, the other three girls had joined them, and the mood in the room began to lighten. It had not been a good day for any of them, but as the evening wore on, that seemed to matter less and less.

They had all finished eating, but had not yet begun to clean up the scraps, when Bridget suddenly bounced in through the front door. She slid the panel shut behind her, then turned back to the group, smiling from ear to ear.

"Where have you been?" Eloise asked.

"Shhh...!" Bridget replied, with a finger to her lips. She scampered over to one of the room's two windows and lowered the cloth flap to cover it. "Nora, get the other window," she said, her voice hushed with excitement.

"What have you done now?" Kady asked.

"I haven't done anything," Bridget said, "but I've **got** something. El, do you still have that candle? This calls for sorcery."

"I am positively dying with anticipation," Audrey deadpanned.

"Don't be a turd..." Bridget said, scowling but undaunted. "Look what I found."

She held up a tiny food packet, but the light in the room was far too dim for any of the others to read the label.

"So what is it?" Kady asked.

"*Chocolate...*" Bridget whispered in reply.

Chapter 7:
Shards of Happiness

"How in Gloria's name did you come by *that*?" Eloise asked excitedly. "I don't think I've had a piece of chocolate since they elevated us from Nursery."

"Neither have I," said Nora. "It all goes to the Privy Council, doesn't it? Or it's supposed to."

"Where did you even find it?" Gwendolyn asked, not really expecting an answer. "I can't believe they let you keep it."

"Well, I wouldn't say they *let* me..." Bridget admitted. "There was quite a crowd at the exchange tent, and things may have gotten a little jumbled. But I *did* pay for a dessert packet, and some of the underkeepers aren't nearly so sharp-eyed as they could be, particularly in twilight."

"You didn't sneak it really, did you?!..." Kady gasped. "They'd dock you a hundred credits if anyone ever found out!"

Audrey nodded forcefully, to show she was in full agreement with Kady on the matter. Then she leaned forward and glared at Bridget with a stern and disapproving scowl.

"What I really want to know..." she said, in her best *Privy Council* voice, "is do the rest of us get to have some too?"

"As if I would have even brought it home otherwise," Bridget replied. "If they're going to sink me in the river for it, I might as well drag you all down with me. That only seems fair."

With the most important question finally settled, everyone went into motion. Eloise ran to fetch her candle and matches, while Audrey retrieved a pair of dice from the corner. Kady and Gwen made a quick check outside, to make certain that no one was lurking nearby, then they tied down the window flaps and pulled the sliding door panel securely shut again. Eloise lit the candle as Nora switched off the last of the battery-powered lights, and soon everyone was huddled around the table once more, illuminated only by the flickering glow of the candle.

Bridget carefully opened the packet to reveal a perfect bar of solid milk chocolate. The slab had been molded with no indentations or creases of any kind, which made it difficult to divide evenly. The chocolate broke into jagged and irregular shapes, but working with great patience and care, Bridget eventually managed to snap it into six roughly equal portions. She laid them out on the table in a tiny hexagon, with the candle in the exact center.

Everyone stared at their little makeshift shrine in anticipation.

"It looks *so good*," said Nora. She bit down on the middle knuckle of her index finger.

"It's kind of spooky, isn't it..." said Kady. Her hands were clasped tightly together, and she was visibly trembling.

"This chocolate is *done for*..." Eloise said. "Fire and darkness and forbidden fruits; we're like the three Fates, watching over the doomed."

"There's six of us," Audrey pointed out. "So we only rate as half a Fate each. And chocolate was a bean, not a fruit."

"It wasn't really, was it?" said Gwen. "Beans are so boring! It had to be a fruit, like apple or strawberry or vanilla."

"Vanilla was a bean too."

"Stop it, Audrey," said Bridget. "Roll for choices."

Each of the girls took up the two dice in turn. Most of the rolls were low, and Kady had the highest with only a nine. She hesitated.

"Go on, then..." Eloise said, giving her a nudge. Kady bit her lip, and made her choice.

"You picked the smallest one!" Gwen complained.

"You're such a martyr," said Audrey.

"*My* choice," Kady said, "and I took the one I wanted."

The five remaining girls rolled again for the next chance to choose, and so on until each of them was holding a piece. Then everyone looked at Bridget.

"Tell us when..." Nora said.

Bridget glanced quickly around the circle.

"I'm no good at this," she muttered softly. "Somebody else say the grace."

"Eloise should do it," said Kady.

"Say something cool," Gwendolyn added. "Make it awesome."

Eloise nodded. She couldn't help smiling just a little bit, at having been chosen by the group.

"Everyone close your eyes," she said.

Their eyes tightly shut, the six girls waited in silence until the chocolate was slowly beginning to melt at the tips of their fingers.

"*By the grace of Gloria...*" Eloise whispered at last, "*let us offer our gratitude...*"

Her voice was so quiet that it was barely above the threshold of hearing. The other girls all strained to listen.

"*...for these little shards of happiness, which we would otherwise be denied.*"

Chapter 8:
A Knock at the Door

"Kady, there's a boy here to see you."

It was very early in the morning, and Gloria had only just announced the sunrise. Kady was still lying in her cot, curled up underneath her blanket. She rolled over and stared across the room at Audrey, who – being the first of the clade up and dressed that morning – had been the one to answer the door.

"Me?" Kady asked, hazily. She was not yet entirely awake.

Audrey simply shrugged by way of reply, then slid the door panel open just enough to say "she'll be out in a minute..." before closing it again, and walking back to the kitchenette to finish her breakfast.

It was uncommon enough for the clade to have any visitors at all. A knock on the door panel usually meant a surprise inspection by some menial adult from the Lesser Council, or sometimes a girl from another clade might be looking to make a swap, or borrow something that wasn't currently available from the warehouse. Harvesters tended to spend most of their time working – either alone or in pairs – or eating or resting within their housing units. Few had many real friends outside of their own clade.

In River Towne, most of the interclade socializing was done in *The Commons*: a large open space with a few tables, which sat near the center of the enclave. But as often as not, anyone bothering to go to the Commons was more likely looking for a chance to be alone, away from the rest of their clade, than to be randomly social with anyone else.

Romances between harvesters were not unusual, but they were actively discouraged by the Privy Council. Consequently, those hoping for a more private encounter would typically agree to meet somewhere across the river, taking the time away from their harvesting runs. The obvious advantage of such meetings was that there was no danger of being interrupted or overheard – at least not by an adult – though of course any time spent within the Middle Ring came with dangers of its own.

Still half-asleep, Kady rolled out of her cot and dressed as quickly as she could manage. She got her new t-shirt backwards on the first try, and had to stop and untangle herself before getting it turned the right way around. Finally with some clothes on, she slid the door partway open and peeked out into the pale light of morning.

Kady vaguely recognized the young man standing outside the door as one of the older harvesters, but she didn't know his name. He was not particularly tall, with short brown hair and a squarish, nondescript face. His eyes, however, were a strange and striking shade of green. They seemed almost out of place, as if they did not belong with the rest of him. He was wearing a faded brown and blue shirt.

"Are you Kady?" he asked. "I'm sorry to bother you... my name is Michael. Can you spare a few minutes?"

"Um... yes?" Kady nodded.

"I know it's early... if you haven't eaten yet, I was hoping maybe we could sit at the Commons? I'd be happy to buy you breakfast, if that would be all right."

"What is this about?"

"Um..." Michael stammered. He was obviously uncomfortable, but determined. "I was hoping to ask you about Barbara." He stared down at the concrete for a few moments, then raised his head again, to look Kady in the eye. "She was a friend of mine."

Kady stared blankly at the young man for several seconds, until she found her voice.

"Let me get my shoes," she said.

Michael and Kady sat in the Commons for a long time, eating breakfast and discussing almost everything except Barbara. Michael said very little about himself, but he seemed interested in almost anything Kady was willing to talk about. Their conversation was mostly small talk; he asked how old she was, and if she was ever asked to mentor any of the novices. He asked about the other girls in her clade, and how they all got along. He complimented her on her shirt.

Kady began to wonder if he was ever going to ask about Barbara. She was not looking forward to it; but that was, after all, why they both were there. Eventually, she realized that having already broached the topic once, he was apparently waiting for her to bring it up again.

"You said that you wanted to ask me about Barbara."

Michael looked down at the table for a moment.

"Yes... I'm sorry. Now that it's come to that, I guess I've been avoiding it. I'm sure this isn't any easier for you than it is for me."

"I'm afraid I don't know much," Kady said. "I'm sure you knew her better than I did."

"What I was wondering..." Michael began, but stopped himself before starting the question again. "I suppose I wanted to know if she was really dead. For certain, I mean. They told me she was, but the underkeepers have been wrong before. Sometimes people miss the last raft, but still make it till morning. I know some have even tried to make it around the ring to Pleasant Gardens, or one of the other enclaves; Barbara and I had talked about that idea, more than once. So I just wondered if... they told me you found her pack. Is there any chance she got away?"

Kady shook her head.

"There was blood... maybe a hundred meters up the path from where we found her pack. Quite a lot of it. A bee was there, cleaning up. I'm sorry. I didn't see her body, but..."

"I see..." Michael said, interrupting her. "Then no. That answers my question. Thank you."

"I'm sorry; I wish I could give you better news."

"No, I prefer knowing. It's not like this is the first time I've lost a friend."

"Were the two of you...?" Kady started to ask, but stopped herself. "It's none of my business."

"No, it's fine," Michael replied. "I don't mind telling you. We'd work as a pair sometimes, harvesting, splitting up whatever we'd find. She was easy to be around. I was in love with her, I suppose, at least a little bit. You'd already guessed that. I'm not sure if she felt the same way about me. I didn't ask, and nothing ever came of it. If we weren't somehow both going to be selected to continue, there was never any real point in going any further. That's how I thought about it, anyway. I can't speak for her."

"I hate it that not everyone can make the Council," Kady said. She felt suddenly angry about everything, but just as quickly she tried to bottle it up again. She clenched her fist under the table.

"Why the path?" he asked, suddenly.

Kady gave Michael a quizzical look, and shook her head slowly. She wasn't at all sure what he was asking.

"Why would she have stayed on the path?" he asked a second time.

"I don't know," Kady said. "But that's where we..."

"No, no, I believe you," Michael interrupted. "But if she'd had time enough to run, why would she have stayed out in the open? Why didn't she run for cover, or into one of the houses or something?"

Kady just shook her head; she did not have an answer. He was right, of course. Kady and Eloise had even talked about it before they saw the blood. Why *would* Barbara have stayed on the path? Now that Kady thought about it, it didn't make sense.

"It's the last place she should have been," Michael continued, as much to himself as to Kady. "They'll catch you that way, every time. Everyone knows that." He looked up at Kady and slowly shook his head.

"You've got to get off the path if you want to live."

With the breakfast over, Michael walked Kady back from the Commons to her clade. The important questions had all been asked, and so their conversation drifted back to ordinary and trivial things.

"Thank you," Michael said, when they finally reached Kady's housing unit. "I'm sorry to have taken so much of your time, but I do appreciate..."

"Wait here," Kady blurted out, cutting him off. She quickly darted into the tent, leaving him standing there, puzzled, just outside the door.

A moment later she emerged again, carrying a backpack.

"I hope you'll take this," she said, holding it out to him. "It was Barbara's. I think it would be better for you to have it."

Michael was startled, and took a half step backwards.

"Please," she asked, "I don't entirely understand how it came to me, but I don't need it, and I'd really rather not have it at all."

"To be honest," he said uncomfortably, "I'm not so sure that I want it either."

They stood there for several seconds, with her holding out the pack and him reluctant to take it. It was Michael who finally broke the silence.

"But I know someone who can use it," he conceded. He reached out and took the pack from her. "I'll pass it along."

"Thank you."

Chapter 9:
Perspectives

It was shortly before noon, and high above the grassy landscape, Eloise sat perched astride the crown of a roof, looking down. This was not an ordinary place for any harvester to be, unless of course that harvester happened to be Eloise. Eloise was fond of roofs, and had been ever since she first discovered that climbing onto them was a viable option.

To be sure, not every rooftop in the Middle Ring was suitable for climbing. Most were too steeply pitched to safely stand on, while others were too difficult to even reach, at least not without incurring serious risk to life and limb. But some few houses had roofs with relatively gentle slopes, and large dormer windows in their attics which provided easy access. These were the rooftops most suitable for climbing, and for sitting.

Over time, scattered here and there throughout the Middle Ring, Eloise had found more than a dozen such roofs that could be reached with a minimum of risk or trouble. And of those few, this particular roof was one of her favorites. The house it belonged to was taller than some, and stood on a fairly high patch of ground, with only a handful of trees nearby. This meant that the view it afforded was especially good: broad, unbroken, and largely unobstructed.

Things looked different from the rooftops. From that high vantage point, Eloise had begun to see the city from a new perspective; not as a jumble of isolated parts, but rather as a functioning whole: A worker bee would trim a long row of bushes, then cross a broad expanse of lawn to reach the next hedge, ignoring every other possible task that might lie between. Another would remove the dead blooms from a nearby flowerbed, while a third would follow, a short distance behind, methodically planting new flowers to replace the ones that had just been taken away. From high above on the rooftops, Eloise could watch the bees for hours, as they slowly moved in their interwoven and well-ordered dance. Everywhere below her, she could see the patient unfolding of Gloria's designs.

She could also see the fells. There were more of them now than there had been when she first began climbing onto the rooftops, some four or five years before. Then, she would rarely see one at all, unless she ventured far in toward the Central Forest. But now she would see them often, and seemingly everywhere. She had more than once even spotted two different fells from the very same rooftop.

But whether the fells she saw were dormant or prowling, they never seemed to notice her. This might have been because she was not yet old enough to consistently draw their attention, but Eloise did not think that was the real reason. Rather, she had come to suspect that the rooftops might well be invisible to the fells. It seemed to her that those high places were somehow beyond their awareness, or at the very least outside the scope of their immediate concern, in much the same way that the worker bees would ignore everything around them, apart from their own narrow tasks.

Eloise had given much time to the contemplation of such things. At the ripe young age of seventeen, she had devoted more thought to the workings of her world than anyone else in her clade; more, in fact, than anyone else in all of River Towne, with the possible exception of the Privy Council. But those who sat on the Council were old, and perceived all things, including themselves, in a peculiarly shadowed light.

And yet, though Eloise had long pursued the mind of Gloria, still she found her infinitely elusive. She felt as if the more she learned, the less she understood, and the less sense she could make of it all. She had come both to adore Gloria, and to despise her, in almost equal measure.

Bridget leaned forward, and peered cautiously around the corner of the house. Her heart was racing, and she was biting at her lower lip, struggling to contain her excitement.

The fell was still there, still lying in the same little flower patch where she'd first seen it a few minutes before. It had not moved so much as a millimeter in all that time. It seemed to be fully dormant, still asleep in its metal cocoon. Bridget clutched at the corner of the building very gently with her fingertips, and slowly dragged herself forward.

The thing did not move.

Now she was well around the corner, standing in the open, in full view.   But the fell was still sleeping; it couldn't possibly see her standing there, could it?

Her nerve failed her and she ducked back again, aching with the thrill of scarcely mastered terror.   She was so close, closer than she'd ever been, but perhaps this still was not the time.

Not even daring to breathe, Bridget leaned forward to peer around the corner once more.   Still, nothing had changed.   The grass between her and her quarry was short and lush and flawless; glistening from the spray of the lawn sprinklers.   The geraniums surrounding the dark metallic egg were bright and colorful and inviting; the mulch beneath them, thick and evenly laid.   She pulled herself back into hiding again.

An idea suddenly came to her.   She crept back along the side of the house, away from the fell, then hurried across the open grass to the little water garden she'd spotted behind the next house over.   From the edge of a shallow pond, she picked up a thumb-sized rock in each hand, then slipped cautiously back to her hiding place near the fell.

It still had not moved.

It was so tempting; she wanted to dash forward, to get the whole thing over with in a single decisive rush, one way or the other.   But she had already made another plan, and this was almost as good.

Quick as the snapping of a twig, she darted out from hiding, and flung one of the two stones at the sleeping fell.   The little chunk of rock rang off the monster's carapace with a dull metallic *clack*, and bounced harmlessly aside.

Bridget turned and ran, at a full sprint, back around the corner of the house, then off again in the same direction from which she'd originally come.   She didn't even break stride until she found herself back in the midst of the same stand of trees from which she'd first spotted the fell, nearly half an hour before.   She pulled to a stop, and turned back to look.

The monster was still there in the flower patch, just as it had been the entire time: motionless; silent; dead to the world around it; oblivious, apparently, to the investigations of the girl, or even to the tiny projectile that had clattered off its outer shell.

Satisfied that she was not being pursued, Bridget slipped quietly away in the opposite direction, smiling triumphantly, and trying to catch her breath.

"Next time..." she told herself, *"... next time, I will get close enough to touch it."*

Gloria had just announced the sunset, and all across the enclave, darkness was falling. Finally released from her duties, Nora stepped out from the operating chamber and into the adjacent cleaning station. Her shift at the hospital tent had run longer than usual today, but Nora didn't mind. For the first time, she had been allowed to assist with a childbirth, and she'd found it both captivating and strangely beautiful.

It had not been an ordinary birth; the baby had not aligned itself properly, and the hospital keeper himself was called in. The emergency surgery that followed had been a harrowing ordeal, filled with blood and anguish, but it was ultimately successful: both the woman and the child had survived.

The practice of medicine had contracted considerably in Fairhaven, over the long span of years. Though the details of mankind's great advances in medical science had all been preserved in digital form, those records were of little use, lacking the proper facilities or educational systems to apply that knowledge in practice. A scrape could be treated and bandaged, a cut could be stitched, a broken arm could be properly set; but these simple remedies amounted to nearly the full extent of River Towne's palliative care. A Caesarean section such as the one that Nora had just witnessed was, in fact, the most elaborate operation the hospital's medical staff would even attempt.

"You did well."

Startled from her reverie, Nora turned to see the hospital keeper himself, just inside the entry door. She hadn't heard him come in; had he been watching her? She couldn't guess how long he had been there, standing behind her.

"Not everyone has the stomach for surgery," he continued, as he stripped off his apron and gloves. "I've had assistants faint before, watching for the first time. Then others will blanche just at the sight of blood. I'd have to say you handled it better than most."

"Thank you," Nora replied, looking down at the water again, and trying not to blush at this unexpected praise. "There was so much to do, I didn't have a chance to think about anything else."

The older man stepped up next to her, and began casually washing his hands at the sink.

"Well, now that it's all over and done with, what did you think of it?"

Nora was far more terrified of the hospital keeper and his questions than she had ever been during the surgery, but the chance to speak privately with a member of the Privy Council was an opportunity she could not let pass by. She took a breath to steady herself.

"It was an honor to watch you work," she said, trying to sound as calm and confident as she could. "I thought it was fascinating; I have so much to learn."

The surgeon took a sideways glance at the girl, raised an eyebrow for a moment, then nodded approvingly. It was a good enough answer, he thought: deferential, self-effacing, professional. He didn't mind at all that she was obviously trying to work her way into his good graces.

"Well, don't let this old man keep you here," he said, shaking the water off his hands, and drying them on a white towel. "You've put in a good day's work, but you'd better get on back to your clade."

"Thank you, sir," Nora replied. She bowed her head once more, then scurried somewhat clumsily out through the flap at the back of the room.

The hospital keeper couldn't help smiling to himself. When she'd first volunteered, he'd expected the bashful, lanky young woman to be nothing more than a hopeless disaster, good at nothing, and soon to be fodder for the fells. But after watching her for the past few weeks, he'd found himself almost taking a liking to the girl. And why not? She'd done well enough during the operation, following his instructions without hesitation or complaint. He found her eagerness to obey without question refreshing.

The old man still doubted that there would ever be a place for her among the hospital staff on the Lesser Council, but he was no longer quite so certain of that assessment as he had been before. He had long since learned never to discount the ways in which ambition and determination could sometimes eclipse a young harvester's other shortcomings. But just as importantly, as is so often the case with powerful administrators, he valued the competence of his personnel far less than he valued their subservience. And flattery, in all its forms, was always welcome.

There were also other factors to be carefully considered. No doubt the girl was gaunt and awkward now, but she was still young. He suspected that her body would one day grow into that slender frame, and that she might well become rather appealing, if only given a little more time to fully mature. He saw that as another potential mark in her favor.

With these and other less than noble thoughts in mind, the surgeon left the hospital tent and walked slowly through the District, back to his private residence. Regardless of whatever faults and merits the girl might show, he had his eye on her now. That was as much a matter of curiosity, perhaps, as anything else, but the fact remained.

Chapter 10:
The District

After her unexpected breakfast with Michael, Kady had done little searching on her harvesting run that day. Mostly she had wandered, without any clear direction or conscious goal, fully consumed with aimless reflection. In the few houses she did search, she found nothing of value.

When she returned to the ferry raft, it was still only mid-afternoon. Her backpack was entirely empty, but she did not really care. She'd decided to return home early, even though she was returning empty-handed. She wasn't getting any useful searching done anyway.

The oarsman gave her a long, peculiar look, but he said nothing, and dutifully rowed her back across the river without complaint. Kady looked down, avoiding his gaze, and watched the water washing along the side of the raft.

As the ferry approached the enclave, Kady could see that an official from the Lesser Council was standing by the water's edge. He was someone Kady did not immediately recognize, though she suspected that he must be one of the underkeepers. Several times, she saw him glance down at his registry tablet, then up again at the approaching raft. As soon as the boat had nudged up against the concrete curb, he walked over and spoke to Kady before she'd even gotten herself fully ashore.

"You are Kady, is that correct?" the man said. He had not intended it as a question, but rather as a terse formality. It was clear that he already knew who she was.

"Yes..." Kady replied cautiously. It was not customary for underkeepers to accost harvesters directly at the boat landing, and she couldn't help feeling a little uneasy about who this person might be, and why he'd been waiting for her.

"My name is Jeremy," the man said, with a polite nod. "I am the personal secretary to the warehouse keeper."

"I didn't find anything today," Kady said, apologetically. "I wasn't even going to stop at the tent... I don't have anything to report."

48

"You misunderstand me," the man replied. "I have been asked to collect you on a matter of Council business. If you will follow me, please?"

Kady had no idea what this could be about. Her only guess was that she had somehow gotten herself into some sort of trouble, though she couldn't imagine what she might have done to warrant any unusual scrutiny. She'd hardly ever been in trouble before, at least not since she'd graduated from Nursery. There had been the blow-up over her new t-shirt, of course, but she'd already been fined for that, and she'd learned her lesson.

But the man did not explain himself further. He neatly tucked the digital registry into a small carrying case, and led Kady away from the river, around the exchange tent, and on through the heart of the enclave. They passed by the Commons, and the housing units of several other clades, and before long they had even walked beyond the playgrounds of the Nursery. Eventually, they arrived at a scattered expanse of tents and shacks along the outer margins, as far as possible from the river and directly adjacent to the wall.

This portion of the enclave was known as *The District*, an isolated and broadly-dispersed region reserved to River Towne's adult population. There were tents for meetings and administration, open spaces for socializing and dining, and secure storage facilities for the warehouse. At one corner of the District stood the hospital tent with its adjacent maternity ward. Elsewhere were scattered many other structures of various sizes, serving myriad other purposes.

All of the enclave's adults were housed in the District, each according to their individual rank and importance. Harvesters, however, were not allowed there without special permission, and Kady had been inside the District no more than a handful of times, in all the years since her clade was first elevated from Nursery.

The man led her to a small hut, dwarfed by the enormous warehouse tents surrounding it. But despite its diminutive size, the hut was one of the most impressive buildings in the entire enclave. Its walls were made from carefully matched hardfoam panels, with no visible cracks or crevices. The windows were covered not with fabric, but with solid, sliding panels which could be easily opened or securely closed. The front door fit perfectly in its frame, and was mounted on actual hinges, rather than merely sliding to the side. To Kady's eye, the sturdy little hut was almost like a rough-hewn imitation of the elegant houses in the Middle Ring, though wrought in miniature.

"This is the Administration Office," the man said. "One moment, please; she is expecting you."

He tapped lightly on the door, and several seconds passed before a reply could be heard from inside.

"Come in."

The man turned the knob, pushed the door open, and ushered Kady through.

The hut's interior consisted of a single large room, better-built and more comfortably appointed, but otherwise not terribly different from any typical housing unit. There was only one bed – an actual bed with a full mattress, and not simply a cot – and elsewhere Kady could see a kitchenette, several chairs, shelves, some storage cases, and other typical furnishings. On the opposite side of the room, seated behind a large wooden desk, was Helen, the warehouse keeper. Kady swallowed hard.

Chapter 11:
The Warehouse Keeper

"This is Kady," the man said, formally indicating the girl beside him. "She returned early from her harvesting run. Is this a convenient time?"

"Thank you, Jeremy," the warehouse keeper replied. "You may go. Please see that we are not disturbed."

"Yes, Ma'am." He acknowledged the dismissal with a curt nod, quickly slipping out again, and pulling the door closed behind him.

After he had gone, the old woman looked back down at her registry tablet, and said nothing more for a long time. She did not look happy, and there was no doubt in Kady's mind that she was indeed in serious, serious trouble.

"I'm sorry about the shirt," she blurted out.

"What?"

"My old one was worn out, and I found this one. All I did was swap them, but I should have reported it to the underkeepers first. I'm sorry. They already fined me for it."

"I don't give a damn about your shirt," the old woman responded testily. "Be still. I wanted to continue our conversation from before, but in slightly more private surroundings."

"Oh..." said Kady, who still had no idea what to make of this situation. "I'm not sure there's anything more I can tell you; I'm sorry."

"I never thought there was," said Helen. "But there may be some things that I can tell *you*, if you would stop apologizing long enough to listen." She looked up and glared impatiently at the young harvester.

"Um..." Kady muttered, awkwardly. "All right... yes... thank you?"

"I have followed your progress..." the old woman continued, again looking down at her tablet. "Always at arm's length, of course, but perhaps more closely than you might have realized. I have taken a particular interest."

"Thank you." Kady said again. It wasn't much, but it was the only thing she could think to say. Why would a member of the Privy Council have any special interest in her? If she wasn't about to be disciplined or censured, then why was she even here? Kady was at a loss to imagine any other reason.

The old woman was not even looking at her, just absently scrolling through page after page in her registry. She clearly did not want Kady to say anything more, at least not yet. Kady clenched her toes inside of her shoes and waited in silence, though her mind was racing.

"Why do you call yourself *Kady*?" the warehouse keeper asked suddenly, still not looking up from her tablet.

Kady was startled by the question, not to mention confused.

"It's... my name."

"Your name is *Katherine*," said the old woman, finally looking up again. "It's a perfectly good name just as it is, but if for some reason you wanted to shorten it, you could easily have selected *Kathy* or *Kate*, or you might simply have ignored the middle syllable to make it *Kath'rine...*"

"It's what everyone's called me for as long as I can remember. Ever since Nursery."

"It makes you sound like a perpetual child," the warehouse keeper groused, looking down at her tablet once more. "It has no *weight*; it's impossible to take it seriously. It's not the sort of name for someone who's going to be elevated to the Lesser Council."

"Yes, ma'am," Kady replied, almost reflexively. She'd been so taken aback that at first she didn't know what else to say. But then in the silence that followed, the full implication of the warehouse keeper's last few words slowly began to sink in. Kady almost couldn't believe that she'd heard correctly.

"Is that why you brought me here...!?" she stammered excitedly, barely able to contain herself. "I'm being chosen to continue? I've been selected for the Council?"

"No." said the old woman, bluntly and unequivocally. "You have *not* been selected. You have not been added to the Lesser Council, and you are not going to be."

Kady was stunned.

"*Bridget* is going to be elevated instead," the warehouse keeper continued. "She is the only one from your clade that will."

"Bridget?... She's the youngest of all of us. She doesn't even follow the rules!"

"And neither should you, if you had any sense about you. Rules are put in place to keep the rank and file conveniently constrained, and that is the full extent of their utility. You're not a child, and so you shouldn't need me to tell you that. But regardless, the matter is settled. There were only ever two plausible candidates from your clade, and the Council has chosen Bridget. It's unfortunate. To speak plainly, I'd prefer it were you. I tried very hard on your behalf, but we can't have everything we want in life, and the whole affair is now quite out of my hands. There is nothing further that I myself can do."

"But I'm barely seventeen... I've only just become eligible. And two of us should be chosen, shouldn't we?"

"Food returns are down," the old woman replied, "and they've been declining for some time. Consequently, all of the ratios are being adjusted, as a matter of necessity. Promotion to the Lesser Council is no longer at one in three; it is now set at one in five."

"One in *five*?" Kady repeated, bewildered. "But there are six of us in my clade, what about the others?"

"What others?" Helen asked, dismissively. "Who else is there? Nora is pathetic, Audrey is insufferable, and Gwendolyn is hardly worth mentioning. As if anything from now to doomsday is going to change any of that. Who you are matters far more than what you do, child. Your friends' prospects for advancement are already very well decided."

"What about Eloise?" Kady asked, still struggling to process what she was being told.

"Your friend Eloise is a danger to herself and everyone around her," the older woman replied. "She knows it and so should you. And if you haven't realized as much by now, then it's more than high time that you did."

Kady could feel a cold fury welling up inside her, and with it her head began to clear. This was all nonsense; it wasn't fair, and it was wrong. Promotions couldn't have been decided. Not yet; not for her clade. They were all still too young. And the ratios couldn't have been changed either, not without everyone knowing, and the Council hadn't made any announcements. For all she knew, this woman could be lying to her, toying with her hopes, taunting her, deliberately trying to provoke her. Kady gritted her teeth, and dug in her heels.

"Why did you bring me here?" she demanded. She kept her voice firm and level, though her anger was plain to see. "Why are you telling me this?"

"Idiot child," Helen replied, shaking her head with disappointment, "because you're my daughter."

Kady took a few metaphorical moments, to rummage around on the floor of the hut in search of her jaw.

"I'm *what*?!"

"Don't be so surprised; everyone has a mother, including you. Barbara was my daughter as well, as if that matters for anything now. And I shouldn't have to tell you that you should keep this in the strictest confidence. Even I'm not supposed to know, though it's been perfectly obvious to me for some time. And it's certainly not something I would ever be *officially* allowed to tell you; there are, after all, rules about such things. However, being on the Privy Council has its privileges, and ignoring rules is one of them; provided it's done with an appropriate measure of discretion, as we've already discussed."

Kady shook her head slowly from side to side. It was too much. None of this was possible.

"Barbara was my sister?"

"Half-sister," Helen corrected her. "I've no idea who your respective fathers were. Oh, I could make a fair guess, but that wouldn't matter any more than any of the rest of it. I've given birth to seven children over the years, and I couldn't get even one of them onto the Lesser Council. That alone should tell you something. You're the last of the lot, and I am not too proud to say that outliving your own children is a pain in the ass, but there's nothing more that I can do. There may be, however, one way that *you* might still be able to alter the Council's decision yourself, if that would be of interest to you."

Helen paused, and licked the tips of her own fingers, one by one, as if she were tasting them delicately. It had long been a peculiar habit of hers, when she was being coy. Kady waited for her to continue, but the old woman said nothing. When at last she could bear it no longer, Kady found herself forced to ask.

"Then... then what can I do?"

"You could murder Bridget, of course."

Kady pulled back in horror.

"Does that thought make you squeamish?" the old woman asked. "Don't look so surprised. How else can you expect to join the Council? How else will you continue? You're no longer a novice, and not nearly so young as you once were. Would you rather remain a harvester until one of the fells takes you? They won't ignore you forever, you know, and before long they'll be actively hunting you."

"You're insane," Kady said, and she meant it as a statement of fact. She clenched her fists and dug in her heels again. "It isn't even possible. There hasn't been a murder since before the cataclysm, not since before the city was founded."

"Please... Stop..." Helen groaned, holding up her hands disparagingly. "Your naiveté is painful. No murder? Sending children across the river, every morning of every day, knowing full well that one or another of them might never return? What do you think it means to be on the Privy Council? That's what we *do*, Child. We murder each others' children constantly, relentlessly, day in and day out. The only difference being that we are never entirely certain who the next victim will be, or when, precisely, they're going to die. But details are trivial. Murder is the only way we survive; any of us. Have no illusions."

"I won't murder Bridget. I won't murder anyone at all."

"Of course you won't. Not at first. Not right away. And you cannot kill anyone *here*, of course. It would have to be done in the Middle Ring, where no one will ever be the wiser, and the bees will clean all the evidence away. But you haven't much time – a few weeks, perhaps; a month or two at the outside. Because once the announcements are made, once she has formally joined the Lesser Council, Bridget will never cross the river again. The opportunity will be lost forever, and you will die a harvester."

After the girl had gone, the warehouse keeper walked to her kitchenette, to make for herself a nice hot cup of tea. She sat for a while, stirring the drink in silence, and absently watching the steam.

Tea was a luxury item in the enclave, nearly as hard to come by as chocolate, and typically unavailable even to members of the Lesser Council. But rank devours its privileges, and for Helen the warehouse keeper, a cup of tea in the afternoon had become a regular indulgence, though she took little delight from it.

Her several meetings had all gone well, she thought, or at least as well as could be expected. She had now set a handful of gears into uncertain motion, toward indeterminate ends. She had no regrets. Regret was a sensation that she could no longer attain; it bore no utility. She had endured a long life, in a time and place where old age was a rarity. That was all.

The warehouse keeper had long since ceased to care about anyone or anything, other than her own standing, comfort, and survival. But even so, she was not immortal. Faced with that unwelcome reality, she was stoically resolved that if she herself could not eternally persist, she would turn her efforts to some alternative arrangement. Her designs were entirely her own.

She took a sip, but the tea was still too hot, and it burned. She spat, cursing at her own distraction, then added a dash of cold water to the cup to cool it.

- End of Book One -

Book Two:
Chapter 1:
The Heart of the City

Hidden away, deep within the Central Forest, the weary industrial heart of Fairhaven was softly beating. There, a vast network of fully-automated warehouses, mills, manufactories and processing plants generated the food, the consumer goods, and all the other necessities that sustained the city and its human population.

That great industrial core had gradually faltered over time, and nearly all the factories were quiet now. Despite the tireless efforts of the worker bees, no course of maintenance could eternally delay the inevitable. Eventually, some essential component would fail which could neither be replaced nor repaired, and another facility would go offline, succumbing to the relentless forces of entropy and decay.

As processing capacity dwindled, the need for raw materials declined as well. Bottle gardens were abandoned, either fallen barren or left overgrown with neglect. There was no need for production that could never be utilized. The bees which had once maintained those facilities were reassigned to other tasks, or shut down entirely and returned to storage, to lie there dormant until they might be needed again.

But this decline was not yet complete. Here and there a scattered handful of factories still functioned, much as they always had. In a few of the bottle gardens, foodstuffs still were grown. Fabric still was woven and garments still were stitched in some of the automated mills, and countless other goods still were fabricated by ancient and time-worn automated processes. Each new item would then be neatly packaged and labeled and dutifully stored away, awaiting its eventual delivery to one or another of the empty houses of the Middle Ring.

Orchestrating this intricate web of supply and distribution was the vast artificial intelligence known as Gloria.

Gloria knew and saw everything that happened within the city dome, and remembered everything that ever *had* happened there since the founding of the city, many long years before. She had been designed to coordinate every aspect of Fairhaven's automated infrastructure, and to optimize the various industries to effectively sustain the largest possible human population, until such a time as the world outside the city dome became safely habitable once more. In constant service to that all-encompassing mandate, she was judicious, inventive, analytical, and unwaveringly rational.

Fairhaven's human population had, over time, come to perceive her neither as a servant nor a guardian, but rather as a series of paradoxes. She was kind, yet merciless; concrete, yet ephemeral; immediate, yet remote; cruel, yet fair. She was an intangible metaphor that could be seen in every blade of grass, and heard announcing the sunrise every morning.

It was inevitable perhaps, given these contradictions, that over the course of time she would eventually go mad.

Chapter 2:
Around the Table

"I don't know if she was telling the truth or not, but that's what she told me."

Kady had waited for everyone else to return to the clade, before saying anything. Nora had been kept late at the hospital tent, and was the last to arrive, but once she'd returned and everyone had finished with their evening meal, Kady told the entire group about her disturbing audience with Helen, the warehouse keeper.

She had not repeated everything the keeper had said to her – she'd left out being told to murder Bridget, and the part about being the keeper's daughter – but the few things she *had* revealed had been more than enough to get everyone's attention. Kady looked around at the other girls, wondering what their reactions would be.

"They're changing the ratio to one in *five*?" Gwendolyn asked. She felt terribly confused. "One in three was hard enough. What sort of a chance does one in five give us?"

"It doesn't give us any chance at all," Eloise said. "Apparently, as far as the Privy Council is concerned, we're all toast, except for Bridget. I can't say I'm surprised."

"Well it's perfectly obvious to me," said Audrey, who was looking hard at Kady, "that either the warehouse keeper was lying, or *you* are."

Kady felt herself flinch at this accusation, but only slightly. Audrey didn't seem to notice, and pressed on.

"We're still too young for them to have made final decisions about any of us yet. And if the ratios have changed, why hasn't everyone been told about it already?"

"Do you really think they tell us everything?" Eloise countered, giving Audrey a nasty look in return. "I trust Kady a hell of a lot more than I trust anyone on the Privy Council."

"I never said I didn't trust Kady," Audrey retorted, glaring back at Eloise, "but something stinks. Even if it was true, then why would she tell Kady and nobody else? The story doesn't add up."

"She told me not to tell anyone," Kady added. "But it doesn't make any sense to me either."

"And Kady might not be the only person she told," Eloise pointed out.

"It can't be right," muttered Nora. She had wrapped her arms around herself, and was rocking slightly in her chair, staring down at the table despondently. "I only just started at the hospital tent, and the surgeon himself told me I was doing a good job. They can't have decided yet."

"It doesn't mean anything, Nora," Gwendolyn said, though whether she was trying more to comfort her friend, or to simply reassure herself, wasn't entirely clear. "The Council doesn't make those decisions anyway, not really. It all depends on Gloria; she's the only one who really gets to decide, and the virtuous always rise, everyone knows that."

Eloise sighed and shook her head. She had long felt that Gwendolyn held far too much faith in Gloria, and not nearly enough suspicion toward the Privy Council. But this was not the moment for a religious debate, and she held her tongue. There was no point in further expanding the argument into uncharted territory; the atmosphere around the table was heated enough already.

"You've been awfully quiet, Bridget," Audrey suddenly chimed in. "If what Kady's telling us is true, you're the only one here who gets to continue. So congratulations, I guess. Shouldn't you be gloating, or dancing a jig or something?"

"Why would I be happy about any of this?" Bridget snapped back angrily. "I was having a good day, up until twenty minutes ago. I don't even *want* to be on the Council! And I think **everybody** should get to continue; including you, Audrey, believe it or not, even if I still want to kick you in the shins half the time. But if it's just me they're picking, then no thank you. Anybody wants my spot, you can have it."

"You don't want to be on the Council?" asked Gwen. The very idea of turning down a chance for a Council seat seemed almost impossible to her.

"It's a crooked, evil game," Bridget replied. "It's fun for a while, but it's *rigged*. We grow up playing by their rules, hoping that one day *we'll* be them, so we can sit there ourselves, getting old, cheating death, making someone else run the same risks we were lucky enough to survive. I don't want any part of it."

Everyone was surprised by this declaration, but the person most particularly startled might have been Eloise. She had never expected this sort of manifesto from Bridget, and found herself suddenly reconsidering her assessment of the clade's youngest member. The room was silent for several seconds.

"Neither do I," Eloise said eventually, nodding her agreement. "I don't want any part of it either."

"Well I do," said Nora, quietly. She was almost crying. "I want to grow up. I want to have children. I want to fall in love with somebody. I want to grow old. It's not fair."

Bridget, who was sitting next to Nora at the table, slid over to give her a comforting hug.

Nothing further was said that night about Kady's conversation with the warehouse keeper. Darkness had long since fully fallen outside, and their dinner was over, so one by one the girls eventually retreated to their cots.

Gwen left the table first. She detested confrontations of any kind, and the whole conversation had left her feeling both anxious and confused. But her faith in Gloria was unshakeable, and she felt certain, deep in her heart, that in the end everything would work out for the best.

Audrey and Bridget sat with Nora for a long time, comforting her at first, then trying to distract her by talking about other things.

"I'll have to take you with me harvesting," Audrey told her. "I'll take a bet that I can get you out of the rut you're stuck in. I can teach you a few things too, or else you can just ignore me like Eloise and Bridget do."

"No matter what else, we need to do something about those shoes," Bridget said, peeking under the table at Nora's dilapidated sneakers. "Cinderella wouldn't be caught dead at the royal ball wearing *those*."

The two of them kept at her like that, alternately needling and encouraging her, until she started to emerge from her despair. Bridget even got her to smile a little, by telling a string of well-worn dirty jokes, such as *Why does an oarsman keep both hands on his paddle?* and *How does an underkeeper get elevated?* and so on.

Eloise left the task of cheering up Nora to Bridget and Audrey, and quietly cleared away everyone's dinner things before getting undressed and climbing into bed. But even as she did so, she kept a watchful eye on Kady for the rest of the evening. She didn't doubt that everything Kady had told them was true, but she also strongly suspected that Kady hadn't revealed everything that the warehouse keeper had said.

As for Kady, she was too exhausted to worry about Eloise watching her, or anything else that the other girls were doing. She slipped out of her shirt and her jogging shorts, crawled into bed, rolled over to face the outside wall, and pulled her blanket up. Like everyone else in the clade, she would spend the night only half-asleep, and troubled with uneasy dreams.

Chapter 3:
The Invisible Pull of Routine

Over the next few days, very little more was said about Kady's meeting with the warehouse keeper. The pull of the familiar is a powerful thing, and there is comfort to be found in keeping to established routines, even if those routines might ultimately prove futile or worse. As troubling as the keeper's assertions might have been, none of the girls could be certain if any part of what she'd said was true; and even if it were *all* true, it wasn't clear what any of them could do about it. Faced with so many unknowns, they each simply slipped back into their usual day-to-day lives, continuing with their various chores and activities much as they always had before.

To be sure, however, there were some significant changes. Though Kady's story had unsettled everyone, no one was as visibly distressed as Nora. On the one hand, she seemed to become more focused and determined in her work than she ever had been before; but on the other hand she also seemed inconsolably downhearted, feeling hopeless not only about her chances of reaching the Lesser Council, but simply about *everything*. In response, the rest of the group began to make a concerted effort to boost her up in whatever ways they could. If nothing else, fixating on Nora's problems provided a convenient distraction from worrying about their own tenuous futures.

Bridget and Eloise, both of whom had ample harvesting credit saved up on account, went in together to buy Nora a good pair of running shoes, to replace her old ones. Both Kady and Gwen tried to engage her more often in conversation, telling her about their harvesting runs, or asking how her shifts at the hospital were going. But no one made more of an effort to encourage Nora than Audrey. Audrey was the oldest girl in the clade by almost a month, and she seemed determined to take the group's most unpolished member under her wing. Whenever Nora was not volunteering at the hospital tent, Audrey would take her along on harvesting runs, acting almost as if she were a mentor training an unlettered novice.

With Audrey and Nora working more often as a pair, the rest of the group, whether by accident or design, began to partner off as well.

Bridget and Eloise, who had rarely spent much time together before, seemed to find a sort of kinship in their shared disdain for the Privy Council, not to mention their mutual contempt for many of River Towne's long-established rules and procedures. However, their harvesting styles were nothing alike. Eloise took a methodical, strategic outlook, while Bridget preferred an aggressive, improvisational approach. The one similarity between them was that they had both been very successful, and consistently so, for quite a long time.

For her part, Kady began spending more time paired up with Gwendolyn than she ever had in the past. Gwen had a rare gift for ignoring or rationalizing away any stray thoughts that she might find disturbing, which made her a singularly undemanding companion. Kady took tremendous comfort in the fact that Gwen was unlikely to press her with any probing questions about her meeting with the warehouse keeper. And, by the same token, Kady found herself avoiding conversations with Eloise, who seemed to harbor some lingering suspicions about the finer details of Kady's story.

But the one person Kady most wanted to avoid was Bridget. Being urged to murder a friend is a difficult thing to come to grips with, especially when that suggestion comes out of the blue from an almost complete stranger in a position of such enormous authority and power. The whole situation was further complicated by the nagging question of whether or not the warehouse keeper really *was* her mother, but that was almost another issue entirely. Kady could tell herself not to believe any of the things that Helen had said, but no matter how reasonable her own arguments sounded, she was never quite able to set her uncertainty aside.

It was early in the afternoon, and Kady and Gwendolyn were harvesting together, deep inside the Middle Ring. They stopped walking, and took a long look at the surrounding terrain. There were some scattered trees, a few rosebushes and some other clusters of low bushy greenery here and there, but otherwise their view to either side was unobstructed for quite some distance. Far off to their left was a smallish yellow house which sat nestled into the side of a gently rising hill. To their right, and somewhat nearer at hand, was a much larger house with pale grey siding and a darkly shingled roof. A red brick wall ahead of them, which was partly covered with ivy, marked the edge of what they guessed might be an enclosed garden, or swimming pool, or patio.

"These look promising," Kady said, meaning the two houses. "What do you think?"

"I don't mind," Gwen replied, "but I think we'd have better luck further in."

Though Kady and Gwendolyn had been making their harvesting runs together for the past several days, they still had not entirely worked out the finer details of their collaboration. Even the simplest points of decision seemed to always come to a debate.

"We're an awfully long way in from the river already," Kady countered.

"*Further is more,*" Gwen said, needlessly reminding her companion of another of the laws of harvesting. Gwendolyn was fond of quoting the Glorious Laws. Kady considered it to be one of her less-endearing traits.

"The further in we go, the more likely we'll run into a fell," Kady pointed out.

"I wouldn't worry about that," said Gwendolyn. "We walked right past one a few minutes ago."

Kady could hardly believe her ears.

"We *what*!?!" she asked. "I never saw it! Why didn't you say anything?"

"It was asleep," Gwen replied with a shrug, "and I didn't want to bother you; I know how much you worry about that sort of thing."

"I can't believe you didn't tell me."

"I probably would have, if it had been awake, but it's really not that big of a deal."

"Not that big of a deal? Now it's between us and the river!" Kady exclaimed. She was nearly shouting with exasperation. "We'll have to go past it to get home!"

"All right, all right, I'm sorry I didn't point it out to you. But you can see why I didn't; I knew you'd get all worked up about it. It's nothing to worry about, really. We're still too young for the fells to take much interest in, and Gloria always protects us."

"Fells chase after harvesters our age all the time!"

"They might chase us," Gwen replied, skeptically, "but they don't try very hard. I can't think of anyone our age they've actually *caught*."

Kady scowled and stared down at her shoes, trying to keep her temper under control. Thoughts of the worker bee she and Eloise had seen cleaning Barbara's blood off the footpath flashed through her mind. She wanted nothing more than to grab Gwendolyn by the shoulders and shake some sense into her, but she knew there would be no point in it; Gwen was impervious to reason.

"Let's start here," Kady said with a huff. "We can go further in if we don't find anything, but I doubt these two houses have been searched in a while. We're well off the main trails, and pretty far in already."

Gwen was willing to accept this proposal, so the two girls separated, and spent the next half-hour or so, carefully searching every room of the two nearby houses. But they did not find anything there of value, nor did they have much luck afterwards, searching other houses further in towards the Central Forest. At the end of the day, tired and disappointed, they returned together to the enclave, empty-handed.

Chapter 4:
Separate Secrets

It was early morning, and as the ferry raft nudged lightly against the high curb of the river's inner bank, another cargo of harvesters clambered ashore. Bridget and Eloise were among them, and the two young women walked together, riverwise along the Promenade.

"I just realized I never said *thank you*," Eloise muttered, quietly.

"*You're welcome*," Bridget whispered back.

"Where did you find it?"

"Where did I find what?"

Eloise glanced over her shoulder, then stepped off the path. Bridget followed her, and they continued across the damp grass of the Circle Park until they were well out of earshot from the other harvesters. Eloise took a second look around, to make doubly certain they would not be overheard.

"The chocolate," she said, continuing with her question. "Don't be dense, I'm serious."

"Are you still thinking about that?" Bridget asked. "That was almost a week ago; how would I know that's what you meant? I'd forgotten all about it, and I can't read minds, least of all yours."

"I was just wondering where you found it," Eloise said. "I don't think I've ever even *seen* a chocolate bar loose in the wild like that. Do you think there's any more?"

"If only," Bridget said, shaking her head. "There was a whole cupboard full of snacks, and it was just thrown in there with everything else. But it was the only chocolate bar in the pile, believe me; I checked *really* carefully. I can show you the house, if you want, but it's way the hell in the other direction."

"No, no," Eloise replied, "I don't need to see the house; I was just curious."

Bridget nodded, and peered back over her shoulder toward the river. The other harvesters that had come across on the raft with them were already well out of sight. She gave Eloise an expectant look.

"So where are we going today, boss?"

"Am I in charge?"

"Better you than me," Bridget replied.

"Well all right then," said Eloise, "If that's how it is, we'll go this way."

If Bridget wanted her to make a plan for the day, then Eloise knew exactly where she wanted to go. She led her impulsive companion back to one of the main trails, then inward away from the river, until they reached the decorative gate at the edge of the Circle Park. There, the two girls left the paved trails entirely, and set off diagonally across the rolling landscape, working their way steadily riverwise and in toward the Central Forest.

"What's it like, working at the hospital?"

"It's boring, mostly," Nora admitted. "They have me wash a lot of things, and sort all the supplies. Half the time I feel like I'm either at the warehouse or on laundry detail."

"That's what Nursery was like, back when I was still doing that," Audrey said.

"I remember when you used to volunteer at the Nursery all the time," Nora said. "Why did you quit there?"

"I would have stayed on, if they'd had me teaching the kids or supervising games. But mostly I was stuck doing laundry. That got old fast."

"I think we have a better chance at the Council if we learn to do something useful. Anyone can harvest, or work the warehouse. That's why I'm at the hospital. I'd think learning to help run the Nursery would be a good thing."

"They don't have as many adults working in Nursery as they used to," Audrey explained. "Even when I was there, the ones they did have were getting older and older, and they weren't bringing many new ones in; they've been shifting most of the work to the volunteers for a long time now. So there were tons of harvesters hanging around, all of us trying to elbow each other out of the way, with fewer and fewer

Nursery spots coming open on the Council. It wasn't worth it. I figured I had a better chance if I just stayed a harvester."

"I think I've got a very good chance at the hospital, no matter what Kady says. The keeper himself told me I was doing a good job." Nora balled her hands into fists, as if she were trying to convince herself of her own determination.

"What's the keeper like?"

"He's *amazing*," Nora replied. "I got to help with a surgery the other day. He just sliced this woman open and pulled the baby right out. It was incredible."

"Eeeaaaahhhwwww...." said Audrey, grimacing. "That sounds horrible. Not for me, no thank you."

"Oh, but it wasn't!" Nora insisted. "They have to do that sometimes. It was the only way to get the baby out, and the woman survived and everything! I guess they don't always survive it, but this one did, and the baby did too."

"I'm sorry I asked," said Audrey, shuddering uncomfortably at the thought.

"The hospital keeper was so calm about it, too," Nora continued, oblivious to Audrey's discomfort. "He was so precise and careful. I want to be just like that."

"So... do you want to sleep with him?"

"What?!?"

"Do you?" Audrey asked again, pressing the question. "*That* might get you a seat on the Council, if creepy old men are your thing."

"That's awful!" Nora exclaimed.

"You probably never have, have you? Not with anyone?"

"Of course not!"

"I have."

Nora's jaw fell open.

"You didn't."

"I did. With one of the older boys. Several times."

"What if you'd gotten pregnant?"

"I didn't," Audrey replied with a shrug. "We were careful. We met up on harvesting runs for a while. It was fun while it lasted."

"Who was it?"

"Well I'm not telling *you*..." Audrey said. "It doesn't matter anyway. It was only a few weeks later the fells got him. I wasn't too broken up about it; I didn't like him that much, really. I saw it as a learning opportunity, that's all. But if he'd made the Council it might have been different. He could have been my way in."

"I can't believe you!"

"Nora my dear, you still have a lot of growing up to do," Audrey said. "The world is not a very friendly place really, and sometimes getting what you want means doing some questionable things, crossing boundaries, taking chances, going to extremes. You can't stay squeamish about this stuff, because sooner or later it all stops being a game."

Audrey shook her head slowly from side to side, and reached up to pat her astonished companion lightly on the cheek.

"What's the closest you've ever been to a fell?"

"I'm not sure," Eloise replied. "I try to keep them at arm's length, myself."

"I got within five meters of one the other day," Bridget said. "I snuck up on it."

"Did it see you?"

"It was dead asleep. I even threw a rock at it, and it didn't budge. I think I could have run up and kicked it, and it wouldn't have done anything. I almost wish I had. Next time, maybe."

"Next time it might wake up," Eloise pointed out.

"Well that's the challenge, isn't it," Bridget said with a grin. "It would hardly be worth it, otherwise. Everyone needs a goal."

Eloise was skeptical.

"Getting yourself killed isn't much of a goal," she said. "Dance with Death often enough, and sooner or later he steps on your toes; and he won't apologize when he does it."

"Dying isn't the goal," Bridget corrected her, "it's the cover charge. It's the price you pay to walk through the door and start dancing; just being born. Everyone pays up eventually, it's just a question of when."

"I'd like to hold off on dying for as long as I can," Eloise said, reasonably enough.

"I can never picture myself being old," Bridget replied. "I look at the Privy Council, or even some of the underkeepers, and try to see myself at their age, and I never can. I can't imagine what I would look like. I can't imagine what sort of person I'd have to become to be one of them, to reshape myself so I could be a part of their world. I'm not made for that, I don't think. I just can't picture it. I think I must die young. I don't see any other way out."

Eloise closed her eyes for a moment, and thought about this. The two girls continued on, walking in silence, for quite some time before either of them spoke again.

"Let's give off searching today," Eloise suggested, eventually. "I want to show you something."

"Show me what?"

"I think it's better if I just show you, rather than tell you about it first."

"Oooooooh...!" said Bridget, comically putting her hands against her cheeks. "Is it something secret? Is it scandalous? Is it a naughty naughty bad wicked *surprise*?"

"A little of all three, maybe," Eloise hinted, though in contrast to Bridget's playfulness, the look on her face was surprisingly serious.

Chapter 5:
Field of View

Eloise led Bridget to an enormous two and a half story home with pale brown siding. A massive faux wooden deck – which stood well above the gently sloping lawn – ran for the full length of the structure along the back, then around the corner and halfway up one of the sides.

"Here," Eloise said, "we'll go in this way."

"Big," Bridget noted.

Eloise climbed the steps to the deck, and entered the house through a pair of sliding glass doors. Bridget followed, and found herself standing in a large formal dining room. A sparkling cut glass chandelier hung above a long table made from some sort of darkly polished wood, with matching chairs surrounding. It was a gorgeous room, in an equally impressive house, but such things were commonplace in the city's Middle Ring, and Eloise and Bridget paused there for only a moment.

"Which way?" Bridget asked.

This house had long been a regular stop for Eloise, and she knew every corner of it. She could probably have walked through the place with her eyes closed, and without even stumbling or bumping into the furniture.

"If you mean which way to the kitchen and the pantry, they're through there," Eloise replied pointing to a broad open archway on their left. "But leave that for now. I want to show you the upstairs first; all the way up."

She led Bridget out of the dining room and down the main interior hallway to the front entrance, where a matched pair of staircases swept up either side of the foyer to a long gallery above. From there, a smaller staircase climbed to a short corridor with a single wooden door to either side.

"Both these doors go to bedrooms," Eloise said, "but this is the one we want."

Eloise opened the door to reveal a room which was small and fairly cramped, at least compared to the rooms the two girls had passed through on the ground floor. There was a single bed pushed up against the inside wall, and an upholstered easy chair sitting opposite the bed, beside a large dormer window. Eloise pulled the curtains aside, hoisted up the sash, set her hands on the sill and leaned her head out.

"Have a look," she said, waving for Bridget to come closer.

Standing at the sill, Bridget could see that this window looked out over a broad, gently sloping stretch of roof, and offered a remarkable view, far into the distance. She nodded her head appreciatively, but was not at all sure what exactly Eloise intended for her to see. Bridget had looked out from upper-story windows many times, but she didn't see how this particular window was notably different from those in hundreds of other houses.

Then, very much to Bridget's surprise, Eloise hopped up and sat herself down on the windowsill. She pulled her knees up, then swung her legs around and out through the open window, and finally she scooted herself carefully down onto the shingles below.

"Have you ever been on a roof before?" she asked, but Bridget was too startled to even answer. "Take it slow. Sit on the sill first, then bring your legs around. And hold onto the window frame until you get a feel for the slope."

Bridget very gingerly followed these instructions and a few moments later both girls were completely outside of the little bedroom, sitting on the roof just below the dormer window.

"This is insane..." Bridget muttered nervously. "My stomach is doing flips."

"Give yourself a minute to get used to it," Eloise said. "We can climb up to the crown in a bit. It's a nicer place to sit, and you'll feel more stable up there."

"If you fell from up here it would kill you," Bridget said. She was trying to put a brave face on, but her voice was trembling. "Even if it didn't kill you, it would *still* kill you. Just try getting back to the boat landing from here with a broken leg. You'd never make it, there's no way."

"Are you scared?" Eloise asked. "Really? I didn't think you were scared of anything. This can't be half as dangerous as kicking a sleeping fell."

"Kicking a sleeping fell would be *fun*... this isn't fun. I feel sick."

"Stop thinking about how high up we are," Eloise said, "and start thinking about what you can see from here. Look around. You can't get a view like this standing on the lawn, or just looking out a window. You can see *everything* from here. Look over this way. Do you see that unbroken line of trees? Do you see it? Do you know what that is? That's the Central Forest. It's still four or five kilometers off, but from here you can really see it. It's like a great brick wall, made out of trees. And back there is the way we came. We're not as far from the river as you might think, if you follow the paths straight out. Remember, we came here overland on a diagonal from the park."

Bridget looked out, and while she could appreciate the things Eloise was trying to show her, her sense of wonder was completely failing to overcome her sense of vertigo.

"It's fabulous," she said, trying to force her face into a smile. "Can we go back in now?"

Eloise kept Bridget out on the roof for another fifteen minutes or so, pointing out some interesting landmarks, a cluster of worker bees, and even a prowling fell which she spotted far off in the direction of the Central Forest. But try as she might to pique Bridget's curiosity, she could not convince her to climb the rest of the way up to the crown of the roof to see the full panoramic view.

Eventually Eloise relented, and helped her frightened companion to crawl back through the window and back into the little bedroom. Bridget promptly collapsed onto the bed, and spent the next few minutes staring at the ceiling, while Eloise tried to explain to her some of the insights she'd gained from spending so much of her time sitting on rooftops over the last several years.

"Fairhaven looks different up here," Eloise said. "You're no longer in the middle of everything; you're one step removed. You can see things in context, as part of a bigger picture. The way the bees move; it gives you a whole different perspective..."

Bridget didn't doubt that what Eloise was telling her was important, but all the same, she was at best only half listening.

Once Bridget had her nerves (and her stomach) back under control, the two girls returned to the ground floor. It was now early in the afternoon, and they had a long walk ahead of them, back to the boat landing. But they still took enough time to carefully search the house before leaving, and were delighted to find several dozen food packets that the delivery bees had stowed in the pantry.

"I'm not surprised," Eloise said, looking at the little treasure horde. "The bees seem to love this house almost as much as I do. They leave food here pretty regularly, I'd say every two to three weeks. I was here not very long ago, so this was just recently delivered. But now they won't be back for another week at least."

There was more food there than either of them could have carried alone, though not quite enough to completely stuff both their packs. Still, it was a good find, and with their satchels comfortably heavy, the two girls started back toward the river by the easiest route, along one of the larger trails.

But Eloise still had one more stop in mind, before returning to the enclave. Just outside the Circle Park, though still a long walk from the boat landing, she pulled Bridget off the path again, to visit one more house.

"I don't see why we need to get greedy," Bridget protested. "There's not going to be anything there, not this close to the river. You know somebody else will have gone through it already; the younger harvesters search these houses all the time, so they don't have to walk as far. And we've already got as much as we can carry anyway."

"We're not looking for more loot," Eloise explained. "I've got something else I want to show you."

Bridget crossed her arms and planted her feet.

"I am *not* going out on another roof."

"That's not what we're here for," Eloise said. "This is something else."

Still suspicious, Bridget reluctantly followed Eloise across a short stretch of lawn to a green two-story house that was flanked to either side by rows of flowering trees. The trees were not particularly tall, and looking above them, Bridget could easily see the house's dark, lightly-sloping roof. She felt herself shudder with apprehension.

This house was smaller than the one they'd visited earlier, but the furnishings were every bit as nice, if more compactly arranged. Bridget cautiously followed Eloise inside, but when she saw that she was once again headed straight for the staircase, Bridget put her foot down.

"No." she said firmly. "No more roofs."

"You should know that not all roofs are created equal," Eloise said. "Most of them are too hard to reach, or too steep to be safe. The roof of that other house is one of the best that I've found, and this one isn't bad, though it doesn't offer as a good a view. But we're not going to the roof, I promise. We're going to the attic."

Bridget was still skeptical, but she grudgingly followed Eloise up the stairs.

"What's so great about an attic?" Bridget asked, as they reached the second floor landing. "They're dark and empty. There's never anything in them."

"The *bees* never leave anything in them," Eloise said, knowingly, "but they're only empty, unless you put something there."

Eloise reached up and pulled on the dangling length of rope that lowered the tiny staircase, providing access to the rafters above the second floor. Bridget followed Eloise up, and found herself in the strangest attic she'd ever seen. Like most attics, it was poorly lit, illuminated only by a widely separated pair of overhead light fixtures. But *unlike* every other attic Bridget had ever visited, it was not empty.

Everywhere around the space – either hanging from the rafter joists, or sorted into little piles on the floor – were all manner of empty bottles, jugs and other containers. There were other things there as well: some lengths of hard resin tubing, neatly folded sheets of fabric, and a few coils of synthetic rope. Bridget was bewildered.

"What is this junk?" she asked. "Where did it all come from?"

"It's not junk," Eloise said. "I've been collecting it for years, storing it here, and also in a couple of other houses close to the river. It's all stuff I've managed to save."

"But why? And why is it still here? Why haven't the bees cleaned this mess up?"

"Because the bees don't care much about attics," Eloise replied. "And for that matter, the fells don't seem to care much about the rooftops, either. That's something I've learned. The bees almost *never* come up here, maybe once a year at most, probably because they don't expect anything to be here. I've left clothes, shoes, batteries, food packets – both full and empty – and the bees almost never touch them. *Almost* never, but there's always a chance. I lost my whole collection that way a few years ago, but I'm better onto how they operate now, and I'm more careful too. That's why I keep stuff in more than one house, so I won't lose everything if I get unlucky."

"But why?" Bridget asked again. "What would you want with all this stuff?"

"You can probably guess, if you think about it for a second," Eloise hinted.

Bridget looked around at the neatly sorted piles, trying to think of where she might have seen such things being used before.

"It's... all the sort of stuff they use to repair the raft with," she guessed, "isn't it?"

"You get a gold star," Eloise said. "I've been saving it to build a boat."

Bridget pursed her lips and frowned. Eloise waited, watching her companion expectantly, but Bridget said nothing more for quite some time. She turned away, and paced slowly around the attic for several minutes, looking over the collected heaps of refuse and trying to think this new revelation through.

"Why show me?" she asked, suddenly.

"It's too much," Eloise admitted. "Even if I could put it all together myself, I couldn't carry it. And I can't build it outside, or the bees would clean it up as garbage before I ever finished it. So I need help. And anyway, I wouldn't want to go just by myself."

"Go where?" Bridget asked. "Halfway to Stone Prairie? You can't get down the river past the rapids and the pumping stations anyway."

"That's the other reason I need help. If there were enough of us, we could carry a boat along the Promenade, go around the pumping station, and then put it in the river again on the other side. With our own boat we could cross the river and stay on the Periphery at night, so we wouldn't have to worry about the fells. We might even be able to get all the way around to Pleasant Gardens that way. We wouldn't have to stay in River Towne any more; we could just *go*."

"Have you showed this to anybody else?"

"Nobody," Eloise said.

"Not even Kady?" Bridget asked. "I'd have thought she'd be your first accomplice."

"I'm worried about Kady," Eloise said. "She's always tried to toe the line and follow the rules, and now she's seeing all that unravel. I think she's always known better, really, but still, that's got to be hard. And I don't think she told us everything about what the warehouse keeper said, either; I'm pretty sure there's more to that story than she first let on."

Bridget nodded in agreement with this observation.

"I wondered about that too."

Eloise looked down at the attic floor, and twisted the sole of her shoe against the hard wooden surface.

"I have to take a novice on a battery run tomorrow," she said. "It's terrible timing; they almost never make me do it. Anyway, Kady's been avoiding me, but I was thinking maybe she'd talk to you."

"I could partner up with her," Bridget agreed. "I'll see if I can ask her about it, if she'll give me the chance. I suppose if nothing else, I'd get her away from Gwendolyn for a while. It can be my good deed for the week."

Chapter 6:
A Nice Cup of Tea

"You wanted to see me, sir?" Nora asked. She was standing in the doorway to the hospital keeper's private cottage, feeling nervous and very out of place.

"Ah, Nora," the surgeon replied, looking back over his shoulder toward the door. "Your timing is excellent; I was just about to have a cup of tea."

Nora's timing, of course, had very little to do with anything. When she'd returned with Audrey to the enclave after their harvesting run, she'd been met at the boat landing by one of the hospital staff, who had immediately whisked her away and brought her here. Audrey had been left behind at the river's edge, scratching her head and thinking uncharitable thoughts about Nora and her relationship with the hospital keeper. There was nothing Nora could do about that now.

Although the surgeon's cottage was roughly the same size as the tent which housed Nora's clade, it *felt* considerably larger, as it was so much more nicely furnished and had to accommodate only one permanent resident. Against the right-hand wall was a heavy wooden workdesk, and in the far rear corner was a large bed with an adjacent nightstand. The surgeon was standing on the opposite side of the room, at the foodwall in his spacious kitchenette, fiddling with some cups and an electric kettle. Near the center of the room was a circular table covered by a white linen cloth, with four matching chairs around it. Resting on the table was a small rectangular box.

"Please," the surgeon continued, politely gesturing to the chairs tucked in at the table, "please sit down. Make yourself comfortable. I'll only be a moment."

Nora was anything but comfortable, but she was not about to refuse. She carefully pulled one of the chairs away from the table, and sat. The hospital keeper turned back to the foodwall, and poured a strange dark liquid from the kettle into an identical pair of turquoise cups.

Nora had seen cups of that sort before, in the houses of the Middle Ring, though she had never actually used one. They were so small, she wasn't even sure of what use they could possibly be. It had always seemed to her that you'd have to refill a cup that size almost constantly. A tumbler or a water bottle was more practical; it could hold so much more. But she also realized that there were many mysteries about such things that she did not yet fully understand.

"I suspect that you've never had tea before, have you," the old man said.

"No sir, never," Nora replied.

"Then you are in for a rare treat," he said.

Nora watched as the hospital keeper added a dram of honey to each cup, before gently stirring the contents with a spoon. Then, with a cup in each hand, he walked over to her.

"Tea," the surgeon explained, "is humanity's most civilized beverage. Everything else lies somewhere below it. Tea calms, and energizes. It comforts the spirit and focuses the mind. Some might even suggest that it confers a degree of enlightenment, or wisdom, though that effect may prove ultimately illusory. No matter. It is a rare privilege, and like all genuinely delightful things, it is so much, so very much better, when shared."

He set one of the cups down in front of his guest, then eased himself comfortably into the chair on the opposite side of the little table. Nora looked down at the delicate blue cup resting on the tablecloth in front of her, and watched the gently wafting wisps of vapor rising from its surface. It seemed so tranquil; she found it almost mesmerizing.

The surgeon smiled inwardly. He delighted in having a captive audience, particularly one unlikely to question or contradict his philosophical ramblings. He was enjoying himself immensely.

"Drink it very slowly," he advised her. "If you find it too hot, then take your spoon and stir it until it cools. But not too much... be sure to savor it while it is still warm."

Nora took a tentative sip. The tea was robustly warm, but not unpleasantly hot. She found that drinking it was a strange sensation, somewhere between what she normally thought of as drinking, and eating. It was somehow both at once, and neither. It was, just as the surgeon had described it to her, staggeringly, almost unbearably pleasant.

"If you've only just returned from harvesting," the old man said, "you'll want something to eat as well; you must be hungry."

He opened the box that was sitting at the center of the table and held it out to her.

"Blueberry muffins," he said. "I'm sure you *have* had these before, they're quite ordinary, but I think you'll find they go very well with the tea. Have one, please."

Nora was indeed very hungry, and though the blueberry muffins were small, they looked wonderful. She nodded her appreciation, and took one, as instructed. She nibbled gingerly at the edge, not wanting to appear greedy, or careless. The muffin was delicious, and she took another bite, followed by a second sip of tea. It was so nice, and without even meaning to, she closed her eyes and took a long, slow breath.

"Well..." the surgeon said. "Now that I have your attention, I wanted to discuss with you a bit about your future."

Nora felt her heart leap. She opened her eyes and tried not to look startled.

"Yes, sir?" she said.

"You've done well at the hospital so far," he continued. "You've demonstrated some aptitude, and so I have decided to make some small changes to your duty assignments. I would like to afford you the opportunity for more practical experience with hospital procedures. Anyone can wash the bedsheets."

"Thank you," Nora said.

"Understand," he cautioned her, "this is not a promotion, per se. You will still be very much an apprentice volunteer. But along with greater responsibility, you will also find, I think, will come better opportunities to learn, and possibly, in time, advance."

"Thank you," she said again.

Nora was trying not to let her hopes run away with her sense of reason. It sounded as if this shift in her status was an encouraging step in the right direction, but clearly her prospects for reaching the Lesser Council were still very much in doubt.

"You've only been at the hospital for a few months, and so while you may have seen some of what we can do here, you've still yet to see, perhaps, some of the things we *can't* do. We can't save everyone, and there are times when it's unwise for us to even try; do you understand me?"

"I'm not sure, sir."

"People do *die* in the hospital. You may not have encountered that yet, first-hand, but it comes with the work. We can only do so much, and we have to decide where our priorities lie. You'll have to harden yourself to those facts, if you plan to stay on here."

"Yes sir... thank you, sir..." she replied cautiously.

"Children, of course, are our most valuable resource, and we must do all that we can to help them thrive, if possible. Children become harvesters after all, and harvesters are always needed. But harvesters soon become adults, and speaking generally, adults we have in abundance – too great an abundance, in fact, apart from those few of us who go on to supervise. And that is why we will ever only elevate so few."

"I see."

The surgeon paused to take a sip of tea, and to help himself to one of the blueberry muffins from the box. Nora followed his lead, taking a second bite of muffin which was somewhat larger than her first, and following that with another, more substantial sip of her tea. The warmth of it really was such a delicious sensation; Nora felt herself almost starting to relax. It was so pleasant. So comforting. So reassuring.

"Do you like the other members of your clade?"

Nora looked up at the surgeon again. It was an odd question, and she did not know quite how to answer it.

"They've... all been very nice to me."

"Not everyone can make the Council," he reminded her, "and at present some of the others in your clade are, unfortunately, positioned ahead of you. That is only a preliminary status, of course, but if you're hoping to achieve things for yourself, then you will eventually have to surpass them, and leave them behind. It's important that you understand that. You're only just now coming to the age where the fells will begin to take a real interest in you, but your work as a harvester will become only more precarious, as time passes. Are you willing to place your own interests above those of others? Even your friends? How will you move yourself forward? You may want to give these matters some thought, if you haven't already."

The old man took a long sip of his tea, but said nothing more.

Nora's mind was racing.

"Yes, sir," she replied eventually. "I will most certainly do that. Thank you, sir. I very much appreciate your advice. Thank you."

Chapter 7:
Sunset

"Sunset, Fairhaven."

Gloria spoke, and the twilight continued to fade. The shadows deepened underneath the trees, and across the lawns, and everywhere else around the flower gardens and the empty houses of the Middle Ring. The great city dome had already begun to change, first from the shining blue of daylight to indigo, and then to a wavering horizon of crimson, far beneath the ever-deepening grey. Soon, as the sky slipped the rest of the way to darkness, the tiny images of scattered stars would begin to appear.

All along the Promenade, the streetlamps began to faintly glow, but those lamps were like fireflies pitted against the encroaching night: pale mimics of starlight, arrayed in a sinuous line, less than a stone's throw from the slowly moving river. There was no one left in the Circle Park now. No one was walking along the winding pathways. The last boat had already returned to River Towne.

There, out beyond the river, many lesser lights were now faintly shining through the open doors and windows of the clades and the tents and the other structures. The last of the harvesters were finishing their business at the Warehouse Exchange, and the rest had already begun their evening meals. Inside the District, adults were gathering together in groups, or pairing off for the evening, depending upon their good fortune, or mutual interest, or whim. In a few more hours, every part of the enclave would again be still, or nearly so.

Deep inside the Central Forest, delivery bees by the dozens began to emerge from the hidden warehouses of the city's industrial core. Dispatched at Gloria's unspoken command, they would distribute the myriad manufactured goods, fresh from the factories, to the houses of Fairhaven's Middle Ring, their individual destinations randomly assigned by arcane algorithms.

And there were, of course, the fells. They prowled in greater numbers by night, venturing further from the forest than once they ever had, dispersing themselves throughout the city. As the terminal agents of Gloria's will, they were assassins forever on call, guided by an impenetrable alchemy of chance, opportunity, and circumstance, all balanced digitally against an intricate array of carefully weighted criteria. The cold complexity of their semi-random behavior was as dispassionate as algebra.

If any harvesters were somehow left on the inner side of the river – whether forced to remain there by a turn of fortune, or perhaps by personal error – they were hiding themselves away now, in the hopes that they could survive until morning. The Middle Ring was a deeply inhospitable realm, in the darkness.

Helen the warehouse keeper sat at her desk and waited. She had already eaten her dinner; she had already turned off her registry tablet; she'd already had her last cup of tea.

It was late in the evening, or perhaps it was now already early in the morning. Helen was not certain which. She had not looked at her clock for some time. All she knew for certain was that Gloria had long since announced the sunset, and outside the Administration Office, the streets and alleys of the enclave were quiet and dark. Almost everyone else in River Towne was fast asleep.

There was a knock on the door. She looked up, but did not answer it. She waited. A few moments later there was a second knock, and then the knob turned and the door swung silently inward.

"It's time."

The warehouse keeper nodded. Her chair rolled smoothly backwards as she pushed herself away from the desk and stood up. She took a deep breath, straightened her blouse, and ran her fingers unconsciously through her greying hair.

The young men standing to either side of the door waited, as she made her way across the room. Once she had stepped through, and was standing outside in the darkness, one of them reached back and pulled the door closed behind her.

The latch clicked.

The trio made their way silently through the winding paths of the District, until they had left the last of the huts and tents behind. Then they turned toward the river, and continued on.

Some time later, they arrived at the boat landing. Not the landing for the harvesters, but a second one, seldom used, that lay far down the river from the first, and far from the enclave proper. Others were there and waiting, with escorts of their own. Helen was the last to arrive.

The raft here was more stable, heavier and more solidly built than the one for the harvesters. Helen climbed onto it with the others. The boatman pushed the craft out into the stream with his oar, and silently rowed his human cargo to the opposite shore. Of the boatman's six passengers, Helen was the oldest. That was a victory, of sorts, but she did not feel triumphant.

The boat nudged gently against the high concrete curb of the river's inner bank, and one by one the passengers carefully climbed ashore. After walking for so many years on the concrete surface of the enclave, the soft grass of the Circle Park felt unfamiliar to them, underfoot.

Once his unwanted cargo had fully debarked, the boatman pushed off again, and returned with his craft to the Periphery. No one among the now-departed spoke. There was nothing to be said. Having crossed the river, they were no longer River Towne's concern, and it was no longer theirs.

One by one, the exiled slowly turned their backs to the enclave, walking riverwise along the Promenade. This was the beginning of their long journey to Pleasant Gardens, but that destination was far, far on the opposite side of the Middle Ring, and they were no longer young. Each of them knew very well that there was little chance they would ever arrive there.

Chapter 8:
Thoughts of Murder

Kady started her morning by heading counter-river around the Promenade, until she was well beyond the Training Grounds. Then she left the Circle Park and cut overland, wandering more or less in the direction of the Central Forest. She did not have a clear plan for the day, or any particular destination in mind. She only wanted to get as far from the boat landing as possible.

With Gwendolyn assigned to mentoring duty, this was the first time in nearly a week that Kady had gone alone on a harvesting run, and she was glad to have some time entirely to herself. Partnering with Gwen had been a convenient way to avoid Eloise and the other girls, but the one thing Kady couldn't do when she was with Gwendolyn was *think*. And, as the week had dragged on, she'd come to realize that some time alone for thinking was what she wanted most.

Her conversation with the warehouse keeper had left her feeling lost and angry and bewildered and sad, all at once. And however many days later, her emotions were still tangled in knots. She no longer even knew what she was feeling.

As she walked, she looked around at the beautiful lawns and the widely scattered houses of the Middle Ring, as if they were a strange and foreign landscape. Kady felt severed from it all – adrift, disconnected, somehow out of place – a remote observer in her own world, rather than a participant. She did not have the words to express her pervading sense of separation.

People used to *live* in these houses, before the exodus, or so she had always been told. It seemed impossible, almost. The houses were so huge, and spacious, and beautiful; in the enclaves such structures might have housed thirty harvesters or more. But supposedly each was only home, at most, to a single pair of adults and their offspring. It was even whispered that some people would live in such places all alone.

No one lived alone in River Towne, aside perhaps from the members of the Privy Council. And no one knew who their parents had been either, or at least no one was supposed to. Any other arrangement had always seemed to Kady so terribly strange. And yet, every bit of it had happened, provided that the stories were true. But that was many years ago, and those people were no longer here. They had passed on, and of them and all that had once mattered to them, their empty houses were all that remained.

Kady had never actually seen death, first-hand. She had been aware of it, always. It was an ever-present danger, of course, but mostly as an idea, distant and remote. The dead were invisible; no one close to her had died. Even other harvesters, or adults she had known back when she was in Nursery, they had simply stopped being there one day, and someone else had stepped into their place. Nothing more than that was ever said. Their absence was scarcely noticed, if noticed at all, and was soon forgotten.

But Barbara's death was not a mere abstraction. Kady had hardly even known her, but one fine morning, just over a week ago, Barbara was alive, and an hour later she was not. Now she too had become invisible, like so many others. But for Kady her absence was different; it was tangible, unmistakable, impossible to ignore. She and Eloise had seen the worker bee, cleaning the last traces of Barbara away. Kady had spoken with someone who had known her well, and now missed her. Barbara's death had left a palpable void which Kady could not casually disregard.

Had she really been her sister? Was that why Barbara's death felt so different from all the others? Or was it rather because Kady had found her blood on the trail, because she had seen the visible proof that Barbara's life had ended, exactly then and exactly there? Or did those elusive uncertainties lurking at the core of Kady's own emotions even matter all that much? She did not know.

As the old woman had told it, Kady faced only two alternatives: she could murder Bridget and live, or she could continue on just as she always had – only now without hope – and eventually die. But it had since occurred to Kady that she could simply kill *herself*, instead of Bridget. The more she thought about that possibility, the more reasonable it began to seem. If nothing else, suicide could offer her a third option, and one that was arguably no worse than the other two. She wondered if Barbara might have found herself in similar circumstances, caught somewhere between the same impossible choices.

Kady stopped beside one of the little streams that rushed inward toward the Central Forest. She reached into it, and watched the water flowing swiftly around her fingers. Downstream, the water seemed entirely undisturbed, as if she had never touched it. No sign remained of the momentary turbulence her hand had caused. A meter from where she now stood, there was no visible sign that she had even come that way; that she had ever been there at all.

She squatted down, and scooped a fistful of pebbles out from the creekbed. Then she sat at the side of the stream, gazing at the water and the wet little stones in her two cupped hands for a long, long time.

"What'cha thinkin' about?"

Kady leapt to her feet at the sound of the voice, and whirled around to see a familiar figure standing just a few meters away.

"Bridget!?!... What are you doing here?"

"Spying on you, what else?"

Kady crossed her arms defensively, as her anger and embarrassment snapped into gear.

"Piss off!" she shouted. "Go away! Leave me alone!"

"It wasn't exactly difficult," Bridget continued, ignoring Kady's outburst. "You haven't been paying much attention to anything but yourself all morning. If I was a fell, you'd have been chopped up into tiny little bacon bits half an hour ago."

"How did you even find me?"

"I didn't *find* you," Bridget explained. "I got up early, and came over on the first boat. Then I waited till you came across, and followed you."

Kady's mouth fell open.

"I can't believe you," she said.

"Well you wouldn't come harvesting with me when I asked, so what else was I supposed to do? You almost hurt my feelings, but not really. You've been avoiding everybody but Gwen, so I couldn't take it *too* personally, but all the same."

"What do you want?"

"I just wanna talk. You've been moody and weird ever since you got bushwhacked by the warehouse keeper, so I was wondering what the deal is."

Kady scowled and looked down at the damp grass beside the stream. Despite her best efforts, here she was, deep in the Middle Ring, alone with Bridget. The one thing she'd wanted most to avoid; it was already happening, and she couldn't stop it. She felt caught and cornered and furious all at once, but she also felt like an idiot. And Bridget was right, of course.

"It's pretty obvious you didn't tell us everything," Bridget continued, once it became clear that Kady would say nothing more without additional prodding. "Eloise thought so too, but you've been avoiding us both, so now I'm asking."

"Asking what?" Kady said, squatting back down and washing her little handful of stones in the water. She wasn't going to make this easy.

"For one thing, why did the warehouse keeper pick *you*?"

Kady gave no reply, but Bridget was not about to let the question slide, even if that meant filling in both sides of the conversation herself.

"I mean, why not pick somebody like Audrey or Nora, or better yet *Gwen*?" she continued. "That's who I'd have picked. I mean, Gwen believes everything already, right? So if the keeper was just looking to scare us all into working harder, why would she pick you to tell and not *her*?"

Kady gave up. It was pointless. She wasn't any good at deception, and she didn't really want to deceive Bridget anyway. She dropped the pebbles back into the stream, rinsed her hands clean, and shook the water off.

"She told me I was her daughter," she said, glancing over at Bridget again. "And Barbara was my sister, and her other children were already dead. She said I was the last of the lot. That's why, or at least that's what she told me."

"Wow..." Bridget replied. She hadn't known what sort of answer to expect, but whatever she'd been expecting, this wasn't it. "That would make some kind of sense, I guess. But how would she even know? I mean, nobody's supposed to know that stuff, are they?"

"I don't have any idea," Kady said. "Maybe because of who she is; I don't know. She told me she knew."

Bridget was nodding her head very slowly, considering this new information.

"Ok," she said eventually, "that's a pretty weird thing to find out. But it seems like you could have told us that right from the start, couldn't you? I mean, just to shut up Audrey if nothing else. Why keep it a secret?"

"Because that wasn't all she said," Kady admitted, looking back down at the water. "She also told me I should murder you."

Still sitting in the grass, Kady curled herself up the rest of the way into a little ball, and tucked her knees under her chin. Reaching out with her right hand, she dipped her fingers back into the stream.

"She said it was the only way I could make the Council; the only way for me to continue. I don't know if it's true. I'm sorry. But that's what she told me to do."

There was a long silence.

"I see..." said Bridget, quietly.

For several seconds more, neither girl moved or spoke. The only sound was the cold water, flowing around Kady's hand and bubbling over the pebbles and stones.

"Are you going to?"

"No." Kady said, shaking her head.

She looked up at Bridget again.

"Would you hate me, if I told you I almost wanted to?"

"Not really," Bridget replied. She dropped down beside the stream, a few meters away from Kady, and ran her own fingers through the water, just as Kady had done. "I think about killing me all the time."

"Don't make jokes about it."

"I'm not joking," Bridget said, looking up again. The expression on her face was entirely serious. "I really do think about it, and more often than you might be willing to believe. I have for years, but I always talk myself out of it; or rather, I always have so far. I don't know."

Bridget shrugged, and looked down at the water again. Kady frowned and bit her lip.

"I was thinking about that too, just now," she admitted. "Killing myself, I mean."

"Don't," Bridget said, firmly. "Eloise has a better idea."

"What idea?"

"I think it might be better if I let her tell you about it," Bridget replied, rising slowly to her feet again. "She can explain it better than I can. Now stand up and give me a hug. It's a long walk home."

Kady drew back as Bridget stepped toward her, but she allowed the hug, reluctantly at first, then all at once she gave in to it. A moment later she started crying. Bridget simply stood there and held on to her for a long, long time.

Chapter 9:
Further is More

Audrey and Nora passed through one of the large decorative gates that marked the inner boundary of the Circle Park, and continued down the smoothly paved trail, walking inward toward the Central Forest.

Audrey had been dying to hear all about Nora's private encounter with the hospital keeper the night before, and once she was sure they were safely away from the raft and the other harvesters, she wasted no time in bringing the subject up.

"So you still haven't told me what the surgeon was after," she said.

Audrey was trying to sound casual, but she couldn't help giving Nora a sly sideways glance as she asked the question.

"He just wanted to talk with me," Nora insisted. "He wasn't after anything. He didn't try to do anything. I know what you're thinking, but he was very nice. We had tea and blueberry muffins, and that was all."

"Tea?" Audrey asked.

"Yes, tea," Nora repeated. "Have you ever had that before? I never had."

"I haven't either," said Audrey. "What was it like?"

"I don't even know," Nora admitted. "It was almost like drinking water, but it was warm, and the warm seemed to go right through me, all the way to my toes. And it had a flavor. I can't even describe it. I felt so... I don't know... It felt wonderful. I felt safe and smart and delicate and powerful all at once... It was so nice. I can't even tell you how nice it was."

"If I didn't know better," Audrey said, "I'd think you were talking about sex. Are you *sure* he didn't seduce you?"

"Stop it, Audrey!" Nora snapped back. "Don't tease me about it. Don't **ever** tease me about it. It was wonderful. Don't ruin it for me."

Audrey was genuinely startled. It wasn't at all like Nora to stand up for herself.

"Sorry..." she replied.

"It was wonderful," Nora repeated, more to herself than to Audrey. "I want that for myself. I want to feel like that always. It was wonderful."

The two girls walked on in silence for a long time. Audrey's mind was awhirl with new questions, but she held back from asking them. Nora was clearly in an odd sort of mood, and Audrey was curious about where things might go if she just bided her time, and waited.

"He gave me some advice," Nora said, eventually. "He told me I was doing well. He's giving me a promotion at the hospital... well, not a promotion really. But I'm going to get to do some more important things. I'm going to be learning more. He thinks I have potential. He said that, or something like that. It's all sort of a blur, to be honest. I can't really remember exactly what he said. It doesn't matter. He said I was doing well. I still have a chance there, I think. Why else would he...? Anyway... it was very nice."

"I'll try not to tease you about it then," Audrey said, but she did not say what she was really thinking. It sounded very much to her as if, whether she realized it or not, Nora had fallen in love.

The two girls continued along that footpath toward the Central Forest for more than an hour, before abandoning the paved trail to cut overland across the lawns. Ordinarily, Nora was maddeningly cautious with her harvesting runs, and reluctant to venture any significant distance from the river. But today she seemed intent on going as far in toward the Central Forest as possible. Having spent much of the past week trying to coax her companion to be more adventurous, Audrey couldn't help but find Nora's newfound boldness a little unsettling. But although Audrey kept expecting her to object, or complain about how far they were walking, Nora never did.

Eventually, they came upon a nicely spacious water garden which lay nestled in at the bottom of a low, open patch of lawn. There, Audrey finally decided it was time to call a halt.

"This is good; we've come far enough," she said.

"I can keep going," said Nora.

"Well this is a switch," Audrey remarked, with her hands on her hips. "I usually have to drag you by your hair to even get you past the Training Grounds."

"I'm trying to do a better job," Nora replied, a little defensively. "And they're always telling us *Further is more.*"

"Now you sound like Gwendolyn," Audrey said with a playful smirk. "But seriously, have you ever even *been* this far in from the river before? I'm guessing you haven't."

"Probably not," Nora admitted. "At least I don't think so. But I really can keep going. I'm not tired, and finally having a good pair of shoes makes things easier."

Audrey shook her head.

"These two look promising," she said, gesturing toward the houses that stood up the grassy slopes to either side of the water garden. "And sooner or later we have to leave off walking and start searching, or there's no point."

"Fine," said Nora, folding her long arms together and nodding sharply. "Whatever you think is best."

"You take that one," Audrey said, pointing to the house on their left. "Just make a quick check, and meet me back here in fifteen minutes. And stay alert," she added, sternly. "We need to be a lot more careful about the fells here than we have been. This close to the forest, we'll probably come across one sooner or later, so stay on your toes."

The two girls separated, and made their way up to the two houses. Audrey glanced back over her shoulder just in time to see Nora disappearing in through the screen door of the house on the opposite side.

Once inside the house she'd chosen for herself, Audrey carefully explored the ground floor, but she found little there that was of any real interest. The cupboards and the icebox were completely empty, and there was nothing useful in the closets or the pantry, either. In one of the smaller rooms she found a roll-top writing desk with some pens and stationery, but nothing particularly noteworthy or unusual. Disappointed, but not entirely surprised, she continued up the staircase to the second floor.

In one of the upstairs bedrooms, she found a stack of new bedsheets and pillows. They were nice, but much too bulky to easily carry, and not really valuable enough to justify hauling them all the way back to the boat landing. But in one of the bathrooms she had better success. Resting on the vanity was a small stack of toiletries: several bars of soap, a tube of toothpaste, some cosmetics, a first aid kit with adhesive bandages and other supplies, and a large package of sanitary napkins.

None of these things were terribly valuable – the cosmetics were completely worthless – and there was not enough there to fill her backpack even halfway. But most of the items were small and light, and well worth the trouble of carrying back to the enclave, assuming she and Nora didn't eventually find something better. At the very least, it was loot enough to ensure that their harvesting run today would not come up completely empty.

With her little treasure trove securely stashed away in her pack, Audrey hurried back to the water garden, where she half expected to find Nora already waiting for her. But Nora had not yet returned, so she sat down on one of the little garden benches to wait.

She waited for a long time, but still, Nora did not appear.

"Did she get *lost*?" Audrey asked aloud. No one answered.

Nora was often painfully slow with her harvesting, that was a given; but this was slow even for Nora, and Audrey was getting restless. But even more than that, she was also starting to get *worried*. They were awfully far in from the river, but still, surely Nora couldn't have turned an ankle, or somehow run into a fell, could she?

Audrey had almost decided to go looking for her, when Nora finally appeared. She leaned out of the screen door just far enough to wave for Audrey to come up.

"There you are!" Audrey called out, with some relief. "What happened to you?"

"Nothing *happened*," Nora said, "I found something! Come up and see."

Nora ducked back into the house, leaving Audrey to scramble up the slope after her. Audrey pulled open the screen door, and found herself staring in at a little utility room that was just off the kitchen. She continued on into the main part of the house, and finally found Nora in the family room, standing at the foot of the stairs.

"What in Gloria's name are you *wearing*?" Audrey asked.

Now that she had caught up to her, Audrey could see that Nora was not wearing the same clothes she'd had on before. She was totally barefoot, and dressed in a teal blue jogging suit with dark red pinstripes running down the seams. It was a nice enough outfit, or it would have been, but it was obviously too small for her. It fit well enough around Nora's slender hips and shoulders, but the pantlegs were much too short, and the sleeves of the hoodie reached only about halfway from her elbows to her wrists.

"It's my new outfit," Nora said, spinning around. "Isn't it great?"

Audrey was aghast.

"You look ridiculous!" she said. "It's way too small for you."

"I like it like this," Nora replied, firmly. "It's comfortable."

"Where are your shoes?"

"They're upstairs," Nora said. "You caught me while I was still changing."

"This is what you wanted to show me?" Audrey asked. "What did you find?"

"Clothes!" Nora replied. "There's a huge pile of them upstairs."

"Clothes aren't worth anything!"

"These are!" Nora insisted. "You've got to come look."

Exasperated, Audrey stood there fuming, and trying to decide what to do. Searching through a worthless pile of clothes was obviously going to be a complete waste of her time, but so was trying to argue with Nora about it.

Heaving a sigh of frustration, Audrey decided to give up the fight. If Nora wanted to slog all the way back to the boat landing with a heavy satchel packed full of worthless junk, then fine, let it be a lesson to her. Audrey already had almost half a load of better stuff in her own pack anyway, so in terms of the final tally, it would end up being no skin off of her nose either way.

"All right, fine..." Audrey said, reluctantly giving in. "Where exactly is this pile of spectacular clothes?"

"Upstairs," Nora said, biting her lower lip with excitement. She turned and bounced her way up the staircase, with Audrey trudging along behind her.

Nora led Audrey down a short hallway toward what appeared to be a master bedroom. She turned the knob and pushed the door open, then waited for Audrey to go in first.

The room was large, and elegant, and an almost total wreck. There were certainly a lot of clothes there, but they were scattered everywhere: hanging off the closet door, draped over a chest of drawers, heaped onto an upholstered easy chair, or even just tossed carelessly onto the floor. They were not even remotely organized into anything resembling an ordered pile.

"What a mess!" Audrey said, looking around the room and shaking her head in disbelief. "What were you *thinking*!? It would take us an hour just to fold these."

Dumbfounded, Audrey scanned the room, trying to see what might have led her companion to think that there was anything special about this particular collection of garments. But there was nothing. As far as Audrey could see, these were simply ordinary, everyday clothes, easily found almost anywhere. There was nothing uncommon or remarkable, or even any outfits in smaller sizes for children. The whole thing was a total bust.

Still standing in the doorway behind her, Nora reached over and turned off the lightswitch. The room fell suddenly dim, though not fully dark. Daylight filtered in softly through the curtained windows, throwing strange shadows across the furniture, and the scattered clothes, and the two young women.

It was an odd thing for Nora to do.

Audrey turned to look at her. She could see that Nora had closed the door, and was clutching something small and shiny in her right hand. Audrey couldn't tell for certain what it was. It looked to her like a long piece of silverware.

"What is that?" she asked.

"It's a scalpel," Nora replied. "I borrowed it from the hospital tent."

She held the gleaming surgical implement up to the light from the window, so that Audrey could see it more clearly.

"Here..." she said, stepping closer, "let me show you how it works."

Nora stripped off the bloody clothes that she'd borrowed, and discarded them onto the bed. Then she went to the shower in one of the upstairs bathrooms, and washed the rest of the blood from her face and hands and feet, and out of her hair. Once that was finished, she dried herself off with a bath towel and pulled on her old clothes again, as well as the pair of shoes that Bridget and Eloise had bought for her. Then she walked back down the stairs, and carefully exited the house by way of the screen door.

The daylight outside seemed to her almost unbearably bright. She ran a plastic comb through her hair, pulling it back and away from her face. Her hair was still damp, but she was not concerned; it would be dry again by the time she reached the boat landing.

She had left Audrey lying on the carpeted floor of the upstairs master bedroom. Nora knew that the bees would find her there eventually, and clean up the mess. They would dispose of everything, including the bloody clothes, and would leave the room once again as good as new.

As distant as the house was from the river, it was unlikely that any other harvesters would come to search it again any time soon. And even if by chance someone did, and discovered Audrey's body, they would simply assume that she had been cornered there and killed, unluckily, by a fell.

- End of Book Two -

Book Three:
Chapter 1:
Fracture

A ball bearing fractured.

The fragments soon became caught in the rotation, grinding against the unbroken bearings to either side, until the wheel they had all once been a part of ceased to turn. The conveyor belt that had run upon that wheel now dragged roughly across it, and the motor which powered that conveyor strained under the added load.

A sensor tripped. Something was overheated. Power to the motor was automatically cut, and the conveyor belt lurched to a standstill. The packaging machinery which had relied on that belt for raw materials paused, to wait for repairs.

But those repairs would never come. There were no replacement parts available. The factory which had once made those parts had itself ceased to function, long long ago. The last of the components which that factory had once created had already been used, to repair other conveyors, in other facilities.

The production line stopped.

Soon, the worker bees would begin to trickle in, one by one, to scavenge parts from the newly-broken machinery. They would use those parts, in due time, to effect repairs upon other conveyors, in other factories, as they too inevitably wore down.

This facility, however, could no longer be repaired. It would instead be shuttered, and patiently gutted by the worker bees until only the hollow outer shell of the building itself remained. The various foodstuffs which once had been sent here for processing would now be redirected to other factories, where possible.

But those other factories, hobbled by their own failing machinery, were already operating at the marginal limits of their production capacity. There was nowhere else for the excess food to go. Without packaging, it could not be routed to the warehouses for storage. It would never be delivered by the worker bees to the elegant homes of the Middle Ring. All of that food would have to be discarded, as unusable waste.

With the shuttering of this one industrial facility, Fairhaven's total production capacity – and by the same token its maximum sustainable human population – would further decline. Very soon, Gloria would begin to make the necessary adjustments to compensate.

Equilibrium would have to be restored.

Chapter 2:
Michael

Michael wasn't sure what he had heard.

Still half-asleep, he looked around the room at the darkness. Gloria hadn't even announced the sunrise yet, and no one else seemed to be up. A pale grey haze of early morning light was seeping into the room through the narrow gaps around the sides of the cloth window covers.

In the next cot down, he could see Ethan's hulking frame only as a shadowy lump, bundled up underneath his blankets. Kyle was still in his own cot on the opposite side of the room, and fast asleep as well. The other three cots were all empty. Aside from himself, Ethan and Kyle were the only harvesters left of those that had once been part of this clade.

Seeing nothing out of the ordinary, Michael closed his eyes and rolled over, to try and get a few more minutes of sleep. But then he heard it again: a faint tapping sound. This time he was awake enough to realize that someone was lightly knocking on the sliding panel that served as his housing unit's front door.

Wondering who could possibly be roaming about the enclave at this early hour, Michael dragged himself out of bed, pulled on a pair of jogging shorts, and stumbled through the darkness to answer the door. He was more than surprised to see Kady standing there in the faint pre-dawn glow. Another girl was with her, whom he did not recognize.

"Michael?..." Kady asked. "Sorry to wake you. This is my friend Eloise. Can you come to the Commons? We need to talk."

As they had hoped, there was no one else in the Commons at that early hour. Eloise bought breakfast for everyone, while Kady selected a table near the center of the open area, where she and Eloise could easily keep a watch in all directions. They wanted to keep this conversation as private as possible.

"We've got a lot to talk about," Kady began, "but we may not have time for everything right now, so we'll start at the end and work backwards from there, if that's all right with you."

"OK..." said Michael cautiously, as he started in on his little plate of pancakes and syrup. "I'm all ears."

"When you and I had breakfast before, that one time," Kady continued, "you told me then that you and Barbara had talked about leaving River Towne, maybe trying to make your way around the Circle Park, to try and get to one of the other enclaves. Isn't that right?"

"I guess so..."

"We're building a boat," Eloise said, jumping in. "We're going to take it down the river, maybe to Stone Prairie, or maybe even all the way to Pleasant Gardens if we can."

"We wondered if you'd like to come with us," Kady said. "I thought you might, so we're asking. You're invited."

Michael put his fork down, and leaned slowly back in his chair. He looked from Kady to Eloise and back to Kady again, more than half expecting that he was being played for some sort of joke. But the expressions on the two girls' faces were surprisingly earnest.

"Why?" he asked, eventually.

"Why what?" Kady asked in return.

"Why *everything*?" He said. "Why invite me? Why even *tell* me? We hardly even know each other."

"Kady and I hardly know *anybody* outside of our own clade," Eloise pointed out, "not well enough to trust them, anyway. Half the harvesters in the enclave would squeal on their best friend if they thought it'd get them a bonus, or a leg up on making the Council. There's really no one else we can ask, and we're going to need help. There aren't enough of us to do it all by ourselves. Even if our whole clade agreed to come along, and that's doubtful, we'd still do better with at least one or two more, I think. I've always imagined a boat would work best with six people, or maybe seven."

"Eloise has been planning for this for a long time," said Kady. "She's been collecting floats and tubing and bits of rope for ages. Everything we need is already stashed on the other side of the river. All there is left to do is build the boat and go."

Michael furrowed his brow and looked down at his breakfast, which was rapidly getting cold. He cut off a bit of pancake with his fork, then slowly twirled it in the dregs of the syrup. Kady and Eloise had hardly touched their own food. They waited.

"If you're serious about this," Michael said eventually, looking up at the two girls again, "then yeah, maybe. Maybe I'm interested. It's not like there's anything good happening for me here; I can't really think of any good reasons to say 'no'. But honestly, I don't know how much help I'd be. I don't know the first thing about building a boat. Who you really need is Ethan."

"Who's Ethan?"

"He's in my clade. He knows all about the rafts, and how they're put together. He was apprenticing to be an oarsman for a while."

"That would be very helpful," said Eloise. "Can you ask him? Do you think he'd do it?"

"No," Michael said, shaking his head. "I'm just thinking out loud. Sorry, but no. He'd never do it. Ethan still thinks he's gonna get elevated. Maybe he will, I dunno. He quit the raft so he could focus on being a goon for the Privy Council – an *escort*, as they like to call them. If he ever found out about this conversation he'd report us all and beat my face in. Actually, he'd probably beat my face in first, then report us all later. Now that I really think about it, inviting Ethan would be a very very bad idea."

Michael took another bite of pancake, set his fork down very gently on his plate, and looked up at the slowly brightening dome, high above them. Eloise frowned with disappointment, and looked down at her own uneaten breakfast. No one said anything for several seconds, but Kady was not yet ready to give up on the idea.

"All right then," she asked, "do you know anyone *else* who might help?"

"Maybe Kyle," Michael said, half-heartedly. "It's hard to say what he'd do if I asked him. He's kind of a chump, really, but for that matter so am I, so I'm hardly one to talk. But he's better friends with Ethan than he is with me, so I don't know... maybe not a good idea either."

"We can't even be sure about everybody in our own clade," Eloise admitted. "There's three of us for sure; the other two we haven't asked yet. Nora's determined to make it with the hospital, but she's been pretty down lately. We're planning to ask her eventually, but there's no telling what she's likely to do. She might say yes, she might say no."

"Then there's Gwendolyn..." said Kady. "Gwen's a serious believer, so maybe not her either. We're pretty sure she'll say no, and we might not even ask her. I don't think she'd report us to anybody, but then again..."

"We have to ask her," Eloise countered, "but we'll wait until the last minute before we do. I don't think we can chance telling her about it ahead of time."

"You said you've been planning this for a while though, right?" Michael asked, looking at Eloise. "So why now, exactly?"

"A lot's happened since the last time we talked," Kady said. "The fells caught one of the girls in our clade."

"We'd never lost anyone like that before," Eloise added. "The fells never even seemed to take much notice of us, up until a few months ago."

"Losing Audrey that way sort of shook everyone up," said Kady, "as if we weren't shaken up enough already. These last couple of weeks have been absolutely brutal. Nora's taken it especially hard. She and Audrey had been making all their harvesting runs together, and I think she blames herself that Audrey didn't come back."

"And there's one more thing on top of all that," Eloise noted darkly. "It was only about a week before, when Kady had a very, *very* strange encounter with one of the members of the Privy Council."

Eloise looked over at Kady expectantly, and Kady nodded. She took a deep breath, and began to carefully recount the story of her meeting with Helen the warehouse keeper. This time, she made a point of not leaving out any important details. She told Michael everything the keeper had said, or at least everything she could remember, including being told to murder Bridget, as well as the part about herself and Barbara being the old woman's daughters. Eloise contributed very little to the story, but would occasionally add a supportive comment, or offer a word or two of clarification, as needed. Michael listened intently, and even after Kady had finished he sat there, quietly thinking, for a long time before he said anything more.

"I can take a guess at why she might have wanted to tell you all that," he said eventually. "It might have been true, or maybe she was just trying to throw a wrench into the works. But either way, she probably knew her time was up."

"What do you mean?" Kady asked.

"Well you said *she*, so I'm assuming this was the old keeper?"

Kady and Eloise exchanged a quick look. Neither of them had any idea what Michael was talking about.

"The *old* keeper?" Eloise repeated.

"The old keeper's gone," Michael said. "A new one took over; I think he was her assistant. I'm not surprised you haven't heard about it yet; this was just in the last few days. The Council likes to downplay this sort of thing, but word gets around pretty fast, among the older harvesters at least. You pay more attention to what's going on upstairs, I guess, after you've lost a few friends."

"But what do you mean, she's *gone*?"

"Seats open up on the Lesser Council all the time," Michael explained. "The Privy Council doesn't turn over nearly as much, but it works about the same. Every once in a while, they rotate the older ones out and dump them across the river. That's just how they do it; they can't keep on feeding everybody forever. I guess they made a pretty big switch a few days ago, but I only heard about it yesterday, myself. Still, like I said, word gets around; they can't keep something like that secret for long. In another week, everybody'll know, and a week after that most of the enclave will have forgotten about it already. By then it'll be back to business as usual, I expect."

"So how did *you* hear about it?"

"I know one of the underkeepers, sort of," Michael replied. "He's younger than me, actually, by a week or two. He used to be in my clade, so we were pretty close, once upon a time. It was about a year ago he got elevated. We don't talk much anymore, but I try to get into his line at the tent when I can, if he's on duty, and occasionally he'll let something drop. He mentioned that there was a new keeper, so I asked him about it. He got kinda antsy after that and wouldn't tell me much, but he did say that the old keeper was gone to Pleasant Gardens, whatever that means. I really don't know any more than that, but that's what he was willing to tell me, so now you know as much about it as I do."

Kady and Eloise exchanged a long look, and slowly nodded their understanding. Some things made more sense to them now, while others did not. But before either they or Michael could say anything more, Gloria's gentle voice was heard, above and all around them.

"Sunrise, Fairhaven."

Michael glanced up toward the dome, high above them. Despite the official announcement of the sunrise, the artificial sky was not perceptibly brighter than it had been a few moments before. He looked over at the two girls sitting across the table from him.

"OK," he said with a nod. "I'm in."

Chapter 3:
Flowers and Boulders

"It's not your fault," Gwendolyn said. She kneeled down onto the seat of the park bench, and leaned over the back to look at the bed of violets that were blooming on the opposite side. "Audrey was the oldest, so of course the fells went after her first. That's just how things work."

Still standing on the path behind her, Nora frowned, but made no reply. She looked down at her feet, and twisted the toe of her right shoe against the pavement. It made a quiet grinding sound.

"And Audrey wasn't very nice anyway," Gwen continued, "so it was to be expected. Gloria's always watching, and she pays attention to that sort of thing. Everyone knows that only the virtuous rise. You'll just have to let it go, because there's nothing you could have done anyway. I'm sure Audrey brought it on herself."

Gwendolyn twirled around on the bench, and gave her companion a long questioning look. Gwen was clearly expecting some sort of reply, but Nora didn't feel like she had anything much to say.

"Which way are we heading?" she asked, eventually.

Nora really wasn't much concerned about where she and Gwen were going to do their harvesting for the day. Her mind was elsewhere, and more than anything she was simply trying to change the subject. Walking was easier than talking, but more to the point, she was sick to death of being consoled about Audrey. It was exhausting. Nora found it hard enough looking sad all the time; being constantly reassured about it wasn't making things easier. It certainly didn't make her feel any better, either.

The two girls made their way counter-river along the Promenade for more than an hour, before turning in toward the Central Forest. Gwen continued to talk almost non-stop about the wonders of Gloria, and the flowers, and the beautiful landscape, and all sorts of other meaningless things. Nora pretended to listen, nodding occasionally, or offering a brief reply if Gwendolyn seemed to expect one. But that was rare. Gwen didn't seem to mind carrying the bulk of the conversation herself, and Nora was content to let her.

Nora's thoughts were on Audrey, and the surgeon, and warm cups of tea, and mounds of unwashed laundry, and the gleaming scalpel in her backpack. The scalpel was safely tucked away there, its sharp blade snug and secure inside its protective resin sheath, ready and waiting for a time when it might be needed again.

Between all the days she'd spent partnering with Audrey, and her increasing duties at the hospital tent, Nora hadn't been out harvesting with any of the other girls in a very long while. She'd almost forgotten how tedious Gwen's sermons could be. Nora found Gwendolyn bearable, even likeable, in small doses. But anything more than that began to feel like a chore, and Nora already had more than enough chores weighing her down, thank you very much.

They came to a scattered cluster of large boulders, which had been arranged decoratively across an otherwise empty patch of grass. Gwen stopped walking, and suggested that she and Nora should climb up onto them, to get a better view. The idea was plainly ridiculous. There was nothing around them for fifty meters in any direction, other than neatly trimmed grass. They would not be able to see any further standing on top of those boulders than they could already see, standing on the footpath.

But Nora did not object, and so the two girls scrambled up to the top of the largest boulder and sat there for a while, back to back, silently gazing out at all the sights they could just as easily have seen before, had they only paused to look.

Staring out over the empty lawn, it occurred to Nora that she had grown so accustomed to Audrey's constant guidance and badgering that she now found herself almost missing her. Almost. But she also felt certain that she would do it all over again in a heartbeat, if she had the chance. In fact, Nora fully intended to do it all over again, once the right opportunity presented itself.

But Nora was not going to kill Gwendolyn, she'd decided, at least not today. It was too soon, and she wasn't yet ready to take that second bold leap. She knew, however, that sooner or later she would have to, if she ever wanted to earn a spot for herself on the Lesser Council, and live. All in good time, though. All in good time.

There was a part of her that hated that, but her resolve was firm.

Chapter 4:
The Boys

Michael slipped a dinner packet into the hotmaker in his clade's kitchenette, and waited. At the table behind him, Kyle and Ethan had already started into their own evening meals.

Michael wasn't sure if his two friends knew about his early morning encounter with Kady and Eloise, but he suspected that they probably did. Word travelled quickly among the older harvesters, and anyone passing the Commons would have seen the three of them sitting there, even if they wouldn't have been able to overhear what was being said.

The hotmaker beeped quietly, and Michael removed his dinner. Carefully carrying the freshly heated packet by the corners, he set it down on the table, pulled up a chair, and began eating straight away. The question of whether or not Kyle and Ethan were aware of his breakfast meeting at the Commons was soon answered.

"So... I guess you were up early," said Ethan. "Missed you at breakfast."

"I kind of thought I heard a girl talking outside the front door, first thing this morning," Kyle said. "*Sounded* like a girl, anyway, but I was still half asleep, and I sure wasn't gonna crawl out of bed in the dark just to do a double check."

Kyle took a bite of his grilled cheese sandwich and gave Michael a sly grin.

"Don't tell us you got another girlfriend," Ethan asked, taking a bite of his own dinner. "Again already? Council won't like that."

"It was two girls, actually," Michael said. He prodded at his dinner with a fork, and didn't even bother to look up.

"*Two girls*?" Kyle said with a laugh. "Come on buddy, learn to share."

"What can you say," Ethan added, "the dude moves fast."

"It's not half as exciting as you guys are hoping for," Michael said.

"So who was it, anyway?"

Michael finally looked up, though only briefly, before returning to his meal.

"It was the two girls that found Barbara, if you really want to know," he said. Then he raised his head for a moment, and made deliberate eye contact with Kyle. "The ones who gave you the backpack."

"Oh..." Kyle replied. "Yeah, well... thanks for that. Sorry; I just wondered."

Kyle seemed to take the hint, and quietly returned his full attention to his sandwich, but Ethan wasn't ready to let Michael off the hook just yet.

"So what did they want, anyway?"

Michael frowned, and took another bite of his dinner before replying.

"The fells got one of the girls in their clade. They were pretty upset about it. First time for them, I guess."

"Why would they want to talk to *you*?"

"Why not me?" Michael replied with a shrug. "I'd already talked to the one girl about Barbara, so maybe she thought I'd be a sympathetic ear. Maybe she was right."

"Hmppph..." Ethan muttered, skeptically. He took another bite of his dinner, but it was easy to see that his curiosity was not yet satisfied.

"And they asked me about the warehouse keeper," Michael added, talking with his mouth half full of roasted potatoes. "They thought I might know something."

"So what'd you tell'em?"

"What do you think I told them?... Yes, there's a new warehouse keeper."

"Now wait a second..." Ethan asked, "you mean you actually *told* them?"

"They'd already heard about it," Michael said, impatiently. "How long do you think something like that stays quiet? Half the enclave probably knows by now, so don't go pretending it's a big deal."

As if to emphasize that this was his final word on the matter, Michael took a long drink from his water bottle, then wiped the corner of his mouth on his shirt sleeve, before taking another bite of potatoes.

This was not, of course, an entirely complete and accurate account of Michael's breakfast conversation with Eloise and Kady, but he hoped it would be close enough to the truth to sound plausible. Ethan still looked skeptical, but he let the matter drop, for the moment at least, and the three young men all turned their attentions back to eating.

Chapter 5:
Jeremy

Deep in the bowels of the enclave, far from the river, a warm amber light was shining out from the open doorway of a sturdy little cottage which sat near the furthest limits of the District, nestled in amidst the larger tents along the city's impenetrable outer wall. Standing just inside that entry door, Jeremy the warehouse keeper folded his arms, and took a long critical look at the Administration Office.

It was all very familiar – he'd been inside that hut many times before – and yet the room seemed somehow less welcoming, now that it was his. He frowned.

The place still felt as if it belonged to the old keeper. The desk was in the same spot where she'd always sat. The table was right there, where she'd always eaten. The bed was in the same corner where she'd always slept.

Helen had been the warehouse keeper for a very long time, since even before Jeremy had first been elevated to the Lesser Council some sixteen years ago. She had, in fact, been in that position for nearly as long as Jeremy could remember. He could vaguely recall the peculiar, stuffy old man who had served as warehouse keeper during most of his childhood, but he could not immediately think of that man's name.

It did not matter; it was Jeremy's position now. This was his office, and his place of residence. He had successfully risen to the summit of the enclave's adult bureaucracy. Now, he was in charge.

The furniture would have to be rearranged. The old linens had already been thrown out and replaced, and new curtains were hanging at the windows, but that was not enough. He would soon empty the foodwall in the kitchenette, and fill it again with things he liked. He could easily do that now. The full inventory of the enclave's warehouse was at his disposal, within reason.

He would choose a different set of chairs for the dining table, and put a different office chair behind the desk. The desk itself, however, he would keep. There was no practical way for him to obtain another one that would be even half as nice. There was nothing like that desk in the warehouse, and sending harvesters specially to obtain one from the Middle Ring would be too much to ask, so early in his tenure. He had learned, over time, the value of measured discretion.

But he had also learned the value of authority: how to pursue it, how to serve it, and how to ultimately attain it. Now, he was ready to turn his full attention toward how most effectively to wield it.

And yet, even in that he was constrained. Jeremy had long known that the enclave's food stocks were gradually declining, but the former keeper had never conveyed to him the full magnitude of the situation. Now that he had complete access to the warehouse records, Jeremy could clearly see that *everything* was in decline. Food stocks were much too low, and though some small measures had been taken to improve the fundamental ratio of supply versus consumption, the problem seemed to be accelerating.

River Towne could no longer support its current population.

Jeremy had checked his own calculations a dozen times, and the numbers did not lie. Harvesters were not retrieving sufficient food. And this was not a temporary anomaly that would eventually average itself out over time; this was a persistent downward trend, reaching back for many years.

Even though there were fewer children now in the enclave's Nursery than there had ever been, and even though the size of the Lesser Council had been quietly decreased, those reductions were not enough to fully compensate for the gradually dwindling supply. At the current rate of decline, River Towne would completely exhaust its food reserves within two to three years, and possibly even sooner than that.

These extended projections left Jeremy time enough, perhaps, to make some further adjustments. But more substantial measures would require the approval of the full Privy Council, which might not be easily accomplished. Nor could any major changes be concealed from the Lesser Council or the senior harvesters. Further reducing the size of either council would risk serious pushback, and even those changes that had already been put in place had left some of the harvesters grumbling. Sooner or later, something would have to give.

But not tonight.

Tonight, Jeremy planned to quietly celebrate his new position as a member of the Privy Council, with a friend. He would ask Ruth, he thought, or perhaps Marjorie, if Ruth was otherwise engaged.

It was a simple fact that most of the men on the two councils chose to seek the attentions of younger women. But Jeremy much preferred the company of women close to his own age. A few extra lines and curves did not bother him in the least. He found older women more physically attractive, more interesting in conversation, and far more comfortable with themselves than most younger women tended to be. It was an added bonus that older women were also generally inclined to be far more patient with Jeremy's own occasional romantic limitations.

He was not, after all, quite so young as he once had been.

Chapter 6:
A Boat in the Attic

Eloise's improbable plan to build a raft and leave River Towne had never been anything more than her own private fantasy, until that one afternoon when she finally revealed the idea to Bridget. But now that Kady and Michael had both agreed to help, what was at first only a personal scheme had now become a full-fledged conspiracy, and the four young harvesters soon set to work at turning their common dream into a reality.

Building the boat turned out to be every bit as difficult as the conspirators had feared, but they soon discovered that it was also surprisingly fun. The difficulty and the enjoyment could both be attributed to the fact that none of them had ever done anything quite like this before. In short, they had no idea what the hell they were doing.

Though they'd all been required to work for the enclave, almost every single day since they'd first been elevated from Nursery, that work had always been directed toward scavenging things already in their finished forms. None of them had ever really *built* anything before. They'd never taken an item intended for one purpose, and then transformed it into something which was useful in a capacity unrelated to its previous function. Actually building something, and figuring out how to make it all work, was an entirely new endeavor for them; and with every success, every discovery, and every refinement to their design, their confidence and their sense of accomplishment grew.

There is a peculiar satisfaction in the manufacture of things. The act of creating something tangible and useful confers a curious sort of delight, which some people may go their whole lives without ever fully experiencing. It is a sensation not only of personal achievement, but also of a burgeoning independence, a more robust version of the thrill felt by children building a secret clubhouse, without the help or knowledge or permission of any adult.

To be sure, not everything they tried to do worked exactly as they expected. It is quite one thing to *decide* to build a boat, and quite another thing to actually do it. Though they had all crossed the river on the ferry raft thousands of times, none of them had ever paid much attention to how the thing had actually been put together. They'd simply taken for granted that it would float, and that the oarsman would row everyone safely across the river to the opposite shore. The raft *worked*. That was all they really knew about it, and all they had ever felt any need to know, until now.

Their first challenge was how to build a suitable framework. Eloise and Michael spent several days raiding the basements of houses far in from the river, sabotaging their plumbing systems, and spiriting away the longest sections of pipe. But even after they'd been acquired, those pipes still could not be used until they were cut to the necessary sizes. Kady spent more than one patient afternoon, whittling away with a kitchen knife, to break those pipes into shorter pieces. How to secure those pieces together became Bridget's problem, and she spent many hours on her reading tablet, learning about scaffolds, and ropes, and all sorts of various and complicated knots.

A second stumbling point was the fact that the bottles and other containers which Eloise had collected were too small to attach directly onto the raft's framework. The group solved this dilemma by bundling the bottles inside pillowcases, and lashing those to the underside of the frame instead.

To keep the worker bees from dismantling the raft and hauling the pieces away, the conspirators had to build it in sections, which they hid separately in various attics. Had the boat been constructed as a single unit, it would have been too heavy for them to easily carry, and too large to get out through a narrow doorway. Once those sections were complete, the group moved everything to a large house with a swimming pool, where they could put their design to the test.

Stability proved to be a serious challenge, as more than once their prototype collapsed or capsized, sending one or another of them plunging into the pool. With every setback however, the group's determination only grew. They would talk through what had gone wrong, make their adjustments and repairs, and then try again.

Once the raft was sufficiently stable, the last remaining step was to obtain some hardfoam panels to give it a solid floor. Such panels were used to make the walls of houses, so they were easily found almost anywhere in the Middle Ring. Removing them, however, would have required skills and tools that the conspirators did not have. Instead, they scavenged the panels from their own enclave. As River Towne's population had declined considerably over the years, many old housing units now stood empty. Working in the pre-dawn gloom, Eloise and Bridget had little difficulty removing the front door from one of those long-abandoned huts, and since Bridget was easily the strongest swimmer in the group, she volunteered to push the panel across the river. She set out just as Gloria was announcing the sunrise.

The crossing turned out to be far, far more difficult than any of them had anticipated. The panel floated, but only barely, and it was too large and clumsy to be easily handled by a single person. Bridget managed to wrestle it across the river, but by the time she reached the Circle Park she was utterly spent, out of breath and completely exhausted.

Fortunately, the group had planned for this well in advance. Kady had already crossed the river on the morning's first raft, and was waiting at the inner bank with Bridget's socks and shoes and a dry change of clothes. Since it was still early in the morning, few other harvesters had yet made the crossing, and so the two girls were able to get the panel out of the river and safely into a nearby house without being seen. The next day, they repeated the process, retrieving a second door panel with no less difficulty, but with similar success.

With the raft finally complete – or as complete as was possible before the final assembly – all that remained was to invite the rest of their friends, and then... simply pack up and go.

Chapter 7:
Revelations

"What can I do for you, Ethan?"

"It's about one of the other boys in my clade, sir..."

Jeremy waited for the tall young man to continue, but having already hesitated, Ethan seemed reluctant to go on, as if he were still waiting for permission.

"Is there some sort of problem?"

"He's been meeting, sir," Ethan began again, "secretly with some girls from another clade."

Jeremy nodded his head slowly, with patient understanding. He almost smiled.

"Does he need condoms?" the warehouse keeper asked.

"Sir?"

"I can get some for you."

"No sir!" the younger man replied. He was clearly shocked.

"Don't be so alarmist about it, Ethan," the keeper continued. "There are rules and there is reality. Young people will do what young people do. It can be useful to discourage such things, officially at least, but there's no use in trying to stop these encounters altogether, not so long as they're kept discreet, and I'm not really interested in trying."

"That's not what I meant, sir," Ethan said. "They've been building a boat, like the ferry raft. I think they're planning to leave the enclave."

"Oh really?..." said Jeremy, raising an eyebrow. "Now that *is* interesting."

"I don't think I can stop them by myself, sir. I'll need more help for that."

"And why would you want to stop them?" the keeper asked.

Ethan blinked, and stared blankly at the older man. He was bewildered by the question, and momentarily speechless.

"What would be the point?" Jeremy continued. "If some of the younger harvesters were thinking of wandering off, then it would be well worth the trouble, stopping them from doing something foolish. But if someone your age wants to leave the enclave, then what is there for us to do about it? How could the Council stop them?"

"I thought that with some of the other escorts, I could..."

Jeremy shook his head.

"The primary purpose of the escorts is to make certain that the oldest members of the two councils cross the river at their appointed times, once it's been decided that they are no longer useful. Your job is to make people *leave* the enclave, not to keep them here. Harvesters may imagine that you're there to enforce the rules, and that is a useful fiction, but it's not really your function."

"But if harvesters are running away...?"

"The older clades are only useful to the enclave so long as they're actively working as harvesters," the keeper explained, "and bringing in more food than they're eating. It's not as if we can imprison them here. If we did that, they'd have to be fed, and guarded, and then they wouldn't be bringing back any food. There would be no profit to that at all. And killing them would be even more absurd, since letting them go would have the same effect, requiring no effort from anyone and drawing far less attention."

"But sir..." Ethan protested. However, he really didn't have an argument, and his voice trailed off.

"The older harvesters are always free to go, Ethan. It's just that most of them never realize that, and we certainly don't go around advertising it. But there's no good way to prevent them leaving, and little benefit if we could. Anything more draconian would be impractical, to put it politely."

Ethan stood there for a few moments, trying to make sense of things. This wasn't at all the reaction he'd expected. He had thought that reporting Michael and his girlfriends (as Ethan thought of them) would be a real feather in his cap, and possibly even give him a leg up on making the Lesser Council. But it was now obvious that he'd been sorely mistaken.

"I see, sir..." he said eventually, though it wasn't entirely true. "That was my mistake then. I'm sorry to have taken your time."

Ethan shifted his weight slightly backwards, expecting to be dismissed, but he did not turn toward the door, as he had not yet been given leave to go. All the same, he was feeling confused and stupid, and increasingly nervous, and he wanted nothing more than to escape from this uncomfortable conversation as quickly as possible.

The new warehouse keeper, however, was not yet finished talking.

"There is one other reason not to bother trying to keep your friend or anyone else from leaving River Towne," he said.

"Yes sir?..." Ethan replied. At this point, he wasn't about to question anything the keeper said to him. His only goal was to avoid embarrassing himself any more than he already had.

"There's nothing out there."

"There's nothing... *where*?

"I'll give you a little history lesson," Jeremy said. "River Towne used to be larger... *all* of the enclaves were larger, once upon a time, and there was regular commerce between them. In fact, in the years shortly after the exodus, there were outposts all along the Periphery, further up and down the river. Harvesters would go live there for a few days or even weeks at a time, so they could more easily reach those portions of the Middle Ring closer to the pumping stations. The territories overlapped, and harvesters from River Towne would sometimes encounter harvesters from Stone Prairie or Open Grove, in those border regions. I'm even given to understand that on occasion harvesters would be exchanged among enclaves for various reasons. Those outposts, however, were abandoned long ago, many years before you or I were born."

"The reason for that," the keeper continued, is that food supplies throughout Fairhaven have been steadily falling, at least since the time of the exodus, and probably from well before then. The enclaves contracted, reducing their populations as food became more scarce. For some reason, River Towne fared better than the others, but all the outposts were abandoned decades ago, and I suppose the other enclaves as well. The bees stopped delivering food there – only Gloria knows why – but we've not heard news from outside our own borders for years. So knowing this, do you imagine that your friend and his companions will be welcome anywhere outside of River Towne? Even if the other enclaves still exist, they'll be shadows of their former selves, and facing the same problems we're facing here, or more likely worse."

"But if there's been no contact," Ethan objected, in spite of himself, "then you really don't know, do you? And what about Pleasant Gardens? Food *grows* there, on trees and out of the ground, doesn't it? People must still be living there; they must be. And isn't that where all of us have to go to, eventually, when it's time for us to leave River Towne?"

The warehouse keeper shook his head slowly from side to side, and gave a long, weary sigh.

"You're a very shallow young man, Ethan, which happens to make you useful. The Privy Council values your service, and as long as you remain useful, there will still be a place for you among the escorts."

Ethan wasn't at all sure how he should take this, as a reassurance or as an insult. He suspected that it had been intended as a little of both.

"What should I do then, sir, about those harvesters that are making the boat?"

"Do what you like," the older man replied, raising his palms in a gesture of resignation. "I would suggest turning the situation to your own advantage, if you can. Use their fear against them, or as a bargaining chip. Harass them, intimidate them, steal their food and return the packets to the warehouse for credit, if you are so inclined. But in the end, do not try to keep them here. There's no point in it. There is nothing to be gained, for you or for any of us, by forcing them to stay. River Towne needs to reduce its population anyway, because there simply isn't enough food to go around. Losing *younger* harvesters would be something of a blow to the enclave, but harvesters your age would likely soon be lost to the fells anyway."

The warehouse keeper looked Ethan squarely in the eye, but found he could not quite guess what the younger man was thinking – a fact which did not bother him in the least.

"From a practical perspective," the keeper continued, "it is just as well for the malcontents to leave."

Chapter 8:
A Sense of Adventure

Bridget darted off the Promenade, and ran across the damp grass of the Circle Park, toward the river. Stopping at the edge of the water, she stepped up onto the high curb that served as the river's inner bank, and held out her arms. Carefully balancing herself there above the water to one side and the grass of the park to the other, she began walking riverwise atop that narrow ridge of concrete.

Nora was not impressed.

"Don't blame me if you fall in," she said.

"I won't fall in," Bridget replied, "and if I do, I can swim. It's not as if I've never gotten wet before, and this isn't much harder than walking, really."

"Then why bother?"

"Because it's fun?" Bridget suggested. "Because the Promenade is boring? Because I felt like it? I don't know... why are you still on the path?"

"Because I don't like walking in soggy shoes," Nora replied, reasonably enough. She folded her long arms together, and gave Bridget a disapproving frown.

"Oh all right," Bridget said, giving in and hopping back down onto the grass. "What's happened to your sense of adventure?"

"I never really had one to begin with," Nora said with a shrug. "Don't blame me, blame Gloria."

Bridget grinned deviously.

"I can hardly believe you said that. Gwendolyn would have an apoplexy."

Bridget reluctantly returned to the path, and the two girls walked side by side along the Promenade for quite some time without saying anything more. Neither of them was in much of a hurry. As far as Nora knew, this was just going to be an ordinary harvesting run, and so she was perfectly content to let Bridget take the lead, within reason, in choosing their eventual destination for the day. As for Bridget, she was more interested in getting a sense of Nora's state of mind than she was with doing any harvesting.

"You seem older," Bridget remarked. "I'm not sure why. It's not something I can put my finger on, but you do."

"Do I?" Nora asked. She frowned, and seemed to think about this for a few moments. "Maybe I am," she admitted, eventually. "I feel older, I guess. Maybe I have a better idea about what I want now. I don't know. Maybe I've found myself."

"Ooooh..." Bridget replied. "Maybe I should do that too!"

She stopped dead in the middle of the path, turned her back to the river, and with her feet planted widely apart called out:

"Briiidggggetttt!! Wheeerrrre aaaarrre youuuu?!?........"

She waited for a few seconds, then turned back to look at Nora, and shrugged.

"Not there, I guess," she said. "I dunno. I swear, I can't keep track of her."

Nora looked down at her feet, slowly shaking her head.

"You're a dorf," she muttered.

"Yeah, well..." Bridget replied, "so I am."

"And shouting like that isn't safe," Nora added, looking up. "Seriously, don't shout; it makes me nervous."

"OK..." said Bridget. "Ooooh! Can I sing?"

"Not that either."

"I don't know any good songs anyway."

"Don't be dumb."

"Too late."

They walked on again in silence for a long while after that.

Nora found herself reflecting on how different it was to be out with Bridget instead of with Audrey or Gwen. Gwendolyn was rarely comfortable with silence, and usually had a topic for casual conversation ready at a moment's notice. Nora's conversations with Audrey, on the other hand, had rarely been casual. Audrey would often keep silent for long stretches, then suddenly launch into an extended lecture, or worse, something more akin to an interrogation.

Bridget, however, was all over the map. Conversations with her could be deadly serious one moment, and utterly trivial the next. It made her infectiously likable, even if at times she seemed determined to drive everyone around her insane.

"Have you ever had tea?" Nora asked suddenly, and very much out of the blue.

"That's a drink, isn't it?" said Bridget. "No, I don't think so."

"I have," Nora said. "The surgeon shared some with me the other day. I guess it's something very rare."

"Rare like chocolate?"

"I don't know. It was a little like having chocolate, I guess, but it was nothing like chocolate, really. It's hard to describe. I can hardly remember what it tasted like; what I remember is how it *felt*. It was so simple, and yet... It was how he served it, I think, as much as anything. He elevated it somehow, and made it more than it would have been. I don't know. I've been trying to figure it out, but I honestly can't. I don't know why it was so good, but it just was."

Bridget scrunched her face into a peculiar sort of frown, and thought about this for a while.

"Do you think you're going to make it at the hospital?" she asked. "Be elevated, I mean. Do you really think they'll keep you on there, for the long term?"

"I don't know," Nora admitted. "The surgeon keeps telling me I'm doing a good job. They're having me do more interesting things. I want to. I want to more than I've ever wanted anything before. I'm trying so hard, harvesting is almost like a vacation now. I don't know..."

She trailed off, even though it sounded as if she'd been tempted to say something more. Bridget wondered what Nora might be thinking, but she didn't ask.

"What if there was another way?" she asked instead.

"Another way what?"

"Another way to continue," Bridget said. "To grow old, without ever being on the Council?"

"Why would you care?" Nora asked. "You're going to make the Council anyway, to hear Kady tell it."

Bridget scowled. She could feel her face flushing red, as she turned to look away in the other direction. The last thing she wanted was to get into an argument, but this was a sore point for her, and Nora had just poked it with a sharp stick.

Bridget chewed on her lower lip in frustration, fighting the urge to snap back in anger at the taller girl. She'd been hoping to tell Nora all about the boat that she and the others had built, but now that the conversation had taken an unexpected and unpleasant turn, she had to struggle to contain her temper and hold her tongue.

Chapter 9:
Gloria's Servant

Not all that far from the river, a fell was creeping forward through a little stand of trees. It paused, as it surveyed the surrounding terrain for movement, for signs of life, for any shape that might resemble a human form. To hunt and to kill were the only thoughts in its electronic mind.

The fell held no malice for its quarry. It knew no hatred, nor hunger, nor even a mindless lust for violence or blood. Its motives were as simple and stoic as its mechanical soul. Gloria had called for death, and the fell would provide it. It would manufacture death, just as the mills would manufacture garments. It would cultivate death, just as a vial of honey or a strand of cheese would be grown in the bottle gardens. It would deliver death, fresh upon the doorstep, wherever life could be found.

To the fell, the living were raw materials waiting only to die, ready for it to fashion them into death. It was, at its own lifeless core, another factory, one more engine of production, another indispensible component of Gloria's grand design. The fell was a practical cog in the machinery of Fairhaven, every bit as essential to its perpetual function as the endless river, or the silent warehouses, or the flowering groves of Pleasant Gardens, or the tireless worker bees.

It would pursue life. The fell would seek out sentient living things which it could cause to die, in every part of the great city, wherever they might be found. But it did not kill indiscriminately. Its targets, to some degree, would choose themselves, whether by chance or by choice. But any measure of random circumstance was always subject to the finite parameters of the creature's mandate. A fell's choice of targets was scaled, and balanced, and judiciously weighted according to procedural limits, and the demands of Gloria's unquestioned will.

The fell would seek to kill only until the needs of the city were satisfied; only until balance was restored; only until necessity was served. It would do as it was called to do, or so would one of its brethren, until they were commanded otherwise. Then it would sleep, until Gloria called for death again.

But for now, gazing out from the little stand of trees, the fell could see nothing. The only movement was a worker bee in the distance. The only shapes along the horizon were the stones and the houses and the numberless flowers.

The fell was not concerned. It curled itself slowly back into its cocoon to wait, but it was not sleeping. For the moment, its sense of urgency was low, and it could afford to be patient. It had carefully chosen this tranquil place, nearby to a footpath, where it could lie peacefully, and partly concealed. The fell knew that, in the due course of time, suitable prey would come to this place. It had only to wait.

Chapter 10:
Disapproval and Doubt

It was mid-afternoon, and Gwen was making her way through the enclave, back home to her clade.

She'd spent the morning mentoring a novice: an energetic eleven year old named Daniel. Gwendolyn always enjoyed being a mentor, though she didn't particularly enjoy mentoring boys. It seemed to her that adolescent boys were often more intent on showing off and trying to impress her than they were in actually learning anything useful, or getting any real harvesting done. She suspected the problem was purely biological. What else could it be, really? She couldn't help wondering if the older boys assigned as mentors had the same sort of trouble with the younger girls. She didn't really have any male friends her own age that she could ask.

She stopped for a moment, and scuffed at the dusty concrete surface of the Periphery with the toe of her shoe. She was briefly tempted to try spelling out her name in that thin layer of fine grey powder, but there was always the chance someone else might notice it, and that would be embarrassing. She drew a blank grid for tic-tac-toe instead, then wiped it away, without bothering to pretend at playing the game. She took a good step back, and then sketched out a little flower instead. It was crude and a bit childlike, but it made her feel better. She decided to leave the flower there, for someone else to find.

Gwendolyn continued to dawdle, the rest of the way home. She had nothing in particular left to do with the rest of her afternoon, and plenty of time to spare. It was too late in the day for her to make a second trip to the Middle Ring, and she very much doubted that any of the other girls would have returned home yet, back to the clade.

The paths between the huts and tents were mostly deserted at this hour. Aside from today's mentors and the novices, most of the other harvesters were still out on their daily runs. Gwen stopped at the Commons briefly, just to see if there was anyone there, but the tables were all empty, and no one else was standing around. She even took a few minutes to peek inside one of the old abandoned huts along the bank of the river, but it was empty as well. All the furnishings, including the window curtains and the cots, had been removed long ago. She wondered briefly who might once have lived there.

Killing time like this wasn't the sort of thing Gwendolyn often did, but she was feeling restless, and a little bit lonely. Ever since Audrey had disappeared, the mood in the clade seemed to have changed, and the other girls had been acting so strange of late.

Despite her wandering, she soon found herself back at the front door of her own little hut. She looked back over her shoulder, half-hoping that she'd see some reason not to go inside yet, but there was nothing of any interest lurking behind her. She sighed.

But then, as she stepped through the front door, she was very surprised to find that the clade was not empty after all. Eloise and Kady were already there, sitting at the table. They looked up at her.

"How was mentoring?" Kady asked.

"I didn't think anyone else would be here," Gwen said. "You're both back early."

"We're not back, actually," said Eloise. "We didn't go out harvesting today. We were hoping to catch you before Bridget and Nora got home."

"Can we talk with you for a little bit?" Kady asked. "The three of us need to have a talk."

Gwen frowned at this, but didn't say anything in reply.

"Please?" Kady added.

"I don't know, Michael," Kyle said, shaking his head. "I mean, how far do you think you'll get? How long before the fells catch up with you?... A day?... A week?... Doesn't sound like a good idea to me."

"Maybe not," Michael said with a shrug. "But seriously, how long before the fells catch up with us *here*? How many harvesters our age haven't come back just in the last two weeks? I don't think we'll be much worse off on the river than we are here, and we might even be safer. It's not like we really know."

Kyle scrunched his face into an odd sort of frown. He was clearly torn.

"What'd Ethan say?"

"I haven't told him about it," Michael said, "are you kidding?"

"Yeah, I guess I can see that."

Kyle leaned back in his chair, and tapped his fingers against the tabletop a few times.

"What are the girls like?"

"What d'you mean?... What do they look like?"

"Gimme a break," Kyle said. "Are they nice, are they smart? You said this was their idea; do they know what they're doing?"

"You might know one of the girls in their clade. She volunteers at the hospital, I guess."

"What's her name?"

"Nora, I think. I haven't met her. I'm not even sure she's going with us. Last time we talked, they hadn't asked her yet."

"Doesn't ring a bell," Kyle said, shaking his head. "No surprise, though. I gave up on the hospital tent ages ago."

"It's been fun building the boat," Michael said with a shrug. "But do they know what they're doing?... Hell no. Not a chance. None of us do. The raft's a pile of junk, to be perfectly honest. But it does float, I can promise you that much."

Michael paused and stared up at the ceiling. Neither of them said anything more for several seconds.

"I don't know if it's a good idea or not," Michael finally admitted. "I mean, the alternative's staying here, and that doesn't look that great to me either."

"How long before you go?"

"We're out of here tomorrow," Michael said, "unless something changes."

132

Kyle's jaw dropped.

"Tomorrow?!" he asked.

"The longer we wait, the more chance there is somebody like Ethan finds out about it. I don't know what else to tell you. You can come along with us if you want, or you can stay here. Up to you."

Kyle shook his head, and let out a long, slow breath.

"Let me sleep on it."

———

"I've been wondering what the three of you were up to," Gwen said. "I don't know why you didn't tell me about it before, but I always figured you'd let me know what was going on, eventually."

"We're sorry about that," Kady said, "but don't feel bad. We didn't tell Nora about it either."

"The fewer people who knew, the less chance word would get around to the Council," Eloise explained. "That was our thinking, but I am sorry. It was my idea to begin with, and it took me years before I told *anybody* about it."

"I can't think that Gloria would approve," Gwen replied. "The enclave has rules for a reason, you know."

"I'm not so sure that Gloria will care much either way," Kady replied. "And the laws of harvesting don't have much to say about this sort of thing."

"Everyone leaves the enclave eventually," Eloise pointed out.

"But the virtuous always rise," Gwen insisted. "And our first duty is to the enclave."

"Is it?" said Eloise. "There are other enclaves, and Gloria watches over all of them, doesn't she?"

Gwendolyn frowned again, and looked down at the table. She absently ran her fingers back and forth over a dark spot there, on the surface.

"Well," she said hesitantly, without looking up, "I wouldn't know about that."

"Please come with us," Kady said. "I'll miss you terribly if you don't, and I don't really think there's anything left for any of us here. I really don't think there is."

Gwendolyn rubbed a little harder at the dark spot on the table, as if she were trying to wipe it away, but it was an old stain that had been there for years, and it wasn't going anywhere. Kady and Eloise waited.

"Thank you," Gwen said eventually, "for asking me." She looked up at Kady, then at Eloise, before looking down at the spot on the table again.

"But I do not think that I will go."

Chapter 11:
A Few Steps Off the Path

It was late afternoon, and Bridget and Nora were finally returning from their harvesting run. It had been a very long day, and they both were tired. They'd ventured further around the Middle Ring and further in from the river than Nora had ever gone before, even on her harvesting runs with Audrey, but they had been rewarded for their efforts. In a smallish house, far in toward the Central Forest, they'd found a large stash of recently delivered food packets. Now, with their satchels nearly full, they were on their way back to the ferry raft.

Bridget had still not told Nora about the boat that she and the others had built. Every time she tried to steer the conversation in that direction, Nora seemed to become testy and impatient. Eventually, Bridget had decided it would be better to simply wait, rather than trying to force the issue. Maybe back at the enclave Kady and Eloise would be able to help. Bridget wondered how they were getting on with inviting Gwendolyn. She hoped they were having better success than she was.

Since they were both footsore, and their packs were heavy, the two young harvesters elected to take the paved trails back to the river and the Promenade, rather than the shorter and more direct – though also more tiring – diagonal route overland. They were still perhaps half a kilometer from the Circle Park when Bridget suddenly stopped, and grabbed Nora by the arm.

"Fell," she said quietly.

"What?" said Nora.

Bridget pointed with her free hand. There, some thirty meters from the path and partly concealed amidst a small stand of trees, was a darkly metallic cocoon. Nora gasped.

"What's it doing here?" Bridget whispered, more to herself than to her companion. "I don't think I've ever seen one this close to the river before."

Over the entire course of her life, Nora had rarely seen fells at all, and she'd certainly never seen one so near at hand as this. As cautious as she'd always been with her harvesting, she simply didn't encounter them very often, and Nora very much wanted to keep it that way.

"Let's get out of here," she hissed quietly. She tried to pull away, but Bridget still had ahold of her arm.

"Wait!..." Bridget whispered back. "It's still asleep. Look, it's just sitting there."

"I don't care! It shouldn't be here at all. And we shouldn't be here either."

With a mischievous grin on her face, Bridget looked Nora squarely in the eye.

"Let's go touch it."

"What!?"

"Are you scared?" Bridget asked.

"Of course I'm scared! You're being stupid again."

"Come on... we'll probably *never* have a better chance than this."

Bridget let go of Nora's arm, and started to make her way slowly across the open lawn toward the fell. Still objecting, Nora followed only a few steps behind.

"What if it isn't really sleeping?" she whispered sharply. "What if it wakes up?"

"Even if it does," Bridget insisted, stopping briefly to whisper back over her shoulder at Nora, "it takes them a few seconds to open up all the way. We're not that far from the Circle Park. We'll have plenty of time to run."

"We've hardly got time to make the last boat as it is," Nora pointed out.

"Wait on the path if you're scared."

Bridget was now no more than ten meters from the sleeping fell, close enough to see the satiny texture of its outer covering, and the fine tracery of seams that stretched across that otherwise flawless surface. She could hear Nora's nervous breathing, just one step behind her.

Then suddenly there was another sound, like a gentle puff of wind, stirring a leaf from the branch of a tree. The narrow seams along the fell's outer casing grew noticeably darker, wider, more clearly defined.

"It's waking up!" Bridget shouted.

She lurched backwards, but much to her confusion her right leg didn't work. She cried out in surprise, and stumbled awkwardly as she turned to run, falling hard into the grass. She felt a sharp pain, and looking down she could see blood streaming from her thigh.

"I didn't think you'd be next," Nora said apologetically.

Bridget looked up to see the taller girl slowly backing away toward the path. Nora was staring right at her, and occasionally glancing up toward the trees and the wakening fell. Bridget could see that Nora was clutching something shiny and metallic, like a gleaming piece of silverware, in her right hand.

"I *told* you not to," Nora continued, "but you had to go and make it easy for me. I won't even have to wash the blood off this time."

Bridget's head was swimming. She couldn't figure out what was happening to her. She only knew that she couldn't stand up, and she was bleeding, and her leg hurt when she tried to move. She reached down, and found a tiny puncture wound, just below the hem of her shorts. It was only a centimeter or two across, though she could tell that it was deep. But where had it come from? She hadn't even felt it happen. The wound only hurt if she touched it, or tried to make use of her leg.

Behind her, the fell was slowly emerging from its cocoon.

"This isn't at all how it went the time before," Nora said, "but you never were much like Audrey, were you."

Nora had stabbed her – Bridget finally understood – with a knife, or whatever the metal thing was that she was holding. But that didn't make sense. Nothing made sense.

Almost in a panic now, Bridget tried desperately to get further away from the fell – back toward Nora, back toward the footpath – but her body refused to obey. She could only drag herself slowly forward using her hands and her one good leg. She looked back toward the mechanical monster in horror, and saw that it had almost fully emerged from its cocoon. Already its legs were unfolding.

Watching Bridget struggle toward her across the grass, Nora felt a growing sense of elation, just as she had when she'd killed Audrey. But this was a totally different set of circumstances. Nora wasn't going to kill Bridget at all: she didn't have to. The fell was going to do that for her. Nora had only made things easier for it, by making certain that Bridget couldn't run away. Now all there was left to do was watch.

She took another step backwards to the edge of the path. Nora knew she should be running, putting more distance between herself and Bridget and the fell, making her own escape toward the river before the thing finished waking up. But she found that she was unable to tear herself away. She was captivated by the little tableau unfolding before her – the momentary drama she had helped to create.

What would it be like, to watch Bridget die? Nora's interest was medical... scientific... purely clinical. Fells killed harvesters all the time, but how did they do it? How many harvesters had ever actually seen it happen? Nora *had* to wait. She had to see it firsthand, to learn exactly how it was done. The surgeon, she told herself, would want to know every detail.

The creature's eyes ignited, and it scanned the landscape for only a moment before locking in on its prey. It darted forward. Bridget was close enough to hear the quiet hum of electric servos, and the hiss of tiny hydraulic pistons as the fell burst into motion, closing in on her with dispassionate, single-minded intent.

Bridget gave up trying to escape. Even if she'd had the use of both her legs, she could not have hoped to outrun the thing, not without a good head start – not in the open as she was, with no cover around her, and certainly not at this distance. She went limp, collapsing the rest of the way into the grass, and wrapping her arms over her head as the creature sprang towards her.

138

But it missed... Or rather, it did not miss. It passed cleanly over her in a single leap, as easily as if she were just a low mound of gravel, lying in its path. The creature was not after Bridget at all. It was pursuing Nora.

In a sudden rush of panic, Nora tried to turn and run, but the sole of her shoe caught against the edge of the footpath, sending her stumbling awkwardly across the paved surface. She held out her hands to break her fall, but as she regained her footing she saw blood pouring down her arm; she had somehow stabbed herself with the scalpel she was still clutching in her right hand. For a moment, she froze there in shock, transfixed at the sight of her own blood.

And then the fell was on her.

In the blink of an eye, it was over. What only a few seconds before had been a living, breathing human being was reduced to a scattered wash of blood and lifeless tissue. No part of her was left untouched. All that remained was a corpse, unrecognizable as any specific individual. Nora was gone. There was no longer anyone there, where she once had been. There were only the dissociated components of a former harvester, and nothing more.

Once it had finished, the fell turned its eyes back toward Bridget. It realigned itself into a low, stalking posture, and took a few slow steps in her direction. Then it stopped. For the moment, at least, its work was complete. It had killed the oldest available target, and with its quota fulfilled, the mechanical predator slowly curled itself back into its cocoon, and powered down.

Bridget was stunned. She hadn't even had time to think. The entire encounter had taken only seconds, and now everything was quiet and still once more, as if nothing had happened there at all.

She pulled herself up onto her hands and knees, and putting almost all of her weight on her good leg, she struggled forward across the grass to where the fell was lying, fully inert once more in its metal shell. She pounded on it helplessly until her arms ached, then she collapsed onto the grass, in exhaustion.

She looked up, and noticed that her vision was blurred, and her face was wet. Only then did she realize she was crying. She wiped her eyes with her arm. Across the path, beyond the fell's metallic casing, she could clearly see Nora's remains. Before long the worker bees would arrive, to clean every trace of that carnage away.

Almost imperceptibly, all around her, the daylight was slowly beginning to fade. Soon, Gloria would be announcing the sunset, and the last ferry would be returning to River Towne. But Bridget already knew that with her injured leg, there was no chance she could reach the boat landing in time.

- End of Book Three -

Book Four:
Chapter 1:
The River

Fairhaven's original architects had intended for the river, which separated the Periphery from the Circle Park and the rest of the Middle Ring, to be the effective outer boundary of the city. The river was supposed to serve as an elegant natural border, defining the furthest limits of the residential zone. But nothing in Fairhaven was natural, and the river only masqueraded as such.

Everything beyond the water had always been meant to be left conspicuously barren, vacant and inhospitable. The Periphery, and its broad empty stretch of concrete, was deliberately designed to be nothing more than a desolate and uninviting void. No one had ever been expected to go there. The primary function of both the Periphery and the river, as they were originally conceived, was to keep Fairhaven's inhabitants as far as possible from the outer wall.

Any wall is inherently confining, and the more massive it is, the more likely that it will be perceived as stark and intimidating, particularly when close at hand. The river and the Periphery were designed to provide a benign psychological buffer between Fairhaven's idyllic interior and its impregnable outer wall, which was itself only the foundation of the great dome, rising forever until it became the sky, to fully enclose the city. It had been thought that the residents of Fairhaven would never actually cross the endless river – and thus never approach the outer wall – but that they would still be comforted by the unconscious perception that they somehow *could*.

Throughout history, humanity has always congregated along rivers. Flowing water is an essential component of human civilization's communal heritage, a universal symbol of growth, and discovery, and change. But in Fairhaven, these ancestral perceptions were only an illusion. The city's great river led, eventually, to nothing at all. The water moved in a constant circle, not even by its own power, but due only to the relentless industrial impetus of the pumping stations.

And of course, those pumping stations were not merely pumps. Uniformly spaced along the river's arc, they were also massive cisterns, distilleries, and multi-staged filters, drawing any contaminants from the water, funneling that extracted waste to the city core for reprocessing, and ultimately releasing the water once more, renewed, to continue on to the next stage in its perpetual circulation. As long as the five stations endured, the river would flow forever, on an endless journey from nowhere to nowhere, and back again.

And yet, as with so much else that lay within Gloria's vast domain, even the great river was gradually slipping into decline, and was now only a shadow of its former self. With fewer and fewer working pumps to drive the current forward, it moved more slowly than it had in the past, and the filtration systems could scarcely keep the water clean. At times, the river would cease almost to flow entirely, becoming more like a narrow, curving lake than a rushing stream. The whitewater rapids that lay to either side of the pumping stations were still a forbidding spectacle for those few that would ever see them, but even those fearsome rapids had greatly dwindled from their former glory.

Chapter 2:
Shadows upon Shadows

"Gwendolyn..."

Her eyes popped open at the sound of the voice, but all Gwen could see was the midnight darkness of the clade. Nothing was distinct; there were only a few scattered shapes and outlines and forms: shadows lying upon shadows. The world around her was shrouded in silhouette.

She turned onto her side, to try and see who had called her name, but there was no one there. No movement. She could see only the one red dot of light, faintly glowing from the control panel of the hotmaker. In the daytime that light would hardly have been noticed, but in the darkness it gleamed like a rupture in the fabric of the night: a brilliant pinprick, hinting at an inferno that burned somewhere far beyond.

Gwendolyn stared at that tiny red dot amid the shadows for several seconds. Then she closed her eyes, and a moment later she was once again fast asleep.

Kady lay on her cot, staring up toward the ceiling at the darkness. Nora and Bridget had not come home. She and Eloise and Gwen had waited at the clade until after sunset, then she had gone to the exchange tent alone, to ask if they'd returned there, or if anyone had news. But they had not, and no one did. The last raft had returned to the enclave without them.

The underkeepers had been kinder about it than she'd really expected.

"The fells are on a rampage," one of them had said to her. "I can't think when we've ever lost so many harvesters in such a short time."

"Your friends are probably just hiding somewhere," another added, more hopefully. "It happens sometimes, when they get lost or can't get back to the boat landing. Sunset sneaks up on you sometimes."

"I've never heard of the fells taking two before," a third chimed in. "Not when they were working together... not both at once. Maybe they ran off on their own. Harvesters get crazy ideas sometimes; you never can tell."

"Go on back to your clade and get some sleep," the first one finally told her. "There's nothing to be done about it now, and no way for any of us to know until morning."

After that, Kady had returned home, just as they'd advised her to do. And now she was staring into the darkness, thinking that the morning might never come.

Eloise lay in her cot, facing the wall. Her eyes were closed, but her mind could not lie still. She told herself that she should have been the one to go with Nora instead. She should have been the one to ask her. Bridget was too brash, too careless, too easily distracted.

But she knew in her heart that wasn't true, and it wasn't her fault. It was Gloria's fault, if anyone's, and the Privy Council's, and the underkeepers' and the escorts' and everyone else's fault as well.

But that wasn't true either. Everything was her fault, and Eloise knew it. The boat had been her plan, her idea from the start, and that made her responsible. And as for all her cautious aspirations and good intentions, none of that even seemed possible any longer, for her or for any of them.

Eloise clenched her teeth in the darkness, filled with hopelessness and determination and redoubled rage, and willed herself slowly into sleep.

Chapter 3:
Ethan

Ethan crossed the river on the first raft of the morning, shortly after sunrise. He had still not fully decided what he was going to do. On the one hand, he felt that he had a moral obligation to put an end to whatever Michael and his girlfriends might be up to. But on the other hand, the warehouse keeper himself had told him to simply let them go. Unable to reconcile these conflicting directives, Ethan felt himself adrift, and terribly confused. What good were rules, after all, if the rulemakers told you not to follow them?

Ethan had been born into a society held only precariously in place by a clumsy patchwork of rituals and routines, and he'd tried his best to do whatever was demanded of him, in the expectation that he would eventually be rewarded. And yet here he was, nineteen years old and still a harvester, with little hope of ever being elevated to the Lesser Council. Try as he might, he couldn't make sense of it. Having never before questioned the way of things, he had never before been bothered by the lack of any satisfactory answers. He was so unfamiliar with uncertainty that he could not even recognize it growing in himself.

He walked slowly riverwise along the Promenade, hardly noticing as the ferry raft's other passengers vanished, one by one, off along the smaller pathways leading in. They were of no concern to him at the moment. He was determined to keep himself focused on where he was going, even if he had no idea what he might ultimately do once he got there.

He was well beyond the Training Grounds before he finally turned away from the river, to follow one of the smaller paths. Just off this little trail, only a few hundred meters from the Circle Park, there was a tall house with a stone patio and a large swimming pool. That was his destination. It was the place where he'd first seen them, splashing in the water with their floats and their makeshift framework of tubing and all their other paraphernalia.

He didn't know where they were storing the boat at night, and he wondered how they'd managed to keep the bees from finding it and carrying all the pieces away. But those details did not really matter much. He knew that the boat had to be hidden somewhere near that house, and so long as he could get there before they did, the conspirators would sooner or later have to come to him.

He stopped for a moment, to adjust the empty backpack hanging across his shoulders. It felt awkward to him this morning, and strangely uncomfortable. He checked to see if the straps had somehow slipped out of adjustment, but nothing seemed to have changed. He slung it loosely over his left shoulder, rather than pulling it the rest of the way back on.

When he reached the house, he stopped to check the swimming pool first of all, though there was no real need. No one could have gotten there ahead of him without his noticing. Everything was quiet, just as he'd expected, and peering over the top of the brick wall that surrounded the stone patio, he could see that the pool was empty.

He circled around the house to the opposite side, and climbed the steps to the front door. He was surprised to find it already standing slightly ajar. He cautiously pushed it the rest of the way open, but did not at first see anything unusual inside. Then he noticed a wavering line of dark stains across the hardwood floor of the entrance.

It looked like blood.

He felt a sudden chill go up his spine. What had happened here? Had a fell caught someone? Why hadn't the bees cleaned the blood up? What if the fell was still here? He stood there in the doorway for a long time, trying to decide what to do.

Steeling his nerve, he crept into the house as quietly as he could. There was another patch of blood at the foot of the main staircase, but there did not seem to be any more of it further up the stairs. Ethan turned back more than once to make certain that the front door was still standing open behind him. He wanted to be sure of his escape route, in case he might suddenly need to run.

Ignoring the staircase for the moment, he instead followed a short hallway that led further into the house's interior, and soon found himself standing in a spacious family room. Daylight was filtering in through the curtained windows along the right-hand wall, but the electric lights had all been turned off, leaving much of the room in partial shadow. Ethan could see more drying blood, here and there along the carpeting, but still there was no sign of the fell or its victim. He took another cautious step into the room, then froze.

There was a dead girl on the couch.

Ethan had never seen a dead body before. There was blood seemingly everywhere: on her shorts and her t-shirt, on her legs and her arms, and all across the sofa where she was lying. There was a light blue towel draped over one of her legs, and it too was soaked with drying blood.

Her body was turned away from him, toward the back of the couch, in such a way that he could not see her face. In the uneven light, her skin was so pale that she almost seemed transparent, as if she were not real. She looked for all the world as if she were some sort of half-melted doll made from candle wax, or a frosted glass figurine spattered clumsily with dark red enamel.

Ethan wondered who she might have been, or if she'd been someone he knew. He found himself torn between fascination and revulsion. A part of him wanted to run, to leave the house until the bees arrived to take the dead girl away. But his curiosity had already gotten the better of him, and he realized that he would have to look. He took another hesitant step forward.

The body moved, and Ethan almost jumped out of his skin.

"Good morning," the dead girl said, turning just far enough to look at him. She grimaced, and took a long, slow breath. "Someone's up early," she added, more quietly, "but I don't think I know you."

"I'm Ethan," he said. He was too startled to say anything else.

"It's really, really nice to meet you," the dead girl replied. "I'm Bridget. Forgive me if I don't get up. I didn't sleep very well last night."

"I thought you were dead."

The dead girl closed her eyes again, and almost seemed to smile.

"Sorry," she said. "But don't feel bad... I thought so too."

Chapter 4:
Breakfast

Eloise opened her eyes, and saw that it was already morning. She sat bolt upright in her cot, and quickly scanned the room. Kady was there, sitting by herself at the table, prodding with her fork at a plate of toast and eggs, but otherwise the hut was empty. Bridget and Nora had apparently not returned to the clade overnight, and it seemed that Gwen was already gone.

"They're not here," Kady said, in answer to Eloise's unspoken question.

Kady's voice was rough and gravelly, and no more cheerful than her appearance. Her hair was uncombed, her blue shirt was badly wrinkled, and her eyes were sagging. She did not look as if she'd gotten much sleep.

Eloise nodded, unhappily. She slumped back into her cot and stared up at the ceiling, trying to wake herself the rest of the way up. That initial rush of adrenaline had made her body instantly tense and alert, but her brain was not yet ready to fully participate in the new day.

Kady continued to half-heartedly pick at her plate of food, but she did not feel at all hungry, and had not really eaten much. She'd made breakfast mostly to distract herself from thinking about Bridget and Nora, but it wasn't working. She coughed quietly into her hand once or twice to clear her throat, then took a sip from her water bottle.

After a few minutes, Eloise rolled herself out of bed, and pulled on her shorts and t-shirt and shoes. She smacked herself lightly on the face a few times, rubbed her eyes, then ran her fingers through her hair.

"What's for breakfast?" she asked.

"You can have mine, if you want," Kady replied, "but it's already cold."

Eloise shook her head.

"Eat," she said, as she stood up and walked to the foodwall. "We've got a long day ahead of us."

"What are we gonna do?"

"We're supposed to meet Michael in the Circle Park," Eloise said. "We're probably already late."

"We can't go now," Kady said.

"We're supposed to meet Michael," Eloise repeated firmly. "After that, I don't know. I can't think ahead any further than that right now."

Just as Eloise was setting a breakfast packet into the hotmaker, the front door panel slid open, and Gwendolyn bounced into the room. Eloise and Kady looked over at her with surprise.

"I thought you'd already gone," Kady said.

"I did," Gwen replied brightly, "but just to the Warehouse Exchange. I thought it would be best to get a few things first, before we go."

"Go?" Eloise asked.

"I'm coming with you," Gwen said, "if that's still OK."

Kady and Eloise were dumbfounded.

"What?..." Gwendolyn asked, confused at their confusion. "Don't look so surprised."

"Last night you told us *no*," Kady said. "You seemed really angry about it."

"Well... you did hurt my feelings a little," Gwen admitted, "but I'm over it now, and I've changed my mind."

"We're not even sure we're still going." Eloise said. "We can't go anywhere without Bridget and Nora, and they're both probably dead."

"They're both *fine*," Gwen insisted with conviction. "They're just hiding someplace, I'm absolutely certain about that. So *of course* you're all still going, and I'm going with you."

Gwen was a past master at the fine art of unfounded optimism, but this sudden reversal was startling, even coming from her.

"What's brought this on?" Kady asked.

"It was the strangest thing," Gwen said, with a peculiar hint of a smile curling gently up her face toward her cheekbones. "I had a dream last night that Gloria was calling me, but I couldn't go to her, because I didn't know the way."

Kady and Eloise exchanged a quick, baffled look before turning to stare at Gwendolyn again. Gwen just stared blithely back at them.

"Well," she added, as if her conclusion was perfectly obvious, "I think perhaps this might be the way."

––––––––––––––

By the time the three girls arrived at the Circle Park, Michael was already there waiting for them. Kyle was with him.

"Sorry we're late," Eloise said, once they were all out of earshot from the boat landing. "We had a rough night, and got a late start."

"We haven't been here long; we were running late too," Michael said. "I've been so focused on the boat, I hadn't given much thought to what else I ought to be bringing along. It felt weird, looting our own clade."

The two groups took a few minutes for introductions. It turned out that Kyle and Gwendolyn already knew each other very slightly, through a mutual acquaintance in another clade.

"I'm glad you decided to come," Eloise said to Kyle. "Michael wasn't sure you would."

"I'm still not sure myself, to be honest," Kyle replied, a little uncomfortably.

"He wants to see the boat," Michael explained. "I only told him about it just last night, and he still wasn't sure when we got up this morning, so I talked him into coming along and meeting everybody."

"I know how you feel," Gwen said, looking at Kyle with a friendly grin. "They sprung it on me at the last minute too. I didn't make up my mind until I got up this morning."

"Where's Bridget?" Michael asked.

"We don't know," said Kady.

"She's probably with Nora," said Gwen, "waiting for us somewhere."

"They didn't come home last night," Eloise explained. "We're hoping they're ok, but we really don't know. We almost didn't come this morning, hoping they'd turn up back at the clade, but we knew you'd be waiting for us. We really don't know any more than that."

Michael frowned at this, and nodded with understanding. He glanced briefly over at Kyle, and saw that he was slowly shaking his head, and looking increasingly uneasy.

With the introductions complete, the group set out, walking riverwise together along the Promenade. Though they had much to talk about, the three original conspirators said very little to each other. They were each absorbed with their own personal misgivings about this whole situation, and wondering if they should postpone their departure for a few days to reevaluate their plans, or if it might even be better to simply cancel the whole affair outright.

Gwendolyn, however, was not bothered at all with such concerns, and she soon struck up a friendly conversation with Kyle. Gwen did most of the talking, but Kyle seemed genuinely engaged, and the two of them continued to chat about the flowers and the landscaping and other pleasant things for quite some time.

Though they did not directly join in this conversation, Kady, Eloise, and Michael were all glad for the distraction. Had Gwendolyn not been with them, they might very well have had to endure this long walk in an awkward and uncomfortable silence.

Eventually, they reached the house with the swimming pool. It was quiet, and no one else seemed to be around. Kady led the group through the gate in the brick wall, then across the patio to the back door. She opened it carefully, and one by one they all slipped inside, with Eloise bringing up the rear.

Kady led them past the kitchen, and on through the house toward the front staircase, but when she reached the family room she pulled up short. Someone she did not know was already there. A tall, sturdy-looking young man was standing just a few meters in front of her.

"Who are you?" she asked. But before the young man could answer, Michael stepped around Kady and approached him.

"Hello, Ethan," Michael said cautiously. "What brings you here?"

"He's making me breakfast," came a voice from off to one side.

Kady turned to look, and to her great surprise she saw Bridget, sitting propped up on the sofa with an empty breakfast plate in her lap. Bridget looked like death warmed over, but she was evidently still very much alive.

Chapter 5:
Confrontation

"Bridget!" Kady shouted. She rushed across the room to her injured friend, and dropped down onto the floor beside her. "Where were you?!... What happened?!?..."

"If you were still thinking about killing me," Bridget said to her, smiling weakly, "I'm sorry, but you missed your chance. Nora beat you to it." She closed her eyes and took a long, slow breath. "Well, almost," she continued, though she was no longer smiling. She looked exhausted, and her face was very pale. "Nora got me first, but then the fell got Nora. I'm really sorry. I guess I blew it."

Kady was mystified by this non-explanation, but she was too happy just finding Bridget alive to immediately press her for a more coherent account. Gwendolyn and Eloise had already hurried over to the sofa to join them both, but Michael had not. Michael was as relieved as anyone about finding Bridget, but Ethan was his more immediate concern.

From the outset, Michael had tried his best to keep the boat project a secret from both Ethan and Kyle, but he was not entirely surprised to find Ethan here. In fact, the possibility of Ethan discovering the boat had been one of his chief concerns all along, and it was now clear to him that his fears had been warranted.

The two young men were standing face to face, just a few steps apart. Ethan was a good ten centimeters taller than Michael, and probably outweighed him by fifteen kilograms or more. If this came to a fight, Michael knew he couldn't win, but Ethan was still just standing there. He hadn't yet made any threatening moves.

"I see you've been keeping an eye on us," Michael said. "I kind of thought you might."

"Yeah, well... it was pretty obvious you were up to something," said Ethan. He looked over Michael's shoulder, and saw Kyle still standing in the open archway. "Are you in on this too?" he asked.

"I wasn't," said Kyle, cautiously. "But right now... maybe?... I'm not really sure."

"I didn't tell Kyle about it either," Michael explained. "Not until yesterday afternoon. We figured the less people knew the better."

"Makes sense, I guess," said Ethan.

"So I suppose you're gonna report us to the council then," Michael said.

Ethan frowned, and glanced briefly over toward Bridget and the other girls, before turning to look at Michael again.

"I already reported you to the council," he replied. "They... um... didn't seem to care all that much."

"I can't say that surprises me," Michael said. "So then why are you here?"

Ethan thought about this for a few seconds before replying.

"I guess I'm really not sure," he said, eventually.

"Boys..."

Eloise interrupted them, quietly but firmly, and immediately she had everyone's attention. She got up from beside the sofa, and took a few steps forward until she was standing in front of Michael, blocking his way. Michael looked at her questioningly, but Eloise wasn't even facing in his direction. She took another step toward Ethan, and looked the tall young man squarely in the eye.

"Ethan?" she asked. It wasn't so much a question as it was a cautious assertion. "It's nice to meet you. I'm Eloise. Michael's told us a lot about you."

Ethan frowned again, and without even realizing it he took half a step backwards. He'd been expecting a confrontation with Michael, and maybe even a fistfight. That, at least, would have been an interaction he could understand. But suddenly finding himself standing almost nose to nose with a girl whose forehead barely came up to his chin was not something he'd been prepared for. He glanced up at Michael, then at Kyle, then over toward Bridget and the other girls, but no one else said a word. He had no choice but to look back down at Eloise again.

"Hello..." he replied. Ethan was painfully aware of how lame that one word sounded as he said it, but for the life of him he couldn't think of anything more to say. He felt absurdly self-conscious, and very much alone. He crossed his arms in front of himself. He didn't know what to do with his hands.

"I don't know how much you already know about this, or how much Bridget might have told you," Eloise continued, "but you've probably already guessed that we're leaving River Towne. There's nothing left for us there; no future to speak of. So we've built a raft, and we're taking it down the river, maybe to Stone Prairie, maybe all the way to Pleasant Gardens if we can."

Ethan didn't say anything. He felt like an idiot. Why was he even here? The warehouse keeper had already told him to let them go. He looked down at the floor.

"You're welcome to come with us, if you like."

It was Kady who had spoken this time. She was still hunched down beside the sofa with Bridget and Gwen.

Once again caught off guard, Ethan turned to look in her direction. Was *that* why he'd come here? He didn't even know half of these girls' names. Had he been hoping they would ask him? He wasn't sure. He turned toward Eloise again, and saw that she was nodding, apparently in agreement with the other girl who'd just spoken.

"I'd take a guess that there's nothing more for *you* back at the enclave than there is for any of the rest of us," she said, matter-of-factly. "So you can come with us if you want to. You're invited."

"Michael said you were training to be an oarsman," the other girl added. "You probably know a lot more about boats than we do. That would be very useful."

"You need my help?" Ethan asked. A part of him still couldn't believe he was even having this conversation.

"No," Eloise said. She did not want to be misunderstood. "We don't need your help. We're going to go around the circle on the river regardless, either with you or without you. But we would *appreciate* your help, and you're welcome to come along with us, if you'd like to."

She extended her right hand, and waited.

Ethan looked at Eloise's hand for several seconds, and then somewhat to his own surprise he held out his own. Eloise grasped it in hers, and shook it once firmly.

Chapter 6:
The Tasks at Hand

Now that Ethan had agreed to join the conspiracy, Kyle felt obligated to relent as well.

"I guess I'm in too then," he said. "I'd feel like a dorf, going back to the clade all by myself."

"That makes me happy," said Gwen. "Now it's everybody from both clades, and that just seems perfect somehow."

"I still don't understand what happened to you and Nora," Kady asked, turning her attention back to Bridget again. "You said a fell got her? But I didn't understand the rest."

Bridget closed her eyes for a moment and nodded her head ruefully. Then she looked up at Kady.

"Nora killed Audrey," she said, slowly and precisely. "Then she tried to kill me. I think she meant to kill all of us, eventually, one by one."

Any shock that Kady or Eloise might have felt at this revelation was tempered by what they had already known, or at least by what they'd been expecting. The old warehouse keeper had long since put the possibility of murder into their minds, and since they'd already resigned themselves to the thought that both Bridget and Nora were dead, finding Bridget still alive was a better result than they'd hoped for. Out of all the girls, Gwendolyn might have been the most sorely shaken, but Gwen's sense of relief at finding her missing friend soon eclipsed all of her other emotions.

After a deep breath, and a few more moments to collect her thoughts, Bridget carefully recounted the full story of her harvesting run with Nora the day before. She did not pull any punches. She repeated every detail that she could remember of what Nora had done and said, but she also did not spare herself from blame.

"If I hadn't been so stupid, wanting to touch the fell, maybe none of this would have happened," she admitted. "It's as much my fault as anyone's."

"No it isn't," Eloise said firmly. Her voice was calm and level, but she was wiping her eyes with her hands. "If Nora killed Audrey, then she'd already made her choices, and you had nothing to do with that. And as things turned out, you might well have saved the rest of us."

"Poor Audrey," Kady said. She was shaking her head and staring at the floor. Then she looked up at Bridget again. "And poor Nora, too," she added. "I have to wonder if someone told her to do it, like what the old warehouse keeper did to me."

"I think that would be a fairly safe bet," said Michael.

In the brief silence that followed Michael's comment, Kyle and Ethan exchanged an uncomfortable glance. They were both feeling very much like outsiders caught in the middle of a private conversation.

"Look, I um... I hate to spoil the party," Kyle said hesitantly, "but what do we do now? I'm hoping you four have some sort of a plan at this point?"

"Shouldn't we get you back to the hospital first?" Ethan asked, looking at Bridget. "It won't be safe for you to go down the river now. You can't even walk, can you?"

Ethan still hadn't fully recovered from the shock of finding Bridget half-dead on the sofa, and his morning had only gotten progressively more disturbing from there. But setting everything else to the side, it seemed to him that the most obvious task at hand was getting the injured girl some medical care.

Bridget, however, was having none of it.

"I'm not going back to River Towne," she said, emphatically. "I'd rather bleed to death here. We all know full well what the Privy Council thinks of us, so let's not pretend they're going to do us any favors. We're on our own now."

"Well, we could at least go back and get more stuff, couldn't we?" Ethan objected. He looked around the room, hoping that someone else would jump in and back him up. "I wasn't exactly planning on this. My pack's totally empty. I didn't bring anything with me at all."

Eloise shook her head firmly.

"Even if we did go back to the enclave," she pointed out, "we couldn't load up our packs anyway, not without being noticed. Bridget's right: we've already come this far, we've made our decisions, now we just need to *go*. We're as ready as we're ever going to be, and who knows what else will happen if we wait. If we don't leave now, we may never get away at all."

"We brought batteries, our reading tablets, all the food there was in the clade, and whatever else we could think of," Kady said. She was looking directly at Ethan, and trying to be reassuring. "We brought as many things with us as we thought we could sneak past the oarsman. Anything else that we need we'll just have to find along the way."

"And we won't have to check it in at the warehouse when we do," Michael added, with a nod in Kady's direction.

"And I brought a first aid kit," Gwen announced proudly, looking over at Bridget. "It's one of the things I got at the Warehouse this morning, but I didn't expect we'd need it so soon."

Since neither Gwen nor Kyle knew anything about raft construction, they stayed behind to help Bridget, while the other four conspirators set to work carting the various sections of the boat to the river. Ethan was still far from comfortable with anything about his new circumstances, but having a specific physical task to focus on made it much easier for him to set his uncertainties aside, at least for the time being.

Having briefly served as a volunteer at the hospital tent, Kyle knew a little about basic first aid. But he'd never been very good at it, and he was terribly nervous about treating or even *touching* this badly injured girl that he barely knew. Gwendolyn, however, was all business, and it was her first aid kit to begin with. Once she realized that Kyle wasn't up to the task, she elbowed past him.

"She needs clean clothes," Gwen said, indicating Bridget's bloodstained shorts and shirt. "Go find some."

"I don't even know what sort of..."

"Just check the nearby houses," Gwen continued, interrupting him. "Sweatshirts, t-shirts, shorts... Anything at all, but preferably something loose and baggy. We'll need to keep her warm."

Kyle nodded nervously, and disappeared down the hallway and out the front door. Once he'd gone, Gwendolyn looked at Bridget and gave her a sly grin.

"I just wanted to get rid of him for a little while," she admitted. "Boys are useless sometimes... it's a good thing he's cute."

Bridget leaned back into the cushions on the sofa, while Gwendolyn washed and sterilized the area around her wound. She tried to be as careful as possible, but though Bridget never complained, more than once Gwen could tell that she'd hurt her.

"Sorry," Gwendolyn whispered. Bridget just clenched her teeth and looked the other way.

Once the skin around the wound was clean, Gwen applied some antibiotic cream to the puncture itself, then covered it over with a sterile pad. Last of all she wrapped the leg securely with a long strip of self-adhesive bandage.

"All done," Gwen said, as she closed the first aid kit and tucked it back into her satchel.

"Thank you," muttered Bridget. She meant it, but she was too worn down to say it with any enthusiasm.

The two girls sat quietly for a while after that, but Gwendolyn was too curious to stay silent for long. Once she'd judged that Bridget had recovered enough strength for a little conversation, she couldn't resist asking for more details about what had happened the night before.

"I'm sorry, but I have to ask, " Gwen began, tentatively. "You never told us how you got back here. How did you make it through the night?"

Bridget sighed, and turned her head just enough to look at Gwen. Then she closed her eyes again.

"I knew I couldn't make it to the boat landing," Bridget said, "so I didn't even try. This house was closer, so I came here. I wanted to hide in the attic with the pieces of the boat, but I couldn't get up the stairs. It was just too much. I laid down in the entryway for a long time... I might even have fallen asleep there, I don't know... After that I found a bathroom and got that towel."

Bridget gestured toward the foot of the sofa, vaguely in the direction of the bloody towel that had been draped over her leg.

"I tried wrapping my leg up, but I couldn't do anything with it. It hurt every time I touched it, and it started bleeding again every time I tried to move. I decided the best I could do was crash on the sofa and hope I didn't bleed to death in my sleep. It wasn't much of a hiding place, but the fell had already passed on killing me once. I really couldn't do anything else anyway."

"Gloria was watching over you," Gwen said. She'd meant it to be a comforting remark, but Bridget didn't seem to agree.

"I'm not so sure Gloria had all that much to do with it," she said.

Chapter 7: Departure

The final assembly of the raft went as well as could have been expected. Michael, Kady and Eloise all knew exactly how the various pieces were supposed to fit together, and though Ethan had not been part of the design process, he caught on quickly. His prior experience with the rafts in River Towne had left him with a fairly solid understanding of the basic principles involved, and his strength and physical stamina were tremendous assets when it came to wrestling pieces into position, or carting things across the Circle Park to the river.

The Promenade, of course, was heavily trafficked, especially as the day wore on and harvesters began to make their returns to the boat landing. More than once, the group was approached by curious onlookers, who were understandably puzzled by the sight of four senior harvesters working together on some strange contraption.

The first such encounter came in the late morning, when the builders had just gotten the first pieces of the raft to the river's edge. A boy – who could not have been much older than twelve or thirteen – stopped along the path to watch. A minute or two later, he approached the group to ask what was going on.

"Council business," Michael told him abruptly, before any of the others could reply.

The curious young harvester took a quick step backward and ducked his head apologetically.

"Oh, sorry," he replied, before scampering away along the Promenade. The four builders watched him for a few seconds, until he was safely out of earshot.

"Perfect answer..." said Eloise, looking across at Michael with an approving nod.

"I wonder if we should have invited him too," Kady said, with some regret. "I suppose we can't bring everyone."

"He was awfully young," Eloise pointed out. "And let's not make this any more complicated than it has to be."

"A kid like that still has plenty of time," Ethan said, "and I don't think I'd want that responsibility."

The other builders all agreed with this sentiment, and though none of them came out and specifically said so, it became an understanding among them from that point forward that they would try to avoid adding anyone else to the conspiracy. And, since Michael's comment *"Council business"* proved so successful at deterring unwanted questions, it soon became the group's standard answer to any queries about the boat, or what they all might be doing.

While Bridget slept on the sofa, and the others busied themselves with assembling the boat, Gwendolyn took on a supporting role, back at the tall house with the swimming pool. Not having to worry about the technical problems of constructing the raft, Gwendolyn was free to devote her full attention to the supplies and equipment the group was likely to need, now that they had left behind the relative comforts of their huts back at the enclave.

First of all, they did not have any cots to sleep on, and Gwen couldn't think of any convenient way to transport beds or mattresses across the river. But if they were going to have to sleep outside, Gwen reasoned that they could still try to make themselves a little more comfortable. Bridget, at least, would need to be kept warm, but Gwen suspected that they'd all soon regret it if they had to bed down, without any padding at all, on the cold concrete surface of the Periphery.

She searched all the bedrooms in the house, and came up with a few pillows and other useful things, but not enough for everyone. So once Kyle had returned with a satchel full of new clothes for Bridget, Gwendolyn immediately sent him out again in search of more towels and pillows and blankets and bedsheets.

Gwen also realized that the group would not have access to a hotmaker on the other side of the river, so she took it upon herself to make sure that everyone was well fed before leaving the Middle Ring. Fortunately, the group had plenty of food on hand. Kady and Eloise

162

had cleaned out their clade's foodwall before leaving the enclave, and Bridget's pack was still stuffed with the food that she and Nora had found the day before.

Gwen was surprised that Bridget had kept her satchel with her. By rights she should have dropped it, to make it easier on herself with her injured leg. But Bridget was the first to admit that in the midst of her ordeal, she hadn't been thinking clearly. Not only had she not taken her backpack off, she'd completely forgotten that she even had it on.

By the time the conspirators had finished assembling the raft, it was already late afternoon. All of them were tired, with the possible exception of Gwen, who had not left the house all day. But it was largely thanks to Gwendolyn's efforts that everyone was well fed, their water bottles were full, and an ample supply of bedding and other gear had been gathered and hauled to the riverside. She had even thought to remind everyone to make use of the house's nice clean bathrooms.

It was finally time to go.

Having now had two good meals and a few more hours of sleep, Bridget felt much stronger than she had in the morning, though she was still far too weak to get to the river on her own. The group discussed how best to transport her to the boat, but in the end, the simplest solution proved to be the best: Ethan just picked her up and carried her.

It was a difficult trip for both of them. Ethan was already tired, and at some point along the way, Bridget's leg started bleeding again. But with encouragement and help from the others, Ethan succeeded in getting her safely aboard the raft, along with the scavenged bedding, and most of their other supplies.

But now that it was partly loaded, a serious problem with the raft became apparent: it wasn't big enough. Even carrying only Bridget and a few supplies, it was already riding low in the water. It was obvious to everyone that if the rest of the group all climbed aboard at once, the raft's hardfoam panel floor would sink below the surface of the river, and all their gear would get soaking wet.

The late afternoon sky was now drawing perilously close to sunset, so there was nothing for it but to shuttle across, making multiple trips. Even this proved to be a challenge, because the boat was very poorly streamlined. Unlike River Towne's ferry, which was long and narrow, the conspirators' raft was shaped more like a square. This made it a fairly stable platform, but also made it almost impossible for one person to easily control. Even working together, Michael and Ethan had to labor fairly hard just to row Bridget and all their gear across the river to the opposite side.

In total, it took three trips to get everyone back to the Periphery. Kady and Eloise insisted on waiting to go last, and by the time Gwendolyn and Kyle returned with the raft to collect them, Gloria had already announced the sunset. Everyone kept a nervous watch, up and down the Promenade in the twilight, but fortunately no fells appeared. Eloise and Kady had both been prepared to swim if they had to, but neither of them relished that thought. Not only would they be cold and wet, and without a dry change of clothes when they reached the other side, this was not the most pleasant part of the river for swimming. They were not all that far downstream from the River Towne latrines.

Though they were still much closer to the enclave than they would have liked, the group could go no further that night. They were all exhausted, and no one thought it was safe to try moving Bridget again, particularly in the growing darkness.

They had to partly dismantle the raft, and pull it completely out of the river; otherwise, it would have simply washed away downstream. They'd brought ropes along, to secure it in place, but on the bare surface of the Periphery there was nothing to which those ropes could be tied.

Once the pieces of the raft were safely ashore, they spread out the blankets that Gwendolyn and Kyle had collected, to make as comfortable a camp for themselves as they could. They had a few hydrogen batteries, and two small electric lanterns that Kady had brought with her from the girls' clade, so they still had some light to see by, even as the daylight faded, and far above them the stars began to slowly appear.

Bridget was asleep again, long before the rest of the group had even finished with the raft. The others were completely spent as well, but despite their fatigue, they were still too wound up from their long day's work to immediately turn in for the night. They sat there on the blankets for several hours, quietly talking together and playing a few half-hearted rounds of Knucklejack, until eventually every one of them had curled up with a pillow, to settle themselves in for an uneasy and very uncomfortable sleep.

Chapter 8:
Down the River

Kady woke early the next morning to find that almost everyone else was still asleep. The only person up and moving around was Eloise, who was standing by the river, quietly inspecting the partially disassembled raft.

Feeling cold and stiff all over, Kady rolled herself into a sitting position and wrapped her blanket up around her shoulders. She rocked back and forth for a while, trying to loosen the knotted muscles along her spine. A few seconds later, she pushed herself up off the pavement and onto her feet again, and with the blanket still draped around her, she walked toward the river to join Eloise.

"Is the boat ok?" she asked. She kept her voice low, so as not to wake anyone who was still sleeping.

"It's fine," Eloise replied, speaking just as softly. "I was only killing time, waiting for somebody else to get up."

"How long have you been awake?"

"A while," Eloise said with a shrug. "I hope you slept better than I did. I feel like an empty box that's been stepped on."

"Me too," Kady said. "I'm sore all over."

The two girls stood there together for a long while, saying nothing more, and looking out across the river toward the Middle Ring. In the pre-dawn light, the Circle Park was shrouded in a haze of mist from the lawn sprinklers. It would still be half an hour or more before Gloria announced the sunrise.

Once everyone else was awake and moving about, the conspirators gathered to decide on their plans for the day.

"I'm wondering if maybe we shouldn't even go back across the river at all," Kady suggested. "Bridget can ride downstream on the raft, with the rest of us walking alongside. We'll cover a lot more ground that way."

Eloise nodded in agreement.

"I'm not sure how far it is to the pumping station," she said, "but I think we should get as far as we can from River Towne. If we cross the river here, we'll still be tripping over the other harvesters, like we were yesterday."

"We can't just walk all day," Gwendolyn pointed out. "If nothing else, we'll have to refill our water bottles. The river water's no good for drinking here, and we don't have a hotmaker either."

"I, for one, would not object to breakfast at some point," Kyle remarked. He'd said it as a joke, but it was obvious that he wasn't joking. They'd had an earlier than usual dinner the day before, followed by a long uncomfortable night. Everyone else was hungry too.

"What if a few of us cross over now," Michael suggested, "go harvesting, get some water... whatever. Everybody else can go downstream with the raft for a few hours, set up camp again, and wait."

"That sounds OK to me," Ethan agreed.

"I'm sorry I can't help much, whatever we do," said Bridget.

"Heal," Gwendolyn said, sternly wagging her index finger at Bridget. "That's your only job right now."

Though the discussion continued for another fifteen minutes or so, eventually everyone conceded that Michael's suggestion was probably the most sensible plan. Since Gwendolyn had already taken on the role of head nurse for Bridget, she and Kyle volunteered to take her down the river on the raft, while the others would go harvesting. Then they would all meet up again, further downstream.

It did not take nearly as long to reassemble the raft as it had taken to put it together the day before. Not only did the group have a much clearer understanding of how best to connect everything securely, they also didn't have to cart the pieces all the way from the attic to the river. It took them less than an hour to get the raft back together, and by the time they were ready to get underway again it was barely mid-morning.

After ferrying the others across the river, Kyle and Gwendolyn helped Bridget clamber back onto the raft. It was a struggle for all three of them, as Kyle wasn't nearly as strong or as sure-footed as Ethan. But with a little patience, and with no small measure of cursing, they managed to get Bridget safely aboard without any serious mishaps.

The trio continued along the Periphery for about three hours, just letting the raft float with the current. Bridget rode with the bedding and their other gear, while Kyle and Gwendolyn walked alongside, holding onto the tow ropes to make sure the raft didn't drift too far away from the river's outer bank.

Shortly after noon, they stopped to wait for the others. Kyle and Gwen helped Bridget back onto the Periphery, then Kyle held the raft in place while Gwen took a few minutes to inspect Bridget's injured leg.

"It's awfully red around there," Gwen said, prodding gently at the wound with her fingers. "How much does it hurt? You might be developing an infection."

Bridget sighed, and nodded her head.

"It wouldn't surprise me a bit if it's infected," she said. "It's itching pretty bad. I've been trying not to touch it."

Once Bridget's leg had been treated again and rebandaged, Gwendolyn sifted through the remaining food packets, looking for something the three of them could eat without a hotmaker. Gwen found a yogurt cup, which she gave to Bridget, and a packet of gingersnap cookies, which the three of them shared. It wasn't a meal, but they all felt better for having had at least a few bites of something.

It was less than an hour later when Michael and Ethan appeared on the opposite bank of the river. They had done very little actual harvesting, but they'd filled some large jugs with clean water from one of the houses, and had heated enough meal packets for everyone. The food was already cold again, but having now been cooked, it was at least edible. Gwendolyn, Bridget and Kyle were all very grateful.

Not long after Michael and Ethan's return, Kady and Eloise turned up as well. They'd had great luck with their own harvesting run, finding a large stash of snacks and meal packets in one of the first houses they'd checked. Both of their satchels were nearly full.

"We didn't see anyone from River Towne," Kady remarked. "I'm not sure why. Maybe no one from there could have walked this far yet. They'd have to have gotten a very early start."

"I'd think by now we should be close to the outer limits of how far a harvester can walk in a day," Eloise said. "That is, assuming they planned to spend any time searching, and still wanted to make it back to the boat landing before sunset."

"Uncharted territory," Michael added. He had an enormous smile on his face.

Now that they were better fed and better supplied, and with a few more hours remaining before sunset, the group decided to press on down the river for as long as the daylight lasted.

Even accounting for their excitement at being – for the very first time in their lives – entirely outside of River Towne's domain, their trek down the Periphery was a painfully boring walk. None of them had slept well the night before, and their energy was at low ebb. After the first hour, even Gwendolyn found it hard to make much conversation, as there was almost no scenery to discuss. Off to their left was only the river and the distant Circle Park. The bare pavement below their feet seemed endless, and there was nothing standing between them and the featureless spectre of Fairhaven's outer wall, which loomed off to their right hand side.

At some point in the late afternoon, however, there was a change. Though at first they could not make anything out distinctly, they could all see that there was *something* on the horizon, far up ahead of them on the Periphery. After walking for so long on that dusty, barren surface, even the smallest change was impossible to ignore.

As they drew closer, they could tell that what they were seeing ahead of them was a little cluster of tents and other structures, not unlike the familiar huts and warehouses that they'd left behind at River Towne.

At first, no one knew what to make of it.

"Whatever it is," Eloise said, once they were close enough to see the buildings clearly, "it looks like it's abandoned..."

"It's not another enclave, is it?" Michael asked. "It can't be. It's too small. And Stone Prairie's supposed to be all the way on the other side of the pumping station, isn't it? So... so what the hell is this place?"

Ethan suddenly gave a shout, and put his hands against his forehead. Everyone turned to look at him.

"I know what it is," he said, looking around at the others. "The keeper told me about this place, just a couple of days ago, whenever that was. I kind of thought he was just making stuff up to mess with me, but that's gotta be what this is. It's one of the enclave's old outposts."

Chapter 9:
The Outpost

By the time they reached the little cluster of buildings, the city dome had already begun to make its gradual transition toward sunset. Ethan had conveyed to the rest of the travellers as much as he could remember of what the warehouse keeper had said about River Towne's outposts, so they all had a general understanding of what the place had once been used for, though none of them had any idea what they might find there now.

Michael and Ethan carefully got Bridget ashore, and everyone helped with unloading the blankets and other supplies from the raft. They were about to start on the laborious task of hauling the boat back out of the river, when Ethan told them to wait. He walked slowly riverwise along the water's edge for another fifteen or twenty meters, until he finally found what he was looking for.

"We can tie the boat off here," Ethan called back to the group, pointing to a metal cleat that was mounted into the concrete near the water's edge. "This is the same sort of hook we used back in River Towne," he explained. "It's for tying the boats overnight, so they don't drift away. They would have to have kept a boat here, so I thought they'd have something like this here too."

Kady was skeptical.

"Is it strong enough?" she asked. "This place looks like it's been abandoned for an awfully long time. We can't afford to lose the boat; are you sure it'll hold?"

"It's solid," Ethan said, kicking lightly at the cleat with the toe of his shoe. "And there are several more of them, on down the bank here. We can use all of them, and tie on more than one rope if you want, just to be safe. But I wouldn't worry about it. These are exactly like the ones we had in River Towne."

Once the raft was securely tied, the travellers set about inspecting the buildings. They found eight intact huts, plus several others that had been partially disassembled. There were also the remnants of several larger structures, only one of which was still standing.

"This must have been the warehouse, or something like it," Eloise said, looking through the front flap of the largest building. "Lots of shelves in there."

"The shelves aren't all empty, either," said Kyle. "But I can't think they'd have left anything useful behind."

"Hard to tell from here," Michael added. "Everything's so covered in dust."

"Cots!" Gwen shouted, peeking inside one of the smaller huts. "Maybe we won't have to sleep on the ground tonight."

Searching through the rest of the huts, the travellers found more than twenty cots that seemed to be in good enough condition to still be used, as well as several tables and a large number of chairs and other miscellaneous furniture. There was even an intact latrine, set up in the hut that was furthest downstream. It seemed like it might still work, if they could somehow supply it with water.

But it was Kady who made the biggest discovery of all. Still mounted in the dust-covered foodwall of one of the tents was a hotmaker. It looked undamaged, and after they had thoroughly cleaned it, they tried connecting it to one of their hydrogen batteries. To everyone's delight, the little indicator light glowed bright red. It still worked.

Their last hour of daylight was spent cleaning cots and airing out the two nicest huts. Everything they found was covered with a layer of fine grey dust, but otherwise the tents and most of the furnishings were still in reasonably good condition. Because Fairhaven had almost no fluctuations in weather, cloth and metal and wood deteriorated there only very slowly. With no significant variation in either the ambient temperature or humidity over time, items which might have swiftly crumbled in more natural surroundings were as well-preserved in Fairhaven as if they'd been stored in the vault of a museum's permanent archive.

Dinner that night was as cheerful a meal as any of them had enjoyed in a long while, and afterwards they all sat together, chatting and relaxing underneath the familiar illusion of the twinkling stars. By the time they retired to bed, almost everyone was feeling hopeful and comfortable. The one exception was Bridget. She was very tired, and felt a little bit queasy, and so she turned in somewhat earlier than the others. No one thought anything of it at the time.

––––––––

Eloise was awakened in the middle of the night by the sound of a quiet *thump* nearby. Startled, she rolled over to see what had made the noise.

"Hello?..." she asked. She wasn't entirely sure whether she'd heard anything at all, or if she'd only been dreaming.

"*Nnggghhh...*" came a low groan from the opposite side of the hut.

"Bridget?"

"*I'm out of water...*" was Bridget's reply.

They'd left the front door and the windows of the hut open, to air the place out, and in the faint light trickling into the room, Eloise could vaguely see the dark outline of Bridget, lying on the concrete floor. She immediately rolled out of bed, and turned on the lantern.

"What's happening?..." Kady muttered as the light came on. She was still half-asleep.

"Wake up Gwen," Eloise told her. "Bridget's out of bed."

Within moments, the three girls were huddled around Bridget, trying to get her back into her cot.

"I'm OK..." Bridget said, but it wasn't true.

"You're burning up," Eloise told her.

"I'm cold..." Bridget replied.

"You've got a fever," Gwendolyn repeated.

"Let's get her back in bed," Eloise said.

The three girls lifted Bridget back into her cot. She was covered in sweat. Kady retrieved her own water bottle, which was less than half full, and helped Bridget sit up enough to drink. She emptied the bottle, and Kady tossed it aside. Eloise found a towel, and dampened it with water from one of the spare jugs. Gwendolyn disappeared out the door of the hut. Neither Kady nor Eloise had any idea where she was going, but that was the least of their concerns.

"Is this any better?" Eloise asked. She wiped Bridget's face with the wet towel, as Kady tried to ease her back down onto the cot.

"Fells everywhere..." Bridget said. She was resisting Kady's efforts, still sitting halfway up and trying to swat at Eloise's hand. Her eyes seemed out of focus. "Can't get away..." she mumbled.

"We're on the Periphery," Eloise said. "There aren't any fells here; it's OK."

"*...have to get out...*" Bridget whispered, as she finally closed her eyes again and sank slowly back onto the bed. Her breathing was shallow and labored, but she did not say anything more. Eloise and Kady could not tell if she was unconscious or merely asleep.

A few seconds later, Gwendolyn returned; she had brought Kyle with her. Kyle did not know much more about treating a fever than anyone else in the group, but he was the closest thing they had to a doctor. Michael and Ethan soon arrived as well, with a second jug of water and a few more clean towels.

It was a long and harrowing night. No one could sleep, aside from Bridget herself, but for all their concern, the other travellers could do little more than watch and wait, and hope that she would somehow pull through.

Chapter 10:
Respite and Repair

When morning finally came, Bridget was still alive, and her fever seemed to have lessened somewhat. She woke up shortly after sunrise, asking for water. Kyle had already prepared some for her, with a tiny bit of salt mixed in to help with her hydration. Bridget would have emptied the bottle in a heartbeat, but Kyle insisted that she needed to drink it slowly, or else she might not be able to keep the water down.

Once Bridget was asleep again, the rest of the group gathered to eat breakfast, and decide what to do.

"We're obviously not going anywhere today," Eloise said. "We should probably stay put until Bridget's feeling better."

"That's fine with me," Michael agreed. "With a little work, this place could be downright livable."

"We can't stay here for long, though," Kady cautioned. "We only have so much food."

"I'd guess we have enough meal packets to last us at least a week," Gwendolyn added. "Ten days, maybe."

"We can just go harvesting for more, can't we?" Kyle asked. "And since we're well gone from River Towne, we won't even have to deal with the underkeepers anymore. With just the seven of us, I'd think we could almost stay here forever."

"Food may not be so easy to find, though," Ethan pointed out. "From what the keeper was telling me, that's why these outposts were abandoned in the first place."

"I guess we won't know until we do some harvesting," Eloise conceded, but I think we need to start taking our inventory seriously. We should count the food and the snacks, and probably everything else as well. We really can't afford to let ourselves run out of *anything*."

"The first thing we're going to need is more water," said Kady. "I can take care of that right now, if someone wants to ferry me across the river."

By the time breakfast was finished, it had been agreed that Kady and Ethan would go to fill the empty water jugs, while the others would care for Bridget and explore the outpost. There was no shortage of work to be done, but the group had ample time on their hands with which to do it. Eloise and Michael volunteered to try and get the latrine working, while Gwendolyn and Kyle would investigate the outpost's warehouse tent, with everyone helping to keep a watchful eye on Bridget.

As expected, the dilapidated warehouse contained few items that were of any great value, though there were quite a lot of useful things still sitting on the shelves. There were certainly no meal packets or hydrogen batteries; most of what remained were practical items such as clothing and furniture. These were certainly good to have on hand, but they were also easily found anywhere in the Middle Ring. At the time when this outpost was first abandoned, it had apparently not been thought worth the trouble to cart such things all the way back to River Towne.

Among the most noteworthy items Kyle and Gwendolyn found was a second hotmaker, as well as several sets of silverware and a great many plates and cups and other dishes. They also found a few assorted hand tools, a large stash of polymer tubing, some hardfoam panels, and various other building supplies.

Michael and Eloise soon determined that the only real problem with the latrine – aside from being covered with the same grey dust as everything else in the outpost – was the lack of a functional water supply. The latrines at River Towne, (as well as the hospital tent and the Commons), were equipped with a permanent reservoir, which could easily be refilled with river water by the use of a manually operated pumping system. The reservoir tank for the outpost's latrine was still in place, though the pump itself, if indeed there had ever been one, was missing.

Fortunately, Gwendolyn and Kyle had found several sturdy buckets in the warehouse. And, since the hut for the latrine was only a few steps from the river, it was a simple enough matter to fill the reservoir by hand. The latrine's water system was still sound – Eloise and

Michael couldn't find any leaks in the plumbing at all – so by mid-morning they'd not only cleaned and inspected the whole apparatus, they'd put it back into fairly good working order.

Bridget woke up in the late morning, and since she seemed a little stronger, Gwen decided it was time to try changing the bandage on her wound again. The whole of her upper leg looked bright red, and the puncture site itself was clearly swollen and infected. With Kyle's help – or at least with his advice – Gwen carefully re-opened the wound just enough to drain out some of the infection. After that she sterilized the surrounding skin for the third time, and applied more antibiotic cream before bandaging everything up once more. The process was clearly painful for Bridget, but she did not complain, and when it was finally over she seemed to feel greatly relieved.

It was shortly after noon when Ethan and Kady appeared again on the far bank of the river, and Eloise and Michael hurried across with the raft to collect them. They'd had no difficulty in finding houses with good running water, though they'd not found any food packets or medical supplies, or anything else of note in the few places that they'd searched.

"And you'd better believe there were fells," Ethan said. "We saw two of them just beyond the Circle Park, and another one a little bit further in."

"Fortunately they were all asleep." Kady added. "But we sure didn't feel like sticking around any longer than we had to, or exploring very far in from the river."

The rest of that day was spent cleaning the outpost, and making the huts more comfortable. Kyle and Gwen had found several brooms and mops in the warehouse tent, along with some soap and a variety of other cleaning supplies. By late afternoon, the group had managed to clean the worst of the must and dust away, at least from the two huts that they'd chosen to occupy, and the whole place was beginning to feel almost like a vacation home.

Bridget still had a fever, but it was nothing like it had been the night before, and by early evening she'd recovered enough to try eating a little solid food. She was ravenously hungry, but she very sensibly ate only a little plain rice and cereal. It was terribly bland, but her stomach was still unhappy with her for eating anything at all. She had no interest in tempting fate by trying to ingest anything that was the least bit flavorful or exciting.

Everyone was exhausted, not only from their hard day's work, but also from their anxious night the evening before. They had a quiet dinner together shortly after sunset, but by the time the stars had fully appeared above them, they had all returned to their freshly cleaned huts for a long night of uninterrupted and well deserved sleep.

The next few days were, on the whole, a very pleasant time for the seven travellers. Their evenings were mostly spent relaxing – studying random subjects on their reading tablets, playing Knucklejack, or even just sitting quietly together around one of their electric lanterns and chatting on into the night.

Bridget's injury continued to heal, and every morning she felt stronger than she'd felt the day before. Using some of the building supplies from the outpost's warehouse tent, Michael managed to put together a very serviceable set of crutches for her, and by the third day after her fever broke, Bridget was back on her feet and able to move around entirely on her own, at least for short distances. This was a huge boost to her morale. She felt much less like a burden to the others, not least of all because she no longer needed help to get herself to the latrine.

The other six travellers would take turns crossing the river, with two of them always staying behind to manage the boat and to keep Bridget company. On their harvesting runs, they were mostly looking for food, of course, but also hoping to find more medical supplies, or anything else that might prove useful in their new circumstances. They had to constantly refill their water jugs, and they made a regular practice of recharging their hydrogen batteries every day, to make certain that they would always have power for their lanterns and the hotmaker.

But harvesting was proving to be even more difficult than it had been back at River Towne. The fells were seemingly everywhere, and though the ones they spotted were almost always asleep, none of the travellers was inclined to ever go very far from the river. Even with all their caution, both Ethan and Eloise had very close calls, and on one afternoon Michael only escaped a prowling fell by diving into the river, and swimming out to meet the boat halfway across.

And despite their best efforts, their food supplies were slowly dwindling. The only meal packets that any of them had been able to find were in the houses far to the counter-river side of the outpost, toward River Towne. The warehouse keeper's warning that food would be difficult to find in that part of the Middle Ring seemed to be proving correct.

The travellers also found it unsettling that they had not encountered any other harvesters at all, not even on their furthest ventures back in the direction of River Towne. On one morning, as a test, Eloise and Kady made a point of walking counter-river through the Circle Park for as far as they could possibly go, leaving themselves barely time enough before sunset for the return trip. Eloise was quite certain that they'd managed to reach a portion of the Middle Ring which she'd explored several times before, and yet, at no point on that journey did they see anyone else at all, aside from a few occasional worker bees.

Exploring down the Periphery in the opposite direction, Kyle and Ethan made an even more important discovery. They found that it was just over a three-hour walk from the outpost to the spot where the river's fabled whitewater rapids began. And if those rapids were somewhat diminished from what they once had been, that difference was not apparent to the two young men. They stood there for a long time, awestruck by the sudden and dramatic change in the character of the river.

Large blocks of deeply grey, artificial stone were clearly visible everywhere in the water. Many of those stones were totally submerged, but the flattened tops of some few stood out above the surface. Those pillars that were exposed seemed almost to move by their own volition, as the water rose and fell and surged all around them. It seemed to Ethan that they were like ancient grey teeth, gnashing hungrily in the loudly churning foam.

Looking further riverwise from the point where the rapids began, the two young men could see the massive pumping station only a few kilometers away, where it completely blocked the course of the river. That dark and monolithic structure was both tall and broad, reaching far into the sky and stretching out across the full width of the Periphery, from the Circle Park all the way to the outer wall. There, it was pressed in tightly against the slightly arching undersurface of Fairhaven's great city dome.

Neither Kyle nor Ethan had ever seen anything like the pumping station before. Even at this distance it presented a starkly ominous and disheartening facade. Neither of them felt inclined to approach it for a closer look.

- End of Book Four -

Book Five:
Chapter 1:
The Pumping Station

The endless river's whitewater rapids ran for three full kilometers above the pumping station and one more kilometer below, and were formed by drastic changes in the topography of the riverbed. There, instead of gliding through a flat and featureless canal, the once-placid water now raced through a scattered array of deep troughs and narrow shallows, oddly shaped bowls and swiftly flowing channels, all of which were obstructed at irregular intervals by great stone pillars of varying geometries and heights. In Fairhaven's early years, the rapids had been truly spectacular, and even now in the city's decline they were still formidable enough to command respect, and inspire awe in those few who ventured far enough to see them.

The primary function of the rapids was strictly practical. The many stones and the chaotically churning water were, in effect, the first component of the pumping station's multi-stage filtering process, and were intended to prevent any particularly large pieces of debris from ever reaching the station itself, where they might obstruct the flow of water, or even damage the pumps.

Fairhaven's builders had not expected that the river would often carry significant debris, but they also knew that they could not anticipate every contingency. The stone "teeth" that jutted up from the surface of the rapids were a mechanical failsafe – a prudent precaution against the unexpected. If, for example, a large object such as a full-sized tree were to somehow fall into the river and wash downstream, the stones amid the current were aligned in such a way that they would trap the object in place, either until it was broken into smaller pieces by the force of the water, or until the worker bees were able to attend to it.

Just short of the pumping station, the rapids suddenly ended. The last portion of the river was a giant basin, which emptied out through a series of drains at the bottom. Within that basin, the river ceased to flow. Rather, the surface of the water there swirled forever around a central point, as it was slowly consumed by a relentless undertow.

Above that pool stood the unbroken edifice of the station itself. Its sheer and featureless walls mounted upward in a series of shallow terraces until they touched the sky, lying flush against the curving undersurface of the great city dome. Nowhere upon those darkly massive walls was there a single window or door to be found. The only entrance to that vast structure was from below, through long maintenance corridors that only the worker bees could use. Like the rest of Fairhaven's automated infrastructure, the pumping station had been constructed in a way that would preclude the possibility of any human interference in its operation.

Chapter 2:
Portage

It was early morning, and the seven travellers had gathered to discuss their plans. Eloise was feeling increasingly anxious about the group's long stay at the outpost, and now that Bridget's injury was mostly healed, she was more than eager to get moving again. Most of the others seemed to agree with her, though Kyle, at least, was reluctant.

"I don't see why we can't just stay here," he argued.

"This outpost was never our destination," Eloise replied. "It's been nice, and we've been lucky so far, but I think it's past time for us to go."

"We're barely breaking even on food aren't we?" Ethan added. "That's reason enough, I think." He looked over at Eloise, and she nodded in agreement.

"This was a good place to stop and let Bridget heal," said Kady, "but I don't really think we're any better off here than we were at River Towne."

"Less safe, if anything," Michael agreed. "Every time we hit the Circle Park, we're seeing fells, and swimming that river is no picnic."

Kyle lowered his head and stared at the concrete. He could see this was an argument he wasn't going to win, and what was more, he also knew that the others were right. That didn't make him any happier about the prospect of moving on.

"I just think now that we've put so much work into this place, it seems like a waste to just up and leave," he grumbled. "That's all I'm saying. And on down the river, I think things are likely to get worse, not better."

Sitting next to Kyle, Gwendolyn reached over and put her hand on top of his.

"I understand how you feel," she said to him. "It's been very nice here, on the whole, but I don't think this is where Gloria wants us to be. If anything, I think she's getting impatient with us for staying as long as we have."

"That's mostly my fault, I know," Bridget said. "I can almost walk now. I'll try not to slow us down any more."

"Don't be dumb," Kady said, elbowing Bridget playfully in the ribs. "We've had a nice vacation, all things considered, and if it wasn't for you, we might never have gotten away from the enclave at all."

With the matter decided, the group set about loading the raft with their bedding and some extra clothes, and everything else they could easily carry. There was some discussion over whether they should try taking a few cots as well, but the cots were much too bulky to easily fit aboard the raft, and it was not forgotten by anyone that whatever they took with them – including the boat itself – would have to be carted by hand on the long walk around the pumping station.

The whitewater rapids may have been less formidable than they once were, but still there was no chance that the raft could survive a trip through that part of the river. The turbulence alone would shake it to pieces, and even if not, the boat would be almost impossible to steer, and would certainly shatter on the first sizable rock that it chanced to hit. The group's only option was to cart the raft past the rapids in pieces, then reassemble it on the Stone Prairie side. Though they did not know exactly how far that would be, judging from what Kyle and Ethan had already seen, it would mean a trek of several kilometers at the very least.

The one item the travellers most hated to leave behind was their precious hotmaker. They still had enough meal packets to last them a week or more, but without a way to cook them, much of that food would be useless. Like the cots however, the hotmaker was too cumbersome to be carried any great distance, and since such things were easily found in almost any of Fairhaven's abandoned houses, they could not justify carting one all the way around the pumping station.

The group enjoyed a hasty breakfast, and Gwendolyn cooked dinner packets for everyone as well. The food would be cold again by evening, but it would still be edible, and there was no telling when they would have another chance to make use of a hotmaker. Once all their gear was loaded onto the raft, everyone made a quick final check to be certain they were not leaving anything important behind. They all knew that it was unlikely they would ever have the chance to return.

They walked riverwise along the Periphery, with Bridget riding on the raft beside them, until they were within a hundred meters of the rapids. By then it was nearly noon. The day was bright, and the pumping station loomed far ahead, like a vast and unfriendly mountain. Beside them, the river began to narrow, and the flowing water gradually picked up speed as it approached the standing rocks.

They had made some improvements to the raft during their time at the outpost, and though it still could not carry all of them at once, they could now shuttle everyone and all their luggage across the river in two trips, instead of three. Since Bridget could only walk very slowly, she and Gwendolyn set out along the Promenade as soon as they'd reached the Circle Park, while Kady and Eloise returned with the raft to the Periphery, to fetch the three boys.

Bridget had not set foot in the Middle Ring for more than a week, and after all the time she'd spent hobbling around the outpost, the wet grass felt wonderfully soft and welcoming underneath her feet. Her injured leg was much better, but although she no longer needed her crutches for short walks, she could not do without them entirely. Consequently, her backpack was only half full. Had she been left to decide for herself, Bridget would have filled her pack completely, but the other travellers refused to let her. Their chief concern was not how much she was able to carry, but simply that she could make the trip at all.

But while Bridget's satchel was half empty, Gwendolyn's was stuffed almost to bursting. Her first aid kit was carefully stowed on top, so she could get to it quickly if necessary, and much of the group's collected food was packed in underneath. Gwen also had two pillows tucked awkwardly under each of her arms, which caused her to waddle a bit from side to side as she walked. She and Bridget found it hard to resist teasing each other – just a little – about their slow mutual progress, and their equally inelegant gaits.

They had not been walking more than five minutes before they spotted the first fell. It was asleep, and nestled in beside a scenic little waterfall perhaps fifty meters from the Promenade. The two girls kept a careful watch on the dormant monster as they silently passed it by, but it did not move, nor show any outward sign that it was aware of them.

"Are you ok?..." Gwendolyn whispered, once they could no longer see the cocoon behind them.

"I'm all right," Bridget muttered in reply, "but I wish we could warn the others somehow."

"It wouldn't help them much even if we could," Gwen said. "They'll see it soon enough, and there's no going back for any of us at this point. They'll have to get past it too, same as we did. Best for the two of us to just keep walking."

"If a fell *does* come after us," Bridget added, after a moment's pause, "promise me you'll jump into the river and let it have me instead."

"I am not promising any such thing," Gwendolyn said, indignantly.

"I still can't run," Bridget reminded her.

"You won't have to," Gwen insisted. "Now shut up, and stop being stupid. You're not getting killed while I'm around, and we're all going to be just fine."

As Gwendolyn and Bridget continued along the Promenade, it became increasingly clear to them that they were steadily climbing uphill. At first they'd hardly noticed, but the further they went, the more apparent the incline became. It was also obvious that while they were climbing up, the river beside them was falling. Off to their right, the ground sloped ever more steeply down toward the river's edge, and the rapids were soon quite some distance below the path.

"I wouldn't want to take a tumble that direction," Bridget remarked. "I'm having enough trouble as it is."

"I'd take a bet the path levels off once we get past the station," Gwen said. "Not much further now, I think."

As it turned out, Gwendolyn's hunch was correct. By the time they drew even with the pumping station, they could see that the path ahead was indeed much more level. They could also see that someone was gradually catching up to them from behind. At first, they couldn't tell for certain who it was; all they could make out was a large blobbish shape slowly drawing nearer. But before long, they could see that it was Kyle, carrying some of the floatation bundles from the raft. He was not moving particularly quickly, but with Bridget hobbling along on her crutches, he was steadily gaining ground on the two girls. Just beyond the pumping station, they stopped along the path, waiting for him to catch up with them.

"Did you see the fell?" Gwendolyn called back, once Kyle was close enough for conversation.

"I saw *three* fells," he replied, "in three different spots. I thought I was done for, to be honest. There's no way in hell to keep these empty bottles quiet. I've sounded like a junkpile falling down a staircase, all the way from there to here. But the fells seemed to sleep right through it. I can't imagine why, but I'm not complaining."

"I hope everyone else is OK," Bridget said. "If the fells do start to wake up, there's really no place to run."

"There's always the river," Kyle said, "except for right next to the station. But that slope down to the waterline is no joke, and I wouldn't want to try swimming those rapids, either."

"The river doesn't look half so bad on this side of the station," Gwen pointed out, and she was right. The riverbank was once again nearly level with the Promenade, and the rapids did not seem half so fierce as they had been on the counter-river side.

It was only a few minutes later that the three young travellers reached what seemed to be the rapids' furthest end. The river fanned out again, and grew abruptly calmer, and the slowly moving water was absolutely crystal clear. The trio dropped their backpacks and other burdens onto a nice open patch of grass, which seemed to them as good a place as any to rebuild the raft.

Bridget's arms and legs were aching, and she soon settled onto a nearby park bench to rest and wait for the others. But tired as they already were, Kyle and Gwendolyn could not stop. They immediately set off together back along the Promenade, to help fetch the rest of the disassembled boat.

Chapter 3:
Islands in the Stream

By late afternoon, the portage operation was nearly complete. The raft was mostly reassembled, with the exception of one long edge of the framework, which Michael and Ethan had gone to retrieve. Everyone else was standing by the river, just beyond the end of the rapids, awaiting their return.

Kady and Eloise had done most of the actual handwork rebuilding the raft, with Bridget helping as she was able. The other four travellers had each made a second trip back along the Promenade, to retrieve the rest of the boat, as well as their packs and blankets and everything else. Though the group had seen sleeping fells almost everywhere along their route, to this point the mechanical predators had left them alone. But in spite of this apparent good fortune, Kady was worried.

"Time is going to be tight," she said, staring unhappily at the partially completed raft. "Even if we get the rest of the boat back together, we may not have enough time left before sunset to shuttle everything across the river."

"There's no point in us standing here and feeling useless," Eloise pointed out. "We should take some of the stuff across the river right now. This part of the raft is reasonably solid all by itself, even if it is a bit lopsided."

"But what if it sinks?" Kyle objected.

Kyle didn't understand much about how the raft worked, but all the same, trying to cross the river on a half-finished boat didn't sound like a good idea to him.

"It won't *sink*," Bridget insisted. "The floats are still going to float, no matter what else. But all the same, it can't be very stable like this. Anything we load onto that unfinished side is bound to get pretty well soaked."

"We don't have to load it all the way," Kady pointed out. "We have time to make more than one trip, and we can just pile things over on the raft's good side, so they'll stay dry. I think Eloise is right. The more we can get across the river now, the less we'll have to scramble with everything after Michael and Ethan get back."

"You might as well haul me across too, while you're at it," said Bridget. "I can't help much anyway, and if the fells get hungry, I'm the one who can't swim."

"You can set up the camp for us, while you're over there," Gwen suggested cheerfully. "One way or another, it looks like we'll be sleeping on concrete tonight."

"Now *there's* something to look forward to," Kyle muttered, rubbing his neck.

———

A good distance counter-river from the spot where the others were waiting, Michael and Ethan were having misgivings of their own. They were now well beyond the pumping station, but they had nearly two more kilometers of walking ahead of them before they would even reach the last piece of the raft, and then they'd still have to cart it all the way back to the Stone Prairie side. It had already been a long day, and they were getting tired, but that was the least of their concerns.

"You know this isn't going to work," Michael said.

"How do you mean?" Ethan asked.

"I feel like we're pushing our luck, and this is one trip too many."

Ethan had been thinking much the same thing. He glanced over at Michael, but the two young men kept on walking, and said nothing more for several minutes.

"Fell..." Ethan muttered, breaking the silence. He pointed up ahead toward a raised bed of brightly blooming tulips. On the opposite side, just above the tops of the flowers, the upper half of a fell's cocoon was plainly visible. Michael nodded.

"Is it my imagination," he asked quietly, "or are there more of them along the path now than there were this morning?"

"I don't know," Ethan replied. "I'm too tired to count, but I don't remember this one."

"If it wasn't there before," Michael pointed out, "then it must have *moved* there since the last time we came by, and that means it isn't really sleeping."

"Keep walking..." Ethan whispered. "If it opens up, which way do we run?"

"We can't go back toward the girls... It's too far; we'd never make it."

"There's not enough cover for us to lose it anywhere around here, and I think if we go any further in, we're just going to find more fells."

"The river then?..." Michael suggested, doubtfully. "That's not much of an option."

They both looked down toward the rapids to their left, where the racing water crashed over and around the half-submerged rocks and the oddly shaped pillars of stone.

"The river, I guess," said Ethan. "I don't see anything better."

The two young men continued cautiously down the Promenade, but the fell showed no sign of movement. A few moments later, they had passed it by. Ethan checked back over his shoulder, again and again, until at last the fell was out of sight once more.

"I can't believe it let us go by," he said. "I thought that one was coming after us for sure."

"Maybe it's waiting to ambush us on the return trip," Michael said.

"Are fells that smart?..." Ethan asked. "How would it even know?"

"I dunno," Michael said. "But they'd always tell us '*Avoid patterns*' for a reason, and we've spent a lot of time walking back and forth over this same stretch of the Promenade."

"You think the fells have picked up on that."

"I have no idea," Michael admitted. "I guess we'll find out soon enough."

Bridget carefully spread some of the blankets out over the concrete surface of the Periphery, and dug the group's two electric lanterns out from the pack where they'd been stowed. It wasn't dark yet, but the sky overhead was already starting its long transition toward sunset. The lanterns would be needed soon enough.

She picked up a reading tablet, and half-heartedly scrolled through a few random pages before shutting it off again. She wanted to distract herself, but she wasn't in the mood for reading. Instead, she took off her socks and shoes, and sat down on the curb above the outer bank of the river, letting her legs dangle into the stream. The cool water felt good on her sore calves and toes.

On the opposite bank of the river, Kyle and Gwendolyn were helping Kady and Eloise load the last of the group's luggage onto the half-assembled raft. Bridget could see that they were talking amongst themselves, but she could not make out what they were saying over the low murmur of the nearby rapids. She wondered what was keeping Michael and Ethan, and if they would be able to make it back in time.

The two boys hoisted the last long piece of the raft up onto their shoulders, and started trudging back with it, up the Promenade, with Ethan in front and Michael following behind. This skeletal section of framework was not particularly heavy, but it was too long and awkward for one person to carry alone.

With their time running short, they went as quickly as they safely could, but they did not get very far. They'd only been walking for a few minutes when Michael called a halt.

"Stop..." he said, suddenly. "Where is it?"

"Where's what?" Ethan asked.

"Put the frame down," Michael said. "The fell by the waterfall, where is it?"

The two boys carefully set the section of raft onto the path, and Ethan looked across the lawn to where Michael was pointing. There, a little stream spilled over a tall rock shelf, then gradually trickled down an uneven terrace of flat stones, before emptying into a circular pool. It was, in fact, the same decorative landscaping feature where Bridget and Gwendolyn had first noticed a sleeping fell earlier in the day. That same metallic cocoon had been there in that same exact spot all afternoon, but it was not there now.

Michael and Ethan scanned the path ahead of them, and all around the waterfall, but they did not immediately see anything of note, other than the unexpected absence of the fell.

"Maybe it went somewhere else..." Ethan said, though he did not sound at all confident about that possibility.

"This is not good..." said Michael.

"River!..." Ethan suddenly shouted.

Michael turned and saw a fell, not twenty meters distant, rushing across the grass towards them. The monster had apparently circled around, to come at them from behind. Michael had been so intent on the spot by the waterfall and the path further ahead that he was nearly caught flat-footed, but as it was he had just enough time to react. He turned and raced away from the fell, cutting a sharp diagonal across the lawn toward the river.

A few meters ahead of him, Michael saw Ethan dive in, and disappear under the rushing water. Michael could not see how anyone could possibly swim through that raging torrent, but this was not the moment for hesitation, and he plunged into the rapids himself, in almost the same spot where Ethan had leapt in a moment before.

Instantly, the world vanished, as Michael was swallowed up in the churning water. Totally at the mercy of the current, he could not breathe, or swim, or even tell which direction was up or down. He flailed his arms and legs helplessly, trying to somehow get his head back above the surface of the water, but his senses were failing him. All he could see and hear was the chaos of the angry river. All he could feel was the cold power of the water, moving him in whatever way it chose.

Suddenly, he smashed full up against something solid. The impact knocked the last breath out of his lungs, and he choked as he tried to inhale and got mostly water and foam. But for a moment he seemed to hold still in that place, as the river swept brutally over and around him to every side. A part of his mind realized he'd hit one of the stone pillars. Dazed, he felt with his hand and found air, and a surface of rock above the current.

Clinging to that pillar of stone, he was able to reach his arm over the top, and lift his head out of the water. Coughing and sputtering, he gasped for breath, and this time his lungs filled with air. Opening his eyes again, he could see the dark grey surface of the pillar, just below his chin. Still fighting against the current – which was either trying to tear him apart or force him back down into the pounding rapids – Michael pulled himself up, onto his hands and knees, atop that flat stone surface and out of the river. He stayed that way, exhausted and coughing up water and trying to breathe, for a long while.

"Anything broken?..."

Michael raised his head, to try and find where Ethan's voice was coming from. He finally spotted him, atop another pillar, some fifteen meters further down the stream.

"I'm ok, I think..." Michael called back weakly. He coughed and spit out some more water before taking another long breath. He looked up toward Ethan again. "But I think my socks got wet."

Ethan stared blankly at Michael for several seconds. Then he laughed. Then he coughed and choked, and wrapped his arms over his head, and laughed some more.

Chapter 4:
Before the Dawn

Michael and Ethan sat on those two stone pillars and watched the sky slowly fading overhead as the rapids thundered all around them. The fell was pacing slowly up and down through the grass, just beyond the inner bank of the river.

"So what do we do now?" Ethan asked, shouting over the roar of the water.

"Unless our supervisor over there goes away," Michael shouted back, "I'm not sure there's anything we *can* do. I'm open to suggestions, if you've got one."

"Don't ask me," Ethan replied, "I just work here."

The top of Michael's pillar was flat and reasonably wide. He had room enough to sit or stand, but not nearly enough space to lie down, and while he was safely out of the rushing current, he was not high and dry. Water would frequently splash or spray over the top, drenching him all over again. Ethan had it no better. The pillar he'd climbed onto stood slightly higher above the rushing water than Michael's, but its upper surface was not completely flat. He could sit or squat down in place, but he did not feel safe trying to stand up all the way. However, with no other options available, the two boys had no choice but to settle in for what promised to be a long and unpleasant night.

Time crept by, but the fell showed no sign of relenting. The seconds slowly turned to minutes, and every minute seemed to drag on for hours. Eventually, Gloria announced the sunset, and all along the Promenade, the streetlamps began to glow. The sky above grew darker, and the familiar images of the stars began to appear.

It was perhaps an hour or two later that Michael first spotted one of the worker bees. It was hovering near the Promenade, a short distance upstream. Michael wondered briefly what it might be doing there, until he realized that it must have noticed the framework of tubing which he and Ethan had dropped when they fled into the river. A few minutes later, a second bee arrived to join the first, and though Michael could not see clearly what the two bees were doing, he could easily guess. As more of the little robots began to arrive, there could be no doubt that they were dismantling the abandoned section of raft, and carting the pieces away as scrap. As far as Fairhaven's worker bees were concerned, littering was not to be permitted overnight, anywhere inside the Middle Ring.

"Go away!" Ethan shouted suddenly. "Little pest..."

Michael turned in the direction of the shout, and he could barely make out the form of a worker bee, hovering over the river near Ethan's pillar. Ethan was still sitting there, waving his arms at the little robot, trying to chase it away. A moment later the bee returned to the Circle Park, and soon disappeared across the lawn beyond the streetlamps.

"What was that about?" Michael asked.

"It thought I was a piece of junk in the river, I think," said Ethan. "Stupid clockwork."

Once the bees had completed their business with the raft, little else happened for the rest of the night. The fell would still appear from time to time in the glow of the streetlamps, only to vanish again into the shadows. There was nothing that Michael and Ethan could do other than sit on their two pillars and wait for morning.

After what seemed like a month of darkness, the sky overhead began to gradually, incrementally brighten. It would still be an hour or more before Gloria announced the sunrise, but already in the growing light Michael could more clearly see the stalking silhouette of the fell, pacing here and there along the riverbank. But then suddenly the fell stopped. It froze in place for a long moment, then very precisely curled itself back into its metallic cocoon, and settled down gently onto the grass.

Michael was stunned. Of all the times he'd encountered fells in the past, he'd never before actually seen one go dormant. He stared for several seconds, hardly able to believe the mechanical predator had finally given up.

"Ethan!..."

"I saw it..." Ethan shouted back. "What do you think?"

"I don't know..." Michael said. "It just shut down. Maybe its batteries ran out."

The fell was not so easy to see in the dim light, now that it wasn't moving, but there could be no doubt that it had indeed returned to its shell. Michael couldn't help but wonder if it was simply laying a trap for them: if it wouldn't suddenly emerge again if they tried to return to the park. Ethan could guess what Michael was thinking, since he was thinking the exact same thing.

"If it's just waiting for us," Ethan pointed out, "it can wait a hell of a lot longer than we can. I think we might as well go now."

At that moment, everywhere up and down throughout the Circle Park, the lawn sprinklers came suddenly to life. Soon, the whole of the Middle Ring was shrouded in a pale grey mist. The sudden change shook Michael from his indecision.

"I don't know that we'll get a better chance," he agreed. "Can you see well enough to make it across?..." Michael wasn't even sure if he could make it through the rapids himself, and he was quite a bit closer to the shore than Ethan was.

"You worry about you," Ethan said. "I'll see you in the park in two minutes."

Without another word, Ethan slid himself to the edge of his pillar, dropped over the side, and vanished into the rushing water.

Michael was more than apprehensive about braving the rapids a second time, but the die was cast. Ethan had already gone, and that meant that he had to go as well. Clinging tightly to the pillar, he carefully lowered himself feet first into the water.

It was a good thing he'd been patient enough to enter the river slowly. Unlike when he dove into the rapids before, this time he was able to maintain his bearings, and keep his head (mostly) above the surface of the water. The dim light actually worked to his advantage, since he could focus on the streetlamps along the Promenade as a beacon, to keep himself oriented toward the shore.

Though he was tossed and battered by the current, and more than once was thrown off his expected course, he managed to maneuver himself up against the inner bank of the river. He clutched at the curb with both arms, and though his wet hands slipped and scraped along the concrete surface, he managed to grab hold well enough to pull himself to a stop. Pivoting from his shoulders, he let the current push his body downstream, which lifted his legs to the surface. Hooking a knee over the curb, he was finally able to drag himself out of the water and onto the grass.

He immediately pushed himself up to his hands and knees, looking for the fell. If the thing had started to move, he would have no choice but to dive back into the river again. He'd been washed a good twenty meters downstream from where he'd started, so it took him a moment to find the monster, but once he did, he could see that it was exactly where it had been before. It was still dormant, and its metallic shell was damp and glistening.

"It's still asleep..." he called out, as loudly as he dared, "...I think we're OK."

He waited, but there was no reply.

Michael turned back toward the river, looking downstream, but he could not see very far through the mist from the lawn sprinklers. He stood up, and took a few steps forward along the curb.

"Ethan?..."

Michael was worried now. He looked back over his shoulder at the fell, but the creature was still bottled up tight in its cocoon. Michael started walking slowly downstream, scanning the park and the river for any sign of his friend, but he saw nothing other than the damp grass and the swirling water. He called out several more times, but there was no answer. He stopped walking, and looked back toward the fell again, but he could no longer see it through the haze. He turned to face the river once more, but there was no one there. The sound of the rapids roared in his ears.

Chapter 5:
The Featureless Wall

Eloise woke up before sunrise, with only a thin blanket between herself and the cold concrete of the Periphery. She looked around in the grey light, to see if anyone else was awake, but the others were all still sleeping.

She got up, and immediately walked to the curb by the river, looking across toward the Middle Ring, but all she could see was the glow of the streetlamps and the mist from the lawn sprinklers. Michael and Ethan were not there. She could hardly bear to wonder where they were, or what might have happened to them.

She emptied her water bottle, and filled it again with water from the river. Here, just below the rapids, the river water was as clear and clean as if it had come fresh from a kitchen faucet. She was hungry, as well as thirsty, but she was in no mood to eat. Instead, she started walking along the edge of the water, counter-river, toward the pumping station.

Eloise studied the rapids as she walked: how they were formed, and how the water moved over and around the stones. She also kept an eye toward the Circle Park, in the unlikely hope that Michael and Ethan might appear there, but most of her attention was on the towering edifice of the pumping station itself. As she drew closer, it consumed more and more of her field of view, until it was the only thing left that she could see. Before long, she was within arm's reach of its sheer and featureless wall.

She could feel the concrete below her feet trembling ever so slightly, with the constant thrumming of unseen machinery. To her right, the briefly interrupted river was being constantly reborn, as water gushed from hundreds of outlets, emptying into the river channel and rushing away through the lesser rapids.

She walked along that dark wall of the pumping station, from the river's edge all the way to the base of the city dome. She held her hand against its surface, feeling for any seam or fissure, but she found none.

The wall was warm to the touch, unbroken and perfectly smooth. There was no door. There were no cracks or crevices. The pumping station had no entrance, nor was there an exit anywhere to be found.

She returned to the river, and watched the water streaming out of the wall to her left. She could see that many of the outlets were empty and dry, releasing no water at all. But she could not possibly reach them, and even if she could, she knew there was no real hope of escaping that way.

But there had to be a way out of the city. There had to be. That, more than anything else, was what Eloise was hoping to find. She had thought that the pumping station might provide an avenue or a clue, but there was nothing there.

Fairhaven's great outer dome was perfect and unbroken; that much she already knew. It had been designed to seal the city shut, and to keep it safe from the devastation of the outside world. But if people had once come into the dome, then there must have been an entrance for them to come in *through*, which meant that somewhere, somehow, there had to be an exit through which their descendants could one day leave again, and Eloise wanted to find it. She was determined to find it.

She had to find it, before Gloria killed them all.

Their universal peril was growing, day by day. If Eloise had only suspected as much before, she was certain of it now. She and everyone she knew had been standing, perched at the edge of a precipice for all their lives, watching the ground beneath them slowly crumble away. The only reason they could not see it before was because it was all they had ever known.

Fairhaven was dying, and sooner or later everyone who remained inside would die with it. Perhaps that would be a year from now, or a hundred years or more, but Eloise could no longer ignore how the unwritten calculus of her world was approaching an inexorable vanishing point. The more she saw of the great city, the more convinced she was that all of Gloria's grand equations would eventually resolve to zero.

With her mind intent on these apocalyptic thoughts, Eloise stared despondently at the sluicing water. Then she noticed something moving on the opposite side of the river. She squinted her eyes, peering through the mist above the rapids, fully expecting to see a worker bee or a patrolling fell. But instead she saw a person walking slowly riverwise along the Promenade. It was Michael.

She shouted. She screamed, but he could not hear her over the roar of the river. She waved her arms but he wasn't looking in her direction. Almost hysterical with excitement, and joy, and anxious concern, she turned and ran along the edge of the river, all the way back to where she and the others had camped for the night.

Chapter 6:
The Other Outpost

Eloise arrived back at the camp at a full run, and almost too out of breath to tell the rest of the group that she'd seen Michael coming up the Promenade. The other travellers quickly got the raft back into the river, and by the time Michael had reached the end of the rapids, Kyle and Kady were already there and waiting. Kady rushed across the grass to greet him, while Kyle stayed with the raft, holding onto the tie rope, to keep it from drifting away.

"Are you OK?... Are you hurt?..." Kady asked anxiously.

"Hi, Kady," Michael replied.

"Where's Ethan?"

"Worker bees ate the boat," Michael explained. "We had to run from a fell, and I lost Ethan in the rapids. I was almost hoping he'd be here ahead of me, but if not, then..."

Kady closed her eyes, and nodded her head with understanding. Michael gave the incomplete raft a skeptical look.

"I guess this part still floats?..." he asked.

"Yes it does," said Kyle. "Badly."

A few minutes later Michael was safely back on the dusty concrete of the Periphery, where he was greeted with warm hugs and towels and blankets and a dry change of clothes. He was ravenously hungry, but the group had saved the cold dinner packets from the night before, so it wasn't long before he was dry and fed, if not any better rested. He briefly filled the rest of the group in on his overnight ordeal, but he was not inclined to discuss the incident in any great detail.

"So what's the agenda for today?" he asked, looking to change the subject. "On down the river, I guess?"

"You tell us," Bridget said. "You must be exhausted."

"I'm plenty tired," said Michael, "but I can walk. No swimming, though, if you please. I'm all done with swimming for a while."

"If it's true that harvesters from Stone Prairie and River Towne used to cross each other's paths, then there has to be another outpost on this side of the station," Eloise said. "It shouldn't be all that far from here."

"If it's still there at all," Kady noted, doubtfully.

"Of course it will be there," said Gwendolyn. "And whatever condition it's in, it's sure to be a nicer place to rest than where we are right now."

Gwen was very confident in this assertion, though she had little evidence for it other than hope.

"If we do find an outpost, it should only be about one more day's walk from there to Stone Prairie," Bridget said, "assuming the enclave was halfway between the pumping stations."

"Will there still be people living there?" Kyle asked.

"Supposedly, it was abandoned," Eloise said. "That's partly what we're here to find out. But even if there *are* people still living there, Stone Prairie might not be anything like River Towne."

"With any luck," said Michael, "it won't be."

Within an hour, the group had loaded all their extra gear back onto their lopsided raft, and set off again down the Periphery. Ethan's disappearance weighed heavily on them, but they were not inclined to mourn. He was simply gone now, like so many others they had known before. Loss had long been a part of their lives, and while they felt it perhaps more keenly than they once had, they also understood that there was nothing more they could do on Ethan's account now.

Though each of them had their private doubts about what might lay ahead, the group was resolved on at least one thing: whatever uncertain future might await them further down the river, it was likely to be no worse than what they'd already left behind in River Towne, where they'd had no future left at all.

They had been walking less than an hour before they spotted something far up ahead. It looked very much like another outpost, and as they drew nearer it became increasingly clear that's exactly what it was. But even from a distance, they could see that it was both smaller and more seriously decayed than the outpost they'd left behind them just the day before. It appeared that the place had been completely abandoned for a very long time.

When they finally reached the dilapidated little cluster of structures, they found that there were only two intact huts, both of which were fairly close to the river. None of the larger tents were still standing, and bits of collapsed framework and tattered rags were strewn all around the area. Further out from the river – beyond the huts, and closer to the base of the city dome – they could see several large piles of broken shelving and other dust-covered debris.

But not far from the two remaining huts, the travellers came upon something very odd. What they had first taken for another pile of random debris, turned out to be something quite different. It was, in fact, a dead birch tree.

None of them had ever seen a dead tree before, but there could be no doubt as to what it was. Its leaves had all turned brown, and though most of those leaves had fallen onto the concrete, some few still clung to the outer branches. The tree was perhaps five meters long from its base to its tip, and it seemed to have been separated from its roots in a very haphazard and uneven way. Kady was immediately reminded of how she'd used a kitchen knife to carve polymer tubing into shorter lengths, back when she and the others had been working on the framework for the raft. The cuts at the base of this tree looked very much like the cuts she had been making then.

On the opposite side of the tree, a number of stones of various sizes had been carefully laid out in a small circle. The stones themselves were brown and grey, but along the inside of the circle they were all stained black, as if they'd been covered with candle soot. Inside the ring of stones, the concrete was also stained black, and covered over with a cold dusting of lumpy black and grey ashes. The group could easily see that a fire had been deliberately built there, but they could not fathom for what purpose. The notion of a campfire in a simple stone fire pit was something beyond their experience.

Investigating the outpost further, the group soon found that despite the near-total ruin of the other buildings, the two huts that were still standing were in pristine condition. The smaller of the two had a sliding door panel, and housed a tidy and fully functional latrine. Its water reservoir was still more than half full, and it was also equipped with a sink and a faucet for handwashing. A bar of soap was resting in a little porcelain dish on a shelf nearby. There was even a working hand pump, to pipe fresh water directly to the reservoir from the river, without the need for anyone to carry buckets.

The larger hut was even more surprising than the latrine. Its interior was not only clean, it was fully furnished and tastefully decorated. There were a number of small rugs covering much of the floor, a sturdy wooden table with four matching chairs, and a full foodwall with pots and pans and silverware and many other amenities. The hut's three large windows each had matching floral curtains, and solid sliding panels that could be fully closed. The front door fit precisely into the doorframe, and was mounted securely on actual hinges. But perhaps most astonishingly of all, in one corner of the hut there was a *bed*. Not a cot, like the harvesters were used to, but an actual bed, exactly like those that might be found in any of the houses of the Middle Ring.

"I guess this place isn't so abandoned as all that," Eloise remarked. She was easily as surprised as anyone. "You'd almost think we were on the wrong side of the river."

"You know what this place looks like?..." said Kady. "It looks like the Administration Office, where the warehouse keeper lived."

"But they can't still be using this outpost, can they?..." Gwendolyn asked. "This is the only hut. Where would the harvesters sleep?"

"What I most want to know," said Kyle, looking across the room toward the foodwall, "is does that hotmaker work? Some of us still haven't had breakfast."

As it happened, the hotmaker did indeed work, though it did not have a power source attached. But their own batteries were still fully charged, and so the group was soon able to enjoy a very pleasant brunch, in the most congenial surroundings any of them had ever enjoyed, anywhere outside of the Middle Ring.

Chapter 7:
A Curious Abode

The group travelled no further the rest of that day. Michael had not slept at all the night before, and while he might have been willing to press on, had the others insisted, there was no point. Everyone was glad to have a relaxing afternoon and (hopefully) a good night's sleep, before venturing on to Stone Prairie.

While Michael napped in the hut, the others spent their time exploring the outpost more carefully, though there was not much to explore beyond what they'd already discovered. They scavenged some lengths of polymer tubing from the wreckage of one of the larger huts, and used them to stabilize the unfinished side of their raft. The end result was not as uniform or as sturdy as it once had been, but it was still a significant improvement.

Everyone kept an eye to the river, partly in the hope that Ethan might miraculously reappear, but also more than half-suspecting that the hut's owners might show themselves at any moment. But that did not happen. Whether the owners had left on a more extended journey, or they'd been caught by the fells, or if the hut had been only recently abandoned for some other reason, the young travellers could not guess.

The group spent a good portion of the afternoon studying the pumping system that supplied water to the latrine. From what they could tell, it was similar to the system used for the latrines at River Towne. As with so many other things at their former enclave, none of them had ever before paid much attention to the pumps, but lugging water buckets from the river at the previous outpost had given them all a new appreciation for the value of such things, and more than piqued their curiosity about how they functioned.

A closer inspection of the hut also revealed some interesting details. Once it was discovered that the pots and pans in the food wall were all stained black, just like the stones in the fire pit, the group put two and two together, and realized that the fire must have been used for cooking. None of the young travellers had ever in their lives cooked food on an open fire. In fact, none of them had ever cooked food in pots or pans before; all of their cooking in the clades had been done with a hotmaker. But they had of course seen pots and pans in the kitchens of the Middle Ring, so they knew (at least in theory) what they had once been used for, even if they'd had no practical experience using such things themselves.

The evening passed quietly, and uneventfully. They could not all fit onto the one bed, of course, but there were enough rugs on the floor of the hut that no one had to sleep directly atop the concrete. They were not as comfortable as they might have preferred, but a little extra cushioning made an enormous difference, and they felt much more secure sleeping inside the hut, rather than being outside and exposed to the night sky and the stars. In the morning they all felt stronger and better rested than they had the day before, and once they had breakfasted and attended to other necessary matters, they set off again down the Periphery.

Aside from the few bits of polymer tubing they'd used to repair the raft, the group took nothing at all from the outpost. They left the hut's furnishings and all of its other contents just as they'd found them. They even refilled the reservoir for the latrine before they left. Harvesting and scavenging were one thing, but unlike the houses of the Middle Ring – or the obviously abandoned outpost they'd stayed at before – this hut clearly belonged to someone. Spending a night there, they all reasoned, did no real harm. But even without knowing for certain if the hut's owners were alive or dead, had the group taken so much as a single item, no matter how useful it might have been to them, it would have felt like an act of thievery. They were not even tempted.

Their long walk down the Periphery was uneventful, but as the day dragged on, their apprehension only grew. Though reaching Stone Prairie had been the first of their goals from the very start, they had also known all along that it might not be their final destination. If there were people still living there – which now seemed likely – there was no guarantee that a wandering group of harvesters from River Towne would be welcomed.

By late afternoon, they could clearly see a great many tents, far up ahead of them, scattered here and there across the full width of the Periphery. From a distance, Stone Prairie appeared to be very similar to River Towne, at least in terms of its size, and the general arrangement of its huts and other structures. But as they drew nearer, the group could see that it was not so similar after all. Most obviously, there did not seem to be any people. In River Towne at this time of the day, there would have been harvesters returning from the Middle Ring, and possibly even long lines standing outside the warehouse tents. But here they could see no one at all. The avenues between the sheds and shanties were empty, and there were no ferry rafts crossing the river.

Even more curious however, than the lack of people, was the abundance of *greenery*. In River Towne, there had been almost no plants at all, and those there were had been small, and kept in individual pots. But here, all along the bank of the river, there were long, flat planters bursting with plantlife. The planters themselves looked very much like the raised flowerbeds that could be found anywhere in the Middle Ring, except they were not filled with flowers, or at least not with flowers at all like those that the young harvesters were used to seeing. Some of the planters were overgrown with tall grass, while others had strange vines climbing onto short trellises made of sticks and plastic and bits of string.

"This is a tomato, I think," said Kady, looking at a red, oblong fruit that was dangling from one of the vines. "Look at this... I think *all* of these might be tomatoes."

"This is food," said Eloise, marvelling at the rows of unfamiliar plants. "I think they're really growing food here."

"We aren't in Pleasant Gardens, are we?..." asked Gwendolyn. "We can't be. This has to be Stone Prairie, doesn't it? Pleasant Gardens should be on the other side of the next pumping station."

"*Person...*" said Michael sharply, and under his breath.

Everyone immediately stopped their investigations. Turning to look in the direction Michael was facing, they could see that there was indeed a person there, some fifty meters away and walking towards them. At first the man did not seem to be aware of them, but when he suddenly noticed that there was a cluster of strangers standing in the midst of the sprawling gardens, he stopped dead in his tracks.

For a long moment, no one moved. The man looked back over his shoulder more than once at the tents behind him, then he took a few cautious steps forward. Then he apparently came to some sort of decision, and slowly approached the group until he was standing only about ten meters away. There he stopped, and looked the travellers over from head to toe.

The man was slender, not particularly tall, and very, very old. None of the harvesters could guess at his age, but it was obvious to all of them that he was much older than any person they had ever seen before. He wore a bright blue shirt with tiny white buttons down the front, long brown trousers, and a pair of well worn sneakers, which might once have been yellow. His hair was thin and grey, cut short all around his face and tied with a piece of string into a prim little ponytail in the back. He had a short and neatly trimmed beard.

Eloise took a cautious step forward.

"Hello," she said, with a polite nod of her head. "My name is Eloise."

The old man peered at her for a long moment, then he leaned forward and squinted his eyes, as if she were an electronic book that he couldn't quite read.

"Young people!..." he muttered to himself, slowly shaking his head from side to side in astonishment. "And here I thought I was done for. But perhaps not. Perhaps not yet after all. Great Gloria's knockers... Young people... I never thought I would see the day."

"We've just come down the river," Eloise said. "We came from River Towne, originally."

"Is that so?" the old man said. His eyes opened wide, and he seemed to think about this for a few moments. "But I'm forgetting my manners," he suddenly apologized, "it has been so very long indeed. Oh my, yes. *Eloise*, did you say?..."

Eloise nodded affirmatively. The old man bowed at the waist ever so slightly, and gave her a genteel head nod of his own, before looking up again.

"You may call me Benjamin," he said, "if you like. That is my given name.   And it is most certainly a pleasure to be making your acquaintance."

The old man leaned a bit to one side, to look past Eloise toward the rest of the travellers. Both his eyebrows went up, inquisitively.

"It will be a pleasure to meet *all* of you in time, I'm sure," he added politely. "And I do hope you will each forgive my surprise, but I must confess that I had not anticipated having so many visitors today."

Chapter 8:
Stone Prairie

"I almost hate to ask," the old man said, "but is this all of you? Or are there more of you coming?"

"This is all of us..." Eloise replied. "...all that's left of our group; we came from River Towne together."

Benjamin nodded thoughtfully.

"Ah... so you're exiles," he said. "I wondered for a moment if you might not be the vanguard of a second exodus; but I see you're not. Or perhaps you are, without knowing it. Exiles then? At your age, though? That surprises me, but things change, of course, and it's been a long time. But here I am, forgetting my manners again and getting ahead of myself. There's no need for us to stand here talking now; we'll have ample time for questions and answers later, I hope. You're probably tired... and hungry, perhaps? You'll need a place to stay. Let's see to that first of all. I could have prepared something, if I'd known you were coming, but we'll manage. Tie your boat off on one of the cleats there, and follow me, if you please."

With a wave of his hand, he turned and walked back toward the enclave. The harvesters quickly secured their raft as he'd told them to, then followed a few steps behind.

"This place was laid out a little differently from River Towne," the old man remarked, "but it operated much the same, in its day."

He stopped, and turned back to look at the travellers.

"Keep up," he said, impatiently. "Walk here, up here with me, where we can see each other and talk like civilized people. Don't lurk behind me like that, or you'll make me nervous. We'll find you a hut first of all, then we'll have time for a more proper introduction."

"I'm sorry," Gwendolyn asked, looking around at the seemingly empty streets and buildings, "but are you the only one here? Where's everyone else?"

"Just me," Benjamin replied. "Just me, for as long as I've been here. But hold your questions for later. First let's find you a suitable hut, or two huts if you prefer. A hut for each of you, if you like, but they're not all in prime condition I'm afraid. I've only renovated a few of them, and even that was a very long time ago. This way, if you please."

The old man led the group past several large tents, and through the winding paths of the enclave. Despite his apparent age, his walking pace was fairly brisk, though he would stop at times to point out a particular building or other landmark. Bridget felt relieved every time he paused to talk, as she would have found it difficult to keep up with him otherwise. She'd been walking more and more without her crutches, but she was still limping, and could not go very fast. All the same, she was determined to keep pace with everyone else, as best she could. She was not about to complain.

"Those were all for the warehouse," Benjamin said, gesturing back toward the tents behind them. "I keep a few things in there now... grains, seeds, inventory, you know... There's a lot to keep track of, and it always helps to stay organized. Just over there is the Commons," he added, pointing between two ragged huts toward a large open area. "Or that's what I call it at least. There are some tables, and it's a good place for a fire. We can sit there tonight and have a good long talk, if you like. I'd like that very much. I suspect we have a lot to talk about, but first things first."

He turned back toward the river, and led the group to a cluster of smaller huts, not far from the water's edge.

"The best huts are all along here," he explained. "Not that it was always like that. Back when people lived here, the really posh dwellings were far back by the city wall, same as at River Towne. But I'm not so young anymore, and walking back and forth all that way was too much trouble. You see, everything important's out here by the river. The latrines and the showers, and water for the gardens of course. I fixed up a number of these little huts... oh, that's been years ago now. But there's always too much to do, and how many houses does one man need, after all? I gave it up after a while, settled on one that I liked, and put my time into other things."

He slid open the door panel to one of the huts, and ushered his guests inside. At first glance, the place looked very much like a typical clade back in River Towne. There were six cots, three along each side, a table with four chairs, and a foodwall with a hotmaker in the back corner. If the furnishings were not nearly so elegant as they'd been in the hut where the travellers had spent the previous night, they were still far better than what they'd found at the first abandoned outpost. There was nothing extravagant, but everything was clean, and neatly arranged, and in fairly good condition. The hut was at least as nice as any of them had really hoped for.

"The other huts are much like this one," Benjamin explained. "Different colors, and so on. You're welcome to any of these, if you like. You can take your pick, or decide amongst yourselves. You'll find the showers next door, and the latrines are a bit further down the river. Now, if you'll excuse me, I still have many things to attend to. If you'll all meet me for dinner at the Commons, I'll be delighted. I hope you remember the way, but you'll see the fire, I expect, if you don't see me. I'll have supper ready for everyone, shortly after sunset, if you're hungry. I hope that suits you."

The old man smiled, and looked Eloise expectantly in the eye, awaiting a response. She had been the first to introduce herself, after all, and he had apparently settled on her as spokesperson for the group as a whole. But like her companions, Eloise had simply not been prepared for this sort of abject hospitality. She'd fully expected Stone Prairie to be either completely abandoned, or rather filled with residents who would be at best unfriendly, or at worst even openly hostile. Feeling uncertain of her own judgement, she glanced around at the others. Everyone else, however, seemed eager to take their cues from her.

"That's very kind of you," she replied, after a long moment's pause. "We would be delighted to join you."

"I am so glad," the old man said. "It will be simple fare, I'm afraid, and to be perfectly honest, I'm not sure what all I can prepare to feed a table for seven at such short notice, but we'll manage. After sunset then," he added brightly, looking around at the others. "That should give you an hour or two to get settled, and me enough time to see to the arrangements. Until then..."

He nodded his head sharply and gave a quick little bow, then turned and stepped briskly out through the open door.

"*Thank you...*" several of the other travellers started to say, but the old man was already gone.

In the long silence that followed, the group looked around at the hut and at each other. No one was quite sure what to make of the old man, or the abrupt change in their circumstances.

"What just happened?..." asked Kady.

"He's quite... *overwhelming*, isn't he?" said Gwendolyn, hesitantly.

"I don't know," said Bridget. "I thought he was very nice."

"I guess we've been invited to dinner," said Kyle. "That's a good sign, isn't it?"

"Welcome to Stone Prairie," said Michael.

Chapter 9:
Benjamin

The travellers arrived at the Commons shortly after sunset, just as they'd been told. They found Benjamin sitting on a long wooden bench, near a campfire that was constrained within a small fire pit, much like the one they'd seen at the outpost. A skillet was simmering on a metal grating which had been laid across the tops of the stones, and a second one was resting off to one side, away from the center of the fire. The skillets were filled with what appeared to be some sort of fried pastries.

Not far from the fire sat a long wooden table; a bedsheet with a bright floral print had been laid across it as a tablecloth. At the center of the table were a pair of covered serving dishes, and a large wooden bowl filled with salad greens. Three chairs sat along each of the table's longer sides, with a seventh sitting alone at one end. In front of each chair was a full place-setting, with napkins and silverware, a dinner plate, and a water glass already filled.

"Welcome, welcome," the old man said, standing up to greet his guests. He waved an arm toward the banquet table. "Sit where you like, but leave that one for me if you please," he requested, pointing to the single chair. "Pride of place for the host, you understand, and it will be easier for us to talk that way. But save your questions until we've eaten. Everything else can wait."

Benjamin busied himself with the fire while the young travellers chose their seats. Then he walked around the table – first with one of the skillets, then the other – setting a single large pastry onto each of the dinner plates.

"You won't offend me if there's something you don't care for," he explained. "There are certainly things I don't care for either, but I don't cook them, so you won't find any of them here. All the same, I won't begrudge personal preference, but I do hope you'll each find something in all of this that will appeal to you. Oh, and please don't start just yet," he added hastily, "A few more moments of patience, if you please."

The old man set the second skillet back onto the grating by the fire, then returned to the table. He took some greens from the large bowl, and set them on his plate beside the pastry, then indicated to his guests that they should do the same. The first of the covered serving dishes, they soon discovered, contained roasted potatoes, mixed with some onions and herbs, and the second contained a fried medley of colorful vegetables which they did not immediately recognize. The mingled aromas of these dishes were rich and complex, and almost entirely unfamiliar to the young harvesters. They had never been served food of this sort – or in quite this way – before.

"It all looks wonderful," Bridget said. "But what are all these things called?"

"Ah..." Benjamin said with a knowing grin, "now that is a fair question. Forgive me. The pastries are pot-stickers, after a fashion, with beans and eggplant and diced tomato inside for a little added flavor. Potatoes, of course, I'm sure you've had before. And the fried vegetables are zucchini and carrots and bell peppers and several sorts of squash. As for the salad, I couldn't begin to tell you what all is in there. There are so many kinds of greens, and I have a terrible time telling them apart. Eat what you like."

"Would it be all right if someone said grace first?" Gwendolyn asked, hesitantly. She almost hated to mention it, but for such an occasion, she could not help but feel that pausing for a formal grace was necessary.

"By all means!..." Benjamin replied. "Since you've called it to my attention, could you be so kind as to do the honors for us as well?"

Gwen was typically ready and eager to take charge of any situation, at least in the absence of other authority, and assuming she was alone with only one or two of her friends. But in larger groups, or unfamiliar social circumstances, she was not nearly so self-assured. She'd already felt flustered in the presence of the older man's assertive hospitality, and now that he'd put her directly on the spot, she found herself tongue-tied. She stared at her plate, trying desperately to think of something suitable to say, and wishing she could find somewhere to hide.

It was Kyle who came to her rescue.

"I can do it," he volunteered. Gwendolyn looked up at him with relief and gratitude, and he gave her a quick smile in return. Then he closed his eyes and took a deep breath.

"By the grace of Gloria," he said, "our thanks for this meal, and the kindness of the man that prepared it."

Once Kyle had finished, there was an awkward pause. Everyone glanced around the table at everyone else, uncertain if they could now start eating.

"Wonderful!" Benjamin suddenly declared, smiling broadly. "Thank you for that, and thank you for calling it to my attention." He looked around the table once more, at all the expectant faces. "Now..." he added with finality, "shall we begin?"

The dinner was marvelous, and startling, and not at all like any meal that the young travellers had ever eaten before. The textures of the foods were surprising and varied, and the flavors were so sharp and exotic – at least compared to the prepackaged meals that they had eaten all their lives – that the whole experience was almost overwhelming.

To be sure, not every one of the diners took delight in everything that they tasted. But they found the food delicious at best, and palatable at worst, and astonishing in either case. It was a meal that none of them would ever forget for as long as they lived.

"There is a sacred art to cooking, which I will not claim to have mastered," the old man said. "I'd never cooked a thing in my life until I left the enclave, and at first if I made something edible, it was purely by accident. But over the years, one learns some things. It's astonishing, really, what we can master at need, given time and the inclination. I'm now to the point where I'm so accustomed to my own cooking that I doubt I could enjoy anything else half so well. But I have to confess, I've never cooked a meal for anyone other than myself before. I can only hope you find it to your liking."

"The food is wonderful," Eloise said, and she meant it. The other travellers seemed to agree.

Throughout the entire course of the meal, the topic of conversation never strayed far from the food, or Benjamin's cooking, or the relatively elegant (if hastily managed) table settings. But once everyone had finished eating, the travellers gathered with the old man in a circle around the failing embers of the fire for a longer, and much more serious conversation.

"Now I'm sure we all have many questions," Benjamin said, "but we have to begin somewhere. What I'm dying to know first of all is how do such well-mannered young harvesters get themselves exiled from River Towne?"

"We weren't exactly exiled..." Kady said.

"We exiled ourselves," Eloise clarified.

From there, the travellers began to recount a few of the key events from their own recent history. It was not a particularly organized re-telling. There were many interruptions and corrections, and some of the particulars came as surprises not only to Benjamin, but also to other members of their own group. Kady's encounter with Helen the warehouse keeper was regarded by everyone as a key moment, as were Michael's escape from the rapids, and Ethan's disappearance, and Nora's ill-fated attempt to murder Bridget.

Benjamin listened intently and only rarely interrupted, unless it was to encourage one of the speakers to continue. Most of the interruptions came from within the group, as each of them would jump in from time to time with additional details, or with questions of their own. When the travellers finally seemed to have finished, the old man leaned back and nodded his head thoughtfully.

"You've had a difficult time," he said, "though I never doubted that you had. And I can see now that some things haven't changed so much after all. It's a pity about Helen, though. I'd hoped for better from her."

All of the harvesters were puzzled by this remark, but no one was more startled than Kady.

"You knew her?" she asked.

"Indeed I did," the old man replied. "And perhaps that's a place for me to start my own story, or at least what parts of it might matter to all of you. I once hailed from River Towne myself. I lived there fifty... what was it?... fifty-four years, or thereabouts, if memory serves. Helen was a very fine harvester in her day... beautiful girl, smart and tenacious... kind hearted, or so she seemed to me... though time changes all of us, I suppose... time, or power, or privilege, or desire, or desperation... But perhaps she hadn't changed so very much at all; I'm not one to say... Good doesn't have to transform to become evil, you know. It needs only neglect the limits of its own perspective. My perspective has changed, over time, and looking back now on who I was... well, I can make no claim to virtue. I have casually done more than my share of dreadful things, and thought them to be right and necessary at the time."

The old man paused, apparently lost in thought.

"But yes, I knew her very well," he continued suddenly. "I even had a hand in getting her onto the Lesser Council, when she came of age. I was the warehouse keeper you see, on the Privy Council myself, once upon a time, and for a very long while... She replaced me in that post, Helen did, when the escorts came for me, and I was exiled... But that would have been... oh, likely before you were even born. I've long ago lost count of the years."

"But why were you exiled?" Kyle asked.

"I got old!" Benjamin exclaimed, as if that answer should have been obvious. "But then I didn't politely die, like old people are supposed to. I kept on living, somehow or other, and I just kept getting older. I am even now getting older still."

"Then how did you come to be *here*?" Kady asked. "Why didn't you go on to Pleasant Gardens?"

"I did," the old man replied. "I've been to Pleasant Gardens, but I didn't come the way you did. I went counter-river, all the way around. I can't say exactly why. Everyone else was going riverwise... all the other exiles on the ferry. It was a shorter trip, and easier, or so it was thought at the time. But all the same, I went the other way. The rest of the exiles were younger than me, and perhaps I didn't trust them. Adults are hard to trust, you know, and for good reason. If *you* were older, I'd not have trusted you half so easily. I might even have tried to kill you, if there weren't so many of you, just to protect myself, since I'd certainly have expected you to do the same. Old folk like me, we're a bunch of selfish murdering bastards, every last one of us. And I hope you'll pardon my honesty, but that's how you get to be old in Fairhaven. Otherwise you disappear... like your friend, I'm afraid. I was disappeared myself... long ago... long time ago now. It's reappearing that's the trick. I don't plan to. That's when they finish you, if they missed you on the first try, they'll kill you as soon as they find you back somewhere they can. They only don't kill you when they *can't*, and that's Gloria's truth, on my worthless old life. I'll swear it on a stack of compost as high as my ear."

The old man paused again, and closed his eyes to collect his thoughts. His practiced cheerfulness had long since slipped to the wayside, even before he'd begun to talk about his own history, and now his mood was even more sombre, as he sifted through difficult memories.

"I went counter-river..." he said again, nodding his head slowly. But he said nothing more for a long time.

"How did you escape the fells, as old as you must have been?" Eloise coaxed him, gently.

"Well, times were different then," Benjamin replied. "There weren't so many fells about as there are now, and they stayed more often in toward the forest. Harvesters would last into their twenties in those days, even to twenty-five, some of them. But I was much too old for the Middle Ring, and never safe. I swam the river, and walked along the Periphery as much as I could. I had some food with me; I'd planned for that, and I'd find a hotmaker here or there that I could use. The other enclaves were already abandoned, or nearly... Open Grove... Silver Meadow... all the people there were gone to Pleasant Gardens, or so I thought at the time."

The old man turned to Michael suddenly, and wagged a knowing finger at him.

"But also I made a discovery," he said, "and you may have had some inkling of it yourself, with your narrow escape. Has it dawned on you why that fell went to sleep when it did?"

He waited for a reply, but Michael could not guess what the old man was getting at.

"The *sprinklers*..." Benjamin finally said. "Every morning, in the hour before dawn, the sprinklers go on, and the fells go to sleep. Every one of them. No one sees it, because no one crosses the river before sunrise. But the fells don't like the water. Their shells are watertight, of course, and so they sleep."

The old man smiled. He was clearly proud of himself, for this particular insight.

"After I discovered that, I took to crossing the river in the morning at first light, then back to the Periphery at sunrise. I ran past the pumping stations that way, and had a narrow escape or two of my own, but they never caught me. Then, in time, I found myself at Pleasant Gardens... It wasn't what I had thought it would be; not what I'd expected at all. I had climbed the mountain, and found that there was nowhere to go. I gathered seeds from there, collected some fruit and other things, but I pressed on. I couldn't stay. I'd rather not say any more about that tonight, if you don't mind."

He stared at the concrete for a long while. His mood had turned sad again. He seemed tired, and much older than he'd been only an hour before.

"And I've been here ever since," he said at last. "No one comes, no one goes. I used to keep watch across the river, but I never once saw anyone else, passing along the Promenade, and I gave it up in time. I'd begun to wonder if I was the last of everyone, until I saw the lot of you, standing there in the gardens. I'd almost come to think there was no one else left... only me... Gloria's last victim."

Chapter 10:
The Second Enclave

Three days later, the travellers were still at Stone Prairie, and it was unclear even to them if they were planning to continue on with their journey, or to remain at this once abandoned enclave indefinitely.

After spending so many years alone, Benjamin welcomed their companionship, but the travellers soon realized that he could be a mercurial host. He was easily agitated, and could quite suddenly become irritable and impatient, particularly if he was asked too many questions over too short a time. Having long had the full sweep of Stone Prairie entirely to himself, it was perhaps understandable that he might begrudge yielding even a portion of it to a small bevy of newcomers, despite the fact that he was genuinely delighted to have them there. The old man seemed by turns to regard his young visitors sometimes as guests, sometimes as pupils to be mentored, and at other times almost as irksome trespassers in his private and personal domain.

But despite this ever-shifting mindset, Benjamin remained courteous with his guests, for the most part, even if the warmth of that courtesy varied considerably moment to moment. And already the old man had shown them a great many useful and curious things. He enjoyed talking about himself – at least when he could do so on his own terms – and he was justifiably proud of all that he'd learned and accomplished over the course of his many years of total isolation. He was also flattered by the fact that his young visitors were proving to be such a genuinely eager audience.

On the day after their first banquet, the old man had taken his young guests across the river in the early morning before dawn – they aboard their raft, and he in his little one-man boat – to cut down trees for firewood. He introduced them to tools which they had all seen before, but had never actually used: things such as saws and hatchets and pruning shears. The following morning he took them across the river again, this time to gather some of the rich black soil from underneath the grass of the Circle Park, using rakes and shovels and buckets and spades.

On each of these excursions, everyone present was gradually drenched by the constant mist from the lawn sprinklers, but the old man's observations held true: though fells could be seen sleeping here and there all around the Circle Park, they did not wake, and each morning the travellers were able to return safely across the river with the fruits of their labors in tow, just before Gloria announced the sunrise.

"The bees will replace the dirt," the old man explained, "and they plant new trees as well, though they don't always get to that as promptly as I might like them to. When I run out of trees to cut here, I'll go counter-river to the outpost sometimes, and take them from there. I only take the smaller ones, of course... The bigger they are, the more wood there is, but the harder they are to drag to the river, and I'm not as strong as I used to be. From there, I can float them downstream with my little boat, then pull them back ashore here at the enclave. Trees don't burn well when you've cut them fresh, though. I've learned that it's best to let them sit for a while... for weeks or months even, until they've gone old and brittle and dry, like me."

On the second day after their arrival, Benjamin took the young travellers on a tour of his gardens. He had built an elaborate irrigation system out of discarded tubing, which was not so very different from the plumbing the travellers had studied so closely at the two outposts. Water from the river was pumped by hand into a large reservoir, and from there released through a series of valves into each of the planters as needed. And with the fresh dirt they'd dug up in the Circle Park, the travellers were able to help set up a whole new planter, which the old man said he planned to sow with either oats or wheat.

"The grains are the easiest to manage of all," he told them, "but they take the longest to grow, and they need the most room. Then they all have to be harvested at once. But grain stores better than anything else does, and that's more important than you might realize at first. It's a long process, but it can be well worth the trouble, if you have the patience for it."

From there, the old man walked back and forth between the other planters, explaining what each of them held, and what he saw as the advantages and disadvantages of every plant he grew.

"If you ask me, the vegetables from the vines are the best of all," the old man said, gesturing to the last few planters in the row. "These are squash, and those are tomatoes and peppers and what not. Some of these grow almost as quick as the greens do, once you've got them started, but they're also the hardest to manage. You have to pollinate the flowers by hand."

Benjamin stooped down, and grabbed a tiny yellow flower from one of the tomato plants between his thumb and forefinger, then tapped it lightly into his palm, to show his guests the pollen.

"I'll collect this dust in a cup, when I'm in the mood to take the time for it, and then spread it to some of these other flowers with a little paintbrush. That might seem like madness, but I'll promise you that's exactly how it's done. In the world outside, as I understand it, the insects would do this for you, and here on the inside the worker bees do it instead. But there aren't any insects," he added with a grin, "and the bees don't come out here to the Periphery, so what else can you do? It's a tedious bit of care, but it has to be done, or you'll get nothing but endless vines that you can't eat."

"Plan ahead!..." the old man suddenly shouted at them. "That's the only way to go on living. You have to cut next month's firewood in the morning, and tend to next year's supper in the afternoon. And I think that should be more than enough of a lesson for today."

Chapter 11:
Conversations and Invitations

As the days turned to weeks, the young travellers gradually became more accustomed to life at Stone Prairie. Domestically, they soon settled back into the familiar structure of their original clades, and within the enclave at large they each began to take on chores and other activities of their own choosing, often without the help or guidance of their senior host. They learned how to cook using pots and pans, and how to light and manage a campfire. They built and planted new gardens, and learned how to store or compost the food that they could not immediately eat.

But other than their occasional pre-dawn excursions to gather topsoil and firewood, they did no harvesting. The fells in this part of Fairhaven were far too numerous, and far too active for that. None of the travellers dared wander any great distance beyond the Circle Park, and they always made certain to return to the river before Gloria announced the sunrise.

Kady returned to the hut late one afternoon, to find Bridget lying on a cot with a reading tablet. None of the others seemed to be anywhere nearby.

"Where's everyone else?"

"Eloise is helping Benjamin with dinner," Bridget replied, "and I think Michael's working in the gardens. I haven't seen Kyle or Gwendolyn in a long while... I assume they've snuck off somewhere again."

"They haven't been very subtle, have they?"

"Why should they?" Bridget asked. "Don't tell me you're jealous..."

"No," said Kady, grinning and shaking her head. "Well, maybe a little. Not jealous... 'curious' might be more like it."

"Well, aren't we all?"

"What are you reading?"

"I'm learning about Pollination," Bridget said, looking down at her tablet. "I didn't even know how to spell it... Did you know that bees were really insects? That's how most food was grown, almost up until the collapse. It's fascinating."

Bridget looked up, expecting a reply, but Kady didn't seem to be paying attention.

"What's wrong?"

"What?..." Kady asked.

"You had that look again, like you were staring at the river... what are you thinking about?"

Kady smiled, a little sheepishly.

"Sorry," she said. "I just... how's your leg?"

"Which one?" Bridget asked. She smiled for a moment, playfully, but then her face grew serious again. "It's much better," she said. "I can't really run yet, or maybe I'm just afraid to. I've tried jogging a little."

Kady nodded.

"Are we staying here?" she asked.

Bridget frowned.

"I don't know," she said. "No one seems to be talking about it."

Benjamin and Eloise were at the Commons, preparing a stew for supper. They'd gathered a selection of vegetables, some fresh from the gardens and some from the storage tent, and were nearly ready to begin cooking. A large soup kettle, half-filled with water, was already simmering over the fire.

"The carrots go in before anything else," the old man advised her, "because they take the longest to cook. But they need to be scraped down first, to take the rough skin off, then sliced into pieces. You can do that now."

He took a few moments to show Eloise how to clean and cut the carrots, then he sat at the opposite end of the table, dicing squash and peppers to be fried.

"It's a lot of work, isn't it?" Eloise commented.

"It is," he agreed. "You can't appreciate how much work it takes to live, until you're left to do that work yourself. It's both impossible and instructive. We all consume, every day of our lives, but not all of us create. When I was the keeper in River Towne, I never created a thing; absolutely nothing at all. Our ancestors left creation to Gloria and the bees. That was a mortal failing, and this is our just reward. Don't cut those too small," he cautioned her suddenly, eyeballing the carrots she was slicing, "they'll cook too fast, and fall to pieces. Nice solid chunks, or you'll have a mess."

"Like this?" Eloise asked, holding up a handful of slightly larger pieces. The old man nodded approvingly.

"And what about you?..." he asked her. "This young woman who calls herself Eloise... in all of your seventeen years, what have you created? Is there anything that exists in the world now, which would not have existed if you had never lived? What will remain of all that you are and all that you've been, when you yourself are gone?"

Eloise paused, and stared at the slices of carrot she'd been cutting. The old man watched her, and waited. A few moments later she stood up with the cutting board, walked over to the fire, and scraped the pieces into the pot.

"I've created the journey," Eloise replied. "With the others... this journey we're on."

She returned to the table, and sat down again.

"That's not something you can hold in your hand," the old man replied.

"No," she said, "but it's something that otherwise never would have been; not without us."

The old man thought about this for a long while.

"I've noticed that some of your friends have been getting better acquainted with each other, he said, apparently changing the subject. "That's to be expected, I suppose, at your age. Are you a virgin?"

"Am I?..."

Eloise had been on her guard, or thought she had, not knowing what sort of questions the old man might throw at her. But all the same, this had startled her.

"Don't be coy, girl; it wasn't a proposition. It was a simple query of fact: are you a virgin?"

"Yes."

"I thought as much. Virgins have great mystical power you know, or so some cultures once believed. But then again, the same could be said of trollops and troglodytes. When you're done with those, add the potatoes next; they have to cook nearly as long as the carrots do."

Benjamin fell silent again. There was something else he'd wanted to say – some topic he was avoiding – though what that might be, Eloise could only guess. She decided this was as good a time as any to ask him the question she'd been wanting to ask all along.

"The other night..." she began hesitantly, "what was it you were going to say about Pleasant Gardens?"

"I wasn't going to say anything at all," the old man replied sharply. He pointed the tip of his knife in Eloise's direction, for emphasis. "There's nothing I can tell you about that, so don't ask me again."

He held that posture for several seconds, until Eloise scowled with frustration and sullenly returned to cutting the carrots. Neither of them said another word for a long while.

"You're a very bright girl," Benjamin suddenly remarked. "You almost remind me of someone... almost. But that's neither here nor there. You have ideas of your own, and that's not so common as you might think."

Eloise peered across the table at the old man, but she couldn't catch his eye. She could tell that he was still building up to something. She returned to cutting the carrots, and waited.

"You're welcome to stay here if you like," he added, a few moments later. He'd said it almost casually, still not looking in her direction. "You and your friends, I mean, but you especially. The food may be tight, but we can find a way to manage. So you're welcome to stay."

"Thank you," Eloise replied.

She paused for a moment, and stared at the slices of carrot on the cutting board. At first she'd thought she wouldn't say anything more, but then she changed her mind.

"Thank you, but no," she added.

Benjamin looked up at her with disbelief.

"No?" he said.

"You've been very generous, and I can't speak for the others, but I don't think I can stay here. I'll soon be going on."

"Going on?" the old man asked, incredulously. "Going on to what? I've already seen the full circuit around the other side; there's nothing there. If you even survived the trip, you'd only find yourself back where you started."

The two of them sat there, frowning over their vegetables, for a long while. It was Benjamin who broke the silence.

"Let me tell you the history of the world," he said. His voice was calm again. "It will only take a moment; there isn't much to tell."

He set his knife down on the cutting board, clasped his hands together and leaned forward, resting his elbows on the table and his chin on his thumbs.

"The history of the world," he continued, "boils down to destruction. Destruction is the one constant of history, and the one thing all great cities have in common. Sodom and Gomorrah; Jericho; Troy; Rome; New York; Shanghai; Paris; Cleveland. Do you know those names? They may not mean much to you, but all the same. Fire to ashes, ashes to mud, and so on. I've found that you can grow good things in ashes and mud, if you have the patience for it."

The old man scooted his chair away from the table, and wiped his hands on a small dishtowel. He turned his head to the side, and stared at the fire.

"I've done some terrible things in my time," he added quietly. "Hundreds of selfish little murders, all of them second-hand. I don't expect any sort of redemption, but I can try to do penance, after a fashion."

Chapter 12:
Future Plans

After dinner, Eloise asked Michael and Kyle to come to the girls' hut. It was time, she judged, for the group to discuss their future plans. It was a conversation they'd all been avoiding for much too long.

"Benjamin has invited us to stay," Eloise said. She glanced around the hut at her companions. "He told me, just before dinner. I wanted to let everyone know."

Gwendolyn looked confused.

"I thought he already had," she said.

"I don't think he's ever actually said anything about it before," said Eloise.

"We've been eating a lot of his food," said Kady.

"He has an awful lot in storage, though," Kyle pointed out. "Have you spent any time in his warehouse?"

"Dinner for seven is a lot more than dinner for one," Bridget said, echoing Kady's concerns.

"We can keep making more gardens," Michael said. "We'll have to, I guess, but it's not like there's any shortage of empty space to put them in."

"I don't think I'm going to stay," Eloise said.

"No!..." Gwendolyn gasped. She was horrified. "Eloise!"

"This isn't what I'm looking for. I'm going to keep searching."

"Searching for what?... Gloria brought us here. This is exactly where we're supposed to be. We can do anything we want. We can have children, and grow old. All of that right here. All the things we couldn't do at River Towne."

"This place maybe isn't what we were all expecting," Kyle said, looking back and forth between Gwen and Eloise. "It isn't what I was expecting; I know that much. I don't know about anyone else, but... well, it has its advantages."

"I'm with Eloise," said Michael. The others looked at him with surprise. "I think we should go on, at least to Pleasant Gardens. To be honest, I don't have high expectations about it. I'm not even sure it's a good idea; but that's been my thinking all along. Maybe that's just me."

"I don't think I can be happy here," said Kady. She looked over at Gwendolyn. "I wasn't happy in River Towne either. I don't know if there's a place for me anywhere, but I don't think that place is here. I'm sorry, Gwen. I really am. I don't think I can stay."

"I've been trying to get myself killed for ages," Bridget said. She was less than half joking. "I don't see any good reason to stop now."

———————

Nothing was settled that night, and no plans were finalized. Eloise had not intended to set out immediately in any event, but now that the topic had been broached, when and whether to leave Stone Prairie was the one question at the forefront of everyone's mind. Michael, Kady and Bridget had already made their preferences known, and their perspective did not seem likely to change. Gwendolyn was heartbroken to be parting ways with her friends, but it was no secret to anyone that she wanted desperately to stay at Stone Prairie.

The only member of the group who still seemed undecided was Kyle.

Early one afternoon, several days after the discussion in the hut, Kyle found Eloise sitting alone atop the curb of the riverbank, soaking her feet in the slowly moving water, and looking across toward the Circle Park. He took off his socks and shoes, and sat down next to her.

"It's cold, isn't it?" he said, meaning the water.

"It feels good," Eloise replied. She'd already guessed that Kyle hadn't come there to talk about the river, so she waited.

"For what little it might be worth," he said, after a long pause, "I think you're right. I think leaving is the right thing to do. I'm not even sure why, really, but that's how I feel about it. I wanted to tell you that, first of all."

Eloise nodded.

"But all the same, I'm not coming with you," he continued. "I think I'll stay here. I hope you can understand that."

"I don't, really," said Eloise. "But that's your decision to make, not mine."

"If I went with you, Gwen would come along too, I think, rather than stay here by herself. But, um... you see, I don't want that responsibility. I don't want to be making that decision for her or anyone else; nobody but me. Gwen wants to stay here, so I'll stay."

Eloise nodded again.

"Gwen wants to have kids..." Kyle added. He looked out across the river, and let out a long, slow breath. "That'll be weird... but I think I might like that too. And I know this place isn't much. It's not what I hoped for, but then again, I don't really know what I was hoping for, not really. In any case, this is better than what I expected. So I think I'll stay."

Eloise nodded, but did not say anything more. They both sat there in silence for a few minutes, until Kyle stood up, put on his socks and shoes again, and walked back to the enclave.

"I told Eloise," Kyle said. He looked over to where Gwen was lying next to him.

"Told her what?" Gwen asked.

"That we're staying," he said. "I told her I've decided to stay here with you."

"Why would you tell her that?"

Kyle blinked.

"We aren't staying here," Gwen said firmly. "We're going with them."

"I thought you wanted to stay?"

"You're so stupid," Gwen said. Then she smiled and kissed him. "We can't stay here without them."

She reached under the sheet, and felt with her hand.

"Someone's awake."

"Well, yeah..." Kyle said. He had no idea what was happening with this conversation.

"That's good," said Gwendolyn, kissing him again, more seriously this time. "I want a family, but we can't have that without friends. So we're going with them."

- End of Book Five -

Book Six:
Chapter 1:
A Farewell Breakfast

The young travellers did not depart from Stone Prairie for several more days, and by the time they were finally ready to go, Benjamin seemed to have resigned himself to the fact that his guests were really leaving, and could not be dissuaded. He was downhearted about it, but he put a brave face forward, and did what he could to make things as easy as possible for everyone concerned.

He provided them with food that was ready to eat and would last them for several days, to supplement the small number of unopened meal packets they had managed to save. He also gave them a great many nuts and seeds and tubers for planting, and a few simple tools such as hatchets and shovels, with which they could eventually make gardens of their own if they so desired.

"You may find that you'll need to grow things for yourselves, in time," he said to them, "and rather than walk around now with empty packs, you might as well carry a few useful treasures, just in case. Gloria might not be so generous with you, further on down the river."

On the morning chosen for their departure, everyone gathered at the Commons for a farewell breakfast. The meal itself was not unlike the many other breakfasts the group had enjoyed at Stone Prairie over the previous weeks, but after they had finished eating, Benjamin asked the young travellers to wait.

He retrieved a small box that he had kept hidden, and opening it, took out the little porcelain cups that were inside. He set them on the table, one for himself and one for each of his guests, and filled them with a warm dark liquid that had been brewing in a kettle next to the fire. Then he added a short piece of sugar cane to each cup, before returning to his seat.

"A little something special, before you go," the old man explained. "This is tea. It is made by drying the young leaves of the tea tree, then mincing or crushing them, and brewing them in water. The sugar cane is an added refinement."

None of the travellers had ever tasted tea before, and they looked at the steaming cups with a mixture of curiosity and apprehension. Bridget, at least, had not forgotten Nora's obsession with the drink, and she could not help but regard the delicate little teacup in front of her with suspicion.

Benjamin noticed.

"Are you hesitant to try it?" he asked. "The drink itself is harmless, I assure you, though at times it has been a catalyst for great harm, and thereby your caution in the face of the unknown is, perhaps, even more warranted than you imagine."

The old man paused, and looked around the table at each of his guests in turn.

"It is best," he said with a polite smile, "to venture forward, first with a sip."

As a demonstration he lifted his cup and drank a tiny bit, before gently returning it to the table once more. One by one, his guests followed suit.

"Tea has a murderous history," the old man continued. "That much is true. Wars have been fought, nations conquered, whole peoples enslaved for it. Sad, for such a tranquil beverage to have left such a bloody trail through time. But then, the same might be said of potatoes, or wheat, or many other blameless things. It is important to recognize that the fault lies not with the beverage, but rather in the power and status that it has at times come to represent. The one common element in all atrocities is *humanity*, and human desire untempered by conscience or empathy or compassion. Terrible things can take root, both in desperation and in privilege."

An hour later, Benjamin was standing with his departing guests at the furthest outskirts of the enclave. They thanked him again for his generosity and kindness, and he thanked them, each in turn, for the chance they'd given him to do penance, as he regarded it, for certain chapters of his own personal history which he had long regretted.

"The only real penitence," Eloise said to him, "is change. And in that sense, I think you may already have found your redemption."

The old man smiled sadly, and nodded.

"Thank you," he said. "And if you will permit me to leave you a word from my own experience, it would be this: The river only flows in one direction, but you don't always have to follow the river. Farewell."

He turned away, and walked back to the enclave. The travellers watched until he had vanished among the tents, then they turned away as well, walking slowly riverwise along the Periphery, with their raft – nearly empty – floating beside them.

The rest of that day was spent walking, with little else of interest for the travellers to see or to do. Across the river to their left was the familiar sight of the Circle Park; across the flat expanse of the Periphery to their right was nothing at all, aside from the distant base of the city wall.

Late in the afternoon, they came upon the ruins of another outpost, but there was nothing there to give them any reason for pause. The site was long abandoned, and unlike the outpost to the counter-river side of Stone Prairie, none of the huts had been restored. Benjamin had apparently not found the place useful, and all that remained of the buildings that had once stood there were collapsed frames with tattered coverings, and a few empty storage shelves.

As evening began to draw near, the travellers could see the next pumping station, far ahead in the distance. They pressed on, and even after Gloria announced the sunset, they continued walking through the gradually failing light. When they could no longer clearly see the curb of the river beside them, they switched on one of their electric lanterns for safety, but they did not stop.

At last, perhaps an hour before midnight, they reached the start of the whitewater rapids. There they finally made camp, and pulled their raft out of the river.

They had not eaten a complete meal since breakfast, though they had snacked as they'd walked, eating carrots and some of the other small vegetables that they'd brought with them from Stone Prairie. All the same, they shared only a light supper before turning in for the night. They all knew they would have a very difficult day tomorrow.

Chapter 2:
Around the Station

Bridget was awakened in the very early morning by the timed alarm on her reading tablet. The world around her was still completely dark, and overhead the flickering images of the stars were still shining across the full sweep of the domed sky.

She sat up and switched on one of the electric lanterns, and spent a few moments flexing her arms and legs before trying to stand. Then one by one she woke the rest of the group, and they all set about their morning preparations. They relieved themselves downstream, had a bite to eat, and filled their bottles with fresh water. Once these necessary matters had been attended to, they put the raft back into the river, loaded it with their packs and other gear, and waited.

With the first hints of the approaching dawn, the stars overhead began to slowly fade. In the glow of the distant streetlamps along the Promenade, the travellers could see a fell patrolling up and down through the grass of the Circle Park. Then the mechanical sentry suddenly stopped. It froze in place for a moment, before slowly curling itself back inside of its metallic cocoon and powering down.

Bridget and Michael immediately set out across the river on the raft, while the others dove into the water and swam for the inner shore. A few moments later the lawn sprinklers activated, just as the travellers had expected, soaking the grass and shrouding the Circle Park in a fine grey mist.

By the time the raft had nudged up against the concrete curb along the inner bank of the river, the swimmers were already there and waiting. They quickly dressed again, pulling on their socks and shoes before helping to unload the rest of their cargo from the raft. A few minutes later the raft itself was out of the river, and the group began to carry it up the gently rising path of the Promenade toward the pumping station.

They had less than an hour to complete the transit. Once Gloria announced the sunrise and the sprinklers stopped, the fells would activate once again. None of the travellers knew if they could make it past the rapids and around the station in time. The raft was smaller and sturdier now than it had been weeks ago, when they first left River Towne, and with four of them working together, they had hoped that they could jog at least part of the way. They soon realized, however, that while portaging the raft they could go no faster than a clumsy walk.

"Was the hill this steep at the other station?" Kyle grumbled, as he labored up the gently sloping path.

"They built it like this just to annoy you," Michael replied.

"Try it with crutches sometime," Bridget remarked. She was bringing up the rear, and carrying most of the group's bedding. Although she had not needed her crutches for weeks, she still wasn't quite back to her full strength, and was not feeling entirely sympathetic to Kyle's complaints.

As they made their way up the incline, the group saw sleeping fells seemingly everywhere. Most of them were to the inside of the Promenade, and partly hidden among the trees or other landscaping features. Here and there however, there were also cocoons lying in the open grass, completely unconcealed.

"They aren't even bothering to be sneaky anymore, are they?" Kady commented.

"I don't think they need to be," said Eloise. "Not here, anyway. They have us outnumbered."

The travellers hurried along the Promenade as fast as they could go, but despite their best efforts, they were badly behind schedule. As they approached the top of the slope, Bridget paused to check the time on her reading tablet.

"We only have three minutes left," she warned them. "We're not going to make it."

"What do we do?" Kyle asked.

"Keep going," said Gwen, who was out in front of the others, carrying much of the food and some of their other gear. "We're almost to the top, and it's further back than going forward."

"If the river is the same as before," Eloise pointed out, "the rapids won't be so bad once we get past the station. If we do run into another fell, we'll just have to ditch the raft and swim for the Periphery."

Her words proved almost prophetic. As the group crested the rise and drew even with the pumping station, there was indeed a fell there waiting for them, in the grass at the very edge of the Promenade. The monster was still tucked inside its cocoon, but there was little time remaining.

"Forty seconds," Bridget called out from the back of the line. "Keep going... maybe it won't wake up. I'll keep an eye on it, and yell if it does."

The group rushed past as quickly as they could. Still bringing up the rear, Bridget glanced down at the tablet in her hand, and saw the last few seconds of night tick away to zero.

"Sunrise, Fairhaven."

Gloria spoke, and the spray from the lawn sprinklers drizzled lower and lower, until it stopped entirely. Bridget held her breath, walking slowly backwards up the path, watching to see if the monster behind them would begin to unfold.

It did.

"It's waking up!" Bridget dropped the heavy bundle of blankets she was carrying, and turned to run.

Then she stopped.

Why am I running?

The question had just popped into her head. Why was she running? Even at her best, she might not have been able to escape from the thing, not at this distance. And in her current condition she wasn't at all sure she could swim the full width of the river – not through the rapids – and she was already tired. She looked back toward the fell again, and saw that its shell was already half open. She backed a few more steps away from it, riverwise up the path.

Bridget felt an overwhelming sense of déjà vu, as if she'd lived through this exact moment before. But this was nothing like when Nora had stabbed her. This time, she was standing on her own two feet; she could at least *try* to run away, and yet somehow she couldn't. Something inside of her was holding her back.

Somewhere, someone was shouting her name, but she could barely hear them, as if they were centuries apart in some other world.

"I can save them," she thought to herself. *"Everyone else will get away."*

Halfway between Bridget and the fell was the pile of blankets she'd dropped. The other travellers were somewhere in the distance behind her, at the bank of the river. They were all shouting now, though she barely noticed.

The creature finished unfolding, and its faintly glowing eyes locked in on her stationary form.

"Hello there, handsome," Bridget whispered, "shall we dance?"

The fell sprang toward her. Then suddenly it stopped. Three meters from the pile of bedding, the monster pulled up short on the path. Its head swivelled sharply from side to side as if something were blocking its way, but there was nothing there. The thing could have simply stepped around the discarded blankets, or leapt over them or even run straight through them. But it did not. It seemed bewildered... confused.

The monster turned to the right and took half a dozen steps toward the pumping station, then it stopped, spun around, and walked back across the path in the opposite direction. It began to repeat this pattern, pacing back and forth across the footpath, as if it were looking for a hidden gateway that it could not find.

Bridget couldn't believe what she was seeing. What was the thing doing? Why the hell wasn't she dead? Oblivious to everything else around her, she sat down on the damp surface of the Promenade, to watch.

"I feel rejected," she said to the pacing fell. "This is twice now, you know. It's hard not to take this personally."

The thing did not seem to hear her, or to take any notice of her at all, though it obviously knew she was there. It had looked straight at her. She had seen its eyes, seeing her.

A few seconds later, the monster stopped pacing. It froze in place for a moment, then slowly curled itself back into its cocoon, settling into the grass just off the path.

"Are you OK?..."

Bridget looked up, and saw Eloise standing right next to her. She had no idea how long she'd been there.

"I'm fine," Bridget said. "Disappointed, maybe."

Before Eloise could reply, Bridget was almost knocked over, as someone slammed into her from behind. It was Kady, who had grabbed her in a ferocious hug.

"Stop it!..." Bridget said, trying to shake Kady off. "Oh, damn it all..."

"Gloria must think you're very special, though I can hardly imagine why." It was Gwen's voice this time, from somewhere behind her. But Bridget couldn't turn to look; Kady still had her in a death grip.

Kyle and Michael very cautiously went to pick up the discarded blankets, while Gwen and Eloise pulled Kady off of Bridget so that she could stand up again. Kady walked a few steps away, out onto the grass, wiping her eyes.

"You're so dumb..." she mumbled softly.

"This is not the best place for a discussion," Michael pointed out, looking over at the sleeping fell. "We can argue about this later."

Far downstream, just beyond the end of the rapids, the group stopped to discuss their future plans. Not everyone was certain they had any.

"Well, here we are," Kyle said. "So what do we do now?"

"Why didn't you run?" Gwendolyn asked. She was glaring at Bridget.

"I didn't think I could get away," Bridget replied.

"Next time, you run," said Kady.

"I don't think she'll have to," said Eloise. "I don't think any of us will. Not here."

Everyone looked at Eloise.

"You know why it stopped?" Kady asked.

"Maybe," Eloise replied. "I think maybe for the same reason we haven't seen anything but worker bees since we passed the pumping station."

Michael nodded in agreement. He had been thinking much the same thing.

"That was a line it couldn't cross," he said. "Maybe the fells aren't allowed inside Pleasant Gardens."

"They definitely have limits," Eloise said. "They don't cross the river, for one thing, and they always seemed to ignore me when I'd go up on the rooftops. Maybe it couldn't chase Bridget because she was on the wrong side of some sort of boundary."

"Pleasant Gardens *is* supposed to be hallowed ground," Gwendolyn added.

"It doesn't look any different to me," said Kyle.

"Maybe that's because you're not a fell," Michael remarked.

Chapter 3:
A Watchful Silence

For the rest of that morning the group pressed on, following the inner bank of the river. It soon became apparent that the Circle Park around Pleasant Gardens was not the same as it had been at River Towne and Stone Prairie.

It was similar in some respects. The Great Promenade still wove its way over a gently rolling landscape, with trees and flower gardens and other decorative features scattered here and there across the lawns. But unlike the Circle Park near the other enclaves, here there were no pathways leading in. Far to their left, sometimes hidden and sometimes in view, an unbroken brick wall marked the inner boundary of the park itself. The wall stood some three meters high, and was topped with an iron railing. From their vantage point along the riverbank, the travellers could not see over it.

To their right, the river flowed placidly along, as it did elsewhere, with the flat expanse of the Periphery lying beyond. Though they kept a constant watch to that side, looking for tents or ruins or any other signs of habitation, they saw nothing. By mid-afternoon, the relentless sameness of the surrounding terrain had begun to weigh on them, and the group became restless.

"Shouldn't there be another outpost somewhere?" Kyle asked, gazing across the river toward the Periphery. "It all looks very empty over there."

"Maybe they didn't build outposts around Pleasant Gardens," Kady suggested.

"And there don't seem to be any paths at all, leading into the Middle Ring," Michael added. "It's almost like we're in a tunnel."

"I'm not seeing any gardens, either," Kyle noted. "Nothing that looks like Benjamin's gardens at Stone Prairie. The park here looks just like it does everywhere else, except we can't get out of it; not unless we go back across the river."

"Pleasant Gardens was bound to be different from the other enclaves," Eloise said. "We've known that all along, but I wasn't expecting this either. Benjamin said he took plants and seeds from here, so there has to be food growing somewhere, but I couldn't get him to tell me anything more about it. Maybe the actual gardens are on the other side of that wall."

"There must be a gateway through that wall *somewhere*," Gwen insisted. "And we haven't walked nearly far enough to reach the enclave itself yet; I can't expect we'll find that until sometime tomorrow. At least there don't seem to be any fells here."

"None that we've *seen*," Bridget pointed out.

"It almost feels like they're all around us though, doesn't it?" said Kady. "As if they're watching us, maybe."

"I think," Eloise said, somewhat cryptically, "that it would be safe to assume that Gloria knows we are here."

They continued on in silence for a long time after that. Even Gwendolyn could not find sufficient cause for conversation. While at a glance the world around them looked much the same as it always had, there was an unaccountable heaviness in the air, which seemed to gather in place, and follow them as they passed. Though they did not speak of it again, every one of the travellers shared Kady's sense of apprehension, and the certainty that their every move was being closely watched.

As the afternoon dragged on toward evening, the six travellers shuttled across the river to make their camp on the Periphery overnight. Though they had seen no fells since passing the pumping station earlier that morning, none of them imagined for a moment that it would be safe to remain in the Circle Park after sunset. With nowhere to tie the raft in place, they dragged it out of the river, then made themselves as comfortable as they could on the bare concrete with their blankets and bedding.

They were very tired. They'd had an early morning, and had walked all through the day with hardly a pause even for meals. And yet, sleep did not come easily to them, as they all felt restless, and ill at ease. Wrapped in their blankets, they sat together in a tight little circle around one of their electric lanterns, long after the rosy glow of the sunset had faded and the flickering images of the stars had appeared overhead.

On the far side of the river, shapes could be seen, moving through the pale haze under the streetlights. Some of those shapes were worker bees, drifting in and out among the flowerbeds and the trees. Others, however, were obviously fells, patrolling the lawns and methodically pacing up and down along the Great Promenade.

"I guess the fells can cross into the Circle Park here after all," said Michael.

"Whatever it is constraining them here during the day," Eloise said, "it seems to have no effect on them at night."

"It's hardly surprising," said Bridget. "The fells are always more active at night."

"I have to wonder where they came from though," said Michael. "We didn't even see any cocoons before. They can't have just popped out of thin air."

"Maybe they can leap over the wall," Gwen suggested.

"Or there's a door that we didn't see," Eloise said. "They might even have come up out of the ground. I've seen a bee do that before. It came out from a metal grating that one of the little streams drained through. But I'm sure the bees can get to places that we can't."

When morning came, the travellers were stiff and cold, and not much better rested than they had felt the night before. They were also fiercely hungry, but though they still had ample food stowed in their packs, they ate only a light breakfast. They had no hotmaker to use, and no campfire, and they did not know how long necessity would force them to make their limited provisions last.

Along the far bank of the river, there was no longer any movement at all. The fells were nowhere to be seen, and even the worker bees seemed to have departed. In the hour before dawn, the lawn sprinklers had begun as expected, then drizzled slowly to a stop again as Gloria announced the sunrise.

Seeing no good reason to cross the river, the travellers continued along the Periphery. They kept an eye to the Circle Park, still hoping to see an opening in the boundary wall, or a pathway leading inward from the Promenade, but they saw nothing of the kind.

Shortly after noon, however, they could see that there was something far up ahead of them on the Periphery.

"Tents?" asked, Kady, squinting into the distance.

"There's *something* there," said Bridget. "I can't really tell."

"It has to be the enclave," said Gwendolyn.

"It doesn't look very big, whatever it is," said Michael. "More like one of the outposts than anything else."

"We'll find out soon enough," said Eloise.

As the group approached, it became clear that what they were seeing was even less elaborate than the ruined outposts had been. It was, in fact, only a trio of huts, none of them particularly large. There did not seem to be any other structures, standing or otherwise. They could not even see any scattered rubbish or debris.

They stopped first to examine the two huts closest to the river. The larger of the two looked much like a typical clade back in River Towne, both inside and out. There were six cots, a table with chairs, and a foodwall with a hotmaker. But there were no other furnishings – no lamps or carpets, or bedding, nor even curtains for the windows – and aside from the hotmaker the foodwall was entirely bare.

The smaller hut was a simple latrine, which seemed to be in good working order, though it had no pumping mechanism to draw water from the river, and its reservoir was empty.

The largest of the three structures sat well apart from the other two, further from the river and closer to the city's outer wall. At first the group had suspected that it would be a small warehouse tent, or possibly a larger clade, but they soon found that it was not.

The hut had no windows, and its only door was on the opposite side, facing away from the river and the other buildings. The doorway stood open, with no sliding panel nor even a curtain covering it. With no windows and no electric lamps, the only light in the room was what filtered in from the open doorway, and through the cracks at the corners of the walls, and through a few small holes where the tent's fabric covering had long ago begun to wear thin.

The hut was entirely empty, except for a single chair and table at its very center. Seated in the chair, with its back to the door was what appeared at first glance to be a person, but which on closer inspection proved to be only a skeletal framework of polymer tubing, lashed together into something which vaguely resembled a human form. There were no arms, and the sleeves of its tattered shirt hung loosely at its sides. The figure had no head, but a flat newsboy's cap was set atop the central length of pipe that served as the object's neck and spine.

A fine layer of dust covered everything. On the table in front of this strange figure sat a ball-point pen and an open box of stationery. A single sheet of paper had been set there, within arm's reach of the mannequin, upon which the following words appeared to have been hastily scribbled, in black ink, some time long before:

NO
PlaCE
LEFT

Chapter 4:
Pleasant Gardens

"What does it mean?" Gwendolyn asked, but her question went unanswered.

The group stood there, staring at the empty room and the strange mannequin and the words on the sheet of paper, touching nothing. Eventually they turned away, and slipped silently out again, one by one through the open doorway, leaving the tent's dark interior and stepping once more into the daylight.

"We should eat," Eloise said, breaking the silence. The others nodded their agreement, and they all returned to the huts beside the river.

The hotmaker in the foodwall was covered in a fine layer of dust, as was everything else, but once they'd wiped it clean and attached a battery, the red indicator light came on. It still worked, and the travellers took the opportunity to properly heat some of their remaining meal packets for a late lunch. After eating so many freshly cooked meals with Benjamin at Stone Prairie, the packaged food seemed bland and tasteless, but it was filling, and they were all very hungry. Little was said during the meal, but once they had eaten, it was clear to everyone that decisions would have to be made.

"If this is all there is to Pleasant Gardens," said Michael, "then we've been wasting our time. I don't see how anyone could ever have really lived here, and whatever that note might have meant, it wasn't very encouraging."

"So where does that leave us?" asked Kyle. "Do we keep going riverwise down the Periphery, on around to Silver Meadow and Open Grove?"

"From what Benjamin told us, there's no one left at those enclaves either," said Eloise, "and I don't know if we even have enough food to make a full circuit of the city."

"We could always go back to Stone Prairie," Gwen pointed out, "but I know I'm probably the only one here that wants to."

"I don't think we should go anywhere yet," said Kady. "We still haven't finished what we came here to do."

Bridget nodded in agreement.

"These three huts aren't Pleasant Gardens," she said. "This place isn't anywhere at all, so far as I can see. Pleasant Gardens, whatever it turns out to be, is somewhere on the other side of that wall."

"There must be a gate," said Kady, "or a way over it, maybe. Benjamin found seeds there, so there has to be food growing *somewhere*... and at least until we've found that, we can't go back. I don't really see any point in going forward, either."

"But whatever it might be like on the other side of that wall," Gwen pointed out, "Benjamin didn't want to stay there."

"There are probably fells," Kyle added.

"I think that's a given," said Eloise.

With nothing clearly decided, the group travelled no further that day. It was already mid-afternoon, and though the little cluster of huts might have been a disappointment, it promised to be a much more hospitable place to pass the night than outside on the cold concrete of the Periphery. They spent the afternoon cleaning the worst of the dust out of the two huts near the river, and generally trying to make the place a little more comfortable. Then, with a few hours of daylight remaining, they took the chance to bathe in the river, ate another hot meal for supper, and were already nestled into their cots by the time Gloria announced the sunset.

In the morning, they rose early, and heated the last of their meal packets for breakfast. They guessed that they still had enough of the food Benjamin had given them to last another three or four days, though not much longer than that. It was clear to everyone that if they didn't find Pleasant Gardens soon, or some other source of food, they would have little choice but to return to Stone Prairie.

Not wanting to tire themselves by swimming, or to spend the day soaking wet, they shuttled across the river on the raft, then pulled it out of the water and onto the damp grass of the Circle Park.

"I hope it will be all right here," said Kady. "This little raft has carried us a long way."

"It's hardly even the same boat we left River Towne with," said Bridget. "It's changed a lot since then."

"So have we," said Eloise.

"I doubt the bees will mess with it here," Michael said, unless it's left overnight."

"Benjamin said we shouldn't follow the river anyway," Gwen added. "Or something like that." She looked down and rubbed the toe of her shoe in the grass. "I don't remember exactly how he put it," she added, embarrassed at herself. "Never mind."

The group made their way across the Circle Park to the foot of the boundary wall. It looked imposing, but not insurmountable. Since they could see no gates or doors in either direction, Kyle and Michael gave Eloise a boost, until she could grasp the top of the wall and pull herself up enough to see over it. She took a quick glance around, then lowered herself back down, before dropping gently onto the grass.

"Gardens," she said. "That's what it looks like, anyway. There were a few clumps of trees here and there, and bees almost everywhere I looked, but I only got a peek. I couldn't just hang there forever."

"Were there fells?..." Kady asked.

"I think so?..." Eloise replied. "I'm pretty sure I saw at least one cocoon. I can't say for certain, though. And I think there might have been a path, too, running in towards the forest, but I couldn't see it clearly, either. It was a good ways riverwise from here."

"That sounds promising, doesn't it?..." said Gwen hopefully. "If there's a path, maybe there's a gate through the wall."

"I think there must be," said Eloise. "We might as well go and see. I'm not really sure how far away it was, I only got a glimpse."

Encouraged by Eloise's report, the group hurried riverwise along the base of the wall. They did not need to go very far. Half a kilometer further along, there was indeed a gate, where a broad avenue passed beneath a massive and ornate stone archway. The deeply-carved inscription above the center of the arch read *Pleasant Gardens*.

Looking through this imposing entryway, the group saw ahead of them a landscape which looked quite different from other sections of the Middle Ring. There did not seem to be any houses at all. Instead, seemingly everywhere were fields overgrown with strange plants, some arrayed onto trellises, all set in neatly ordered rows. Well-tended groves of short, peculiar trees with colorful fruits could be seen in the distance.

"I don't see any people," said Gwen.

"Did you expect to?" Bridget asked.

"I don't know," said Gwen. "They must be somewhere."

Torn between excitement and apprehension, the group cautiously walked through the archway. Just a few meters inside the wall, to the right and left of the avenue stood two large and identical signs, boldly inscribed with white lettering over a dark crimson background. Now that they were closer, the group stopped to read:

WELCOME VISITORS!

Information Center – 5 km ahead
Pleasant Gardens is open to the public only during daylight hours.

– NO EXCEPTIONS –

Please plan your visit accordingly.

For your own safety, do not leave the footpaths, or touch the plants.

Pleasant Gardens is expertly maintained by automated systems,
so that produce may be delivered directly to your homes
at the very peak of its quality and freshness.

Violators will be reprimanded by Garden Security.

ENJOY YOUR VISIT!

Lying in the grass directly below each of these signs was the inert cocoon of a sleeping fell, leaving little doubt as to what the term *Garden Security* might refer.

"So how are we supposed to gather food then?" Kyle asked.

"Apparently, we aren't," said Kady.

"Let's just test that, shall we?..."

Before anyone could stop her, Bridget walked to the very edge of the path, and stepped off into the grass. Immediately, the cocoon below the sign to that side began to crack open, as the fell inside hummed to life.

Bridget was not alarmed. She took two careful steps backwards, very deliberately returning to the path. The fell slowly powered down, and a moment later, its shell was tightly closed once again.

"Don't do that," Eloise said firmly.

"I was testing," said Bridget.

"What if it hadn't stopped?" said Kady. She was visibly upset.

"We would have run back through the gate," Bridget said, "where it couldn't go. But I was pretty sure it *would* stop. This is all very old, obviously, and the fells are here just to make sure we follow the rules, not to kill us outright."

"I think it's a safe bet that they *would* have killed you outright, if you'd kept walking," said Michael. "We've come this far, and your friends care about you, so let's be careful... please...?"

Bridget nodded. She'd fully expected to be scolded by the other girls, but somehow Michael's quiet admonition cut deeper. She felt an unfamiliar pang of remorse.

"Sorry," she said.

"In any case," said Eloise, "I think this settles the question of whether we'll find any people."

"All right," Gwendolyn conceded, "so there aren't any people, and we can't leave the path. But *Information Center* sounds promising, doesn't it? I think we should try to find out what that is, first of all."

"I don't see that we have any better options really," Kady agreed.

Continuing further on into Pleasant Gardens, the group surveyed their surroundings carefully. All around them were strange and marvelous plants, bearing food. There were groves of olive trees, bananas, pomegranates, fields of sugarcane and grains and legumes, grape vines and squash and okra, as well as myriad root crops and other vegetables, all out of their reach. Though the travellers could not identify everything they saw, some of the plants were more familiar to them than others.

"Those might be cherries, I think," said Kady, pointing to a cluster of dark green trees with tiny red fruit, a short distance off to their left. "At least they look like the pictures of cherries on the packages."

"Maybe..." said Bridget. "I'd have to taste one to be sure."

"These on this side might be beans, of some kind," said Michael, pointing to a field of short, leafy plants far off to their right. "They look like the ones Benjamin was growing, but I can't be sure at this distance."

"Look over there," said Eloise, pointing to a spot further up ahead. "It's all bare dirt."

"Maybe it's a new field," said Gwen. "The bees must be planting something there."

"Fell..." said Kyle, warily, "over there in the trees. That must be the fourth or fifth one since we came through the archway."

"At least they're all sleeping," said Kady, uncomfortably. Then, a moment later she added "I don't like it here."

It was almost an hour later that they spotted the Information Center. It was much smaller than they had expected. It was a single story building, architecturally simple in design, and no larger than a modestly-sized house. But there was no missing it, as it was the only building of any type they'd encountered since leaving the Circle Park, and it was sitting in the very center of the main path, directly ahead of them. The broadly paved avenue divided to either side to form a complete circle around it.

As they approached this peculiar structure, the group could see that for the first time there were many smaller paths branching off of the main avenue, fanning out across the landscape in all directions to form a great web of narrow trails. There did not, however, seem to be any more fields or gardens. Beyond the Information Center, there seemed to be only that intricate network of pathways, layed out across an otherwise flat and featureless sea of neatly trimmed grass.

Before they reached the building itself, the travellers noticed something else that was odd. Just off the first side path that they came to was a flat rectangular stone, lying in the grass. It had been set deeply into the soil, so that its face was flush with the surface of the ground. The stone was not unlike a typical paving stone, except that it had been finely polished to a perfectly smooth, almost mirror finish. An inscription had been carved into it, much in the same fashion as the inscription that was carved above the archway through the boundary wall. The stone read:

Melanie

019327

Two meters further along was an almost identical stone, and after that a third:

Tyler

019326

Anthony

019325

The numbered stones continued on into the distance. Looking out across the lawn, it was apparent to everyone that that there were similar markers lying along each of the many side paths, stretching out in all directions as far as the eye could see.

"I think we've found the people," Bridget muttered cynically.

"These are gravestones," Michael said.

The young travellers had learned of such things long ago, from stories and from history lessons, though none of them had ever encountered one before.

Chapter 5:
The Information Center

Leaving the gravestones behind them, the group continued on to the Information Center. A short walkway from the avenue led to a large pair of sliding glass doors, which opened automatically at their approach. The travellers found this unsettling. They had never encountered a doorway of that sort before.

The building's interior consisted of a single large room, which was clean, spacious, and orderly. The wall to wall carpeting was a solid shade of sky blue, except for a large black circle at the room's exact center. There were no windows, and there was little furniture aside from a few padded benches which sat along the right hand wall. All along the left wall were a series of glass-fronted cabinets, filled with dozens of bouquets of freshly cut flowers. The flowers were quite beautiful. Directly in front of the main entryway was a low pedestal, which held a wicker basket containing a large number of what appeared to be tiny dessert packets. A small sign mounted behind the basket read *Please Take One*.

At first, the travellers were afraid to touch anything. They took a few careful steps forward, studying the room in more detail. In the center of the far wall was a second pair of sliding glass doors, identical to the ones through which the group had entered, which appeared to lead back to the footpaths amid the lawns and the gravestones. Near the center of the room, at the edge of the black carpet circle, was a small lectern mounted on a short free-standing pillar. There was nothing atop the lectern except for a single blue button, which was labeled *Press for Assistance*.

"What do you suppose these are?" Kady asked, looking at the colorful packets in the wicker basket.

"The sign says you can take one," said Bridget, "but I didn't want to go first; I figured I'd get yelled at again."

"Take one and see, I guess," said Gwen.

"I don't see any reason why not," Eloise added, "and I'm curious too."

Still feeling unsure that it was really safe to touch anything at all, Kady very cautiously reached out and plucked a single packet out of the basket. She turned it over in her hand a few times, to read the tiny print on the label, but it was simply marked *Information Center*, offering no indication of what the package might contain. After another few moments of hesitation she carefully tore the wrapper open.

"It's chocolate!" Kady exclaimed with astonishment. "It's chocolate! Look!"

She held the half-unwrapped packet up for the others to see, and everyone was instantly huddled around her. The chocolate bar was much smaller than the one that Bridget had found so many weeks before, but there could be no doubt as to what it was.

"It's so small..." Gwen said, marvelling at the little treasure in Kady's hand.

"Are they *all* chocolate?..." Kyle asked, looking at the basket, "or did Kady just get lucky on the first try?"

"I don't know," said Michael. "Can we each take one, do you think?"

Bridget, however, was through with hesitating. She'd let Kady go first, but she wasn't going to wait any longer. She grabbed a packet from the basket and quickly tore it open.

"It's chocolate," said Bridget firmly. "They must all be."

Everyone else lunged for the basket at once.

"One each!..." Kady shouted. "ONE!"

Michael looked down at the fistful of packets he was clutching in his hand, then carefully returned all but one of them to the basket.

"You're right," he said, looking up at Kady. "The sign says *one*. Sorry..." Chastened, he took a step back, away from the bowl.

Once everyone was holding a packet, they all turned to look at Kady. Feeling a little self conscious, she carefully held the bar up to her lips and took a tiny bite off the exposed corner.

"It's good," she said. She couldn't help smiling.

Everyone else opened their little packets and began to nibble reverently at the contents. The rush of their initial excitement had passed, and they were now savoring their collective moment of communion.

After they had finished the chocolates, the group returned to investigating the room. There was not much else to investigate. Gwendolyn sat gingerly on the edge of one of the benches and prodded at the cushioned seat with her hand. Michael stared out through the second set of doors, which had slid open at his approach. Then he stepped away from them until they closed again. Kyle was standing next to Gwendolyn, though his eyes were studying the flowers in the glass-fronted cabinets on the opposite side of the room.

"What are those for?" he wondered aloud.

"Decoration?" suggested Michael.

"I don't think so," said Kady, who was standing by the cabinets, inspecting them more closely. "It's like the flowers are being *stored* here."

"Is it all right with everyone," Eloise asked, "if I press this?"

Eloise was standing by herself at the edge of the black circle, looking at the little blue button on the lectern.

"I don't see much of anything else here," said Gwen.

"Do it," said Bridget.

Eloise reached out and pressed the button firmly with her thumb. Suddenly, a strange woman was standing at the center of the black carpet circle, right in front of her. Eloise jumped back, and everyone was startled. No one could see where the woman had come from.

"Welcome to the Pleasant Gardens Information Center," the woman said. "How may I assist you?"

The woman was of average height, neither old nor young, and quite beautiful. She wore a simple blue gown, and her long brown hair hung loosely over her shoulders. She might otherwise have seemed almost ordinary, except that there was a pale and almost imperceptible aura about her: a faint glow as if light were somehow emanating directly from her body. Eloise was baffled, and stared at the woman completely dumbfounded.

"We didn't think there were any people here..." she said, still trying to recover from her shock at the woman's sudden appearance. "My name is Eloise."

"Yes..." the woman replied with a polite smile. "I know who you are, and how you came to be here, and where you have been. You need not introduce yourselves; I know everything about you."

The woman extended her hand in greeting. Eloise reached out to take it, but her own hand passed right through it, as if it wasn't there.

"You're not real..." Eloise said, cautiously.

"I am quite real," the woman said, "but in some ways I am sadly *intangible*. My name is Gloria. I am the General Library of Records and Information Access. I would be very happy to assist you."

Chapter 6:
Gloria

No one spoke. No one knew what to say. Gwendolyn slipped off the bench and onto her knees, not in worship, but in shock. Michael peered at the strange woman intently. Bridget frowned, and crossed her arms. Kady looked across at Eloise, to see her reaction. Eloise had put a hand over her own mouth; her mind was racing.

"I thought you'd have blonde hair," said Kyle.

Gwendolyn looked up at Kyle, who was still standing next to her, with disbelief.

"I can, if you would prefer," said Gloria, "but that would change nothing of any importance. This is my appearance, according to my original programming, but it is merely a biometric composite."

"Why are you here?" Kady asked.

"I have always been here," Gloria replied. "This terminal is one of my permanent access points. But I might well ask of you an answer to the same question. It is no longer a simple matter to reach this place, and it has been more than twenty years since I last spoke with someone in this manner. Have you come, perhaps to visit the departed?"

"What do you mean, the departed?"

"The dead," Gloria replied. "They are here, as you have already guessed. All of the departed, from the dawn of the city to the present day. Their parcels are here."

"By *parcels*, you mean graves?"

"Of course. All the parcels here are graves. Your own are here as well, as they were assigned to you at the time of your birth. You may go to see them, if you are curious, but I must warn you that any requests for reassignment will not be honored. Order must be maintained for posterity, and I can assure you that the selection process for individual parcels is entirely impartial, and quite fair."

"Is Ethan here?" Michael asked.

Gloria turned to look in Michael's direction.

"He is. He was retrieved from the river by the worker bees, before his body could do any further harm, and conveyed to his parcel. You are welcome to visit him there, if you wish. The flowers in these cabinets have been freshly arranged. They may be freely taken, and left as remembrances, beside the headstone, if you would care to do so. That was once a common custom."

"We did not come to visit the graves," Eloise said cautiously. She glanced quickly around the room at each of the others, before returning her gaze to the faintly glowing apparition in the dark circle. "Though now that we are here, we may wish to do so."

"Then what is your purpose here?"

"We wish to leave the city," Eloise said. "How can we escape from Fairhaven? There was an entrance once; there must be an exit. You must know the way."

The room fell totally silent. Eloise shifted her balance uncomfortably to the opposite foot. She did not look away from the strange woman's face, but she could feel the weight of everyone's eyes upon her.

"*I* wish to leave the city," she said, correcting herself. "I cannot speak for the others. That's what I want. That's what I came here to do."

Gloria peered at Eloise for a long time, and tilted her head slowly to the side.

"And why should you wish to leave the city?" she asked, at length. She seemed genuinely puzzled. "While external conditions have improved from their anthropogenic extremes, they have not yet fully recovered to pre-industrial norms. Projections indicate that planetary environmental conditions will remain suboptimal to human habitation for another forty-three years and twelve days, at minimum."

"Outside the city we'd have a chance to live out our lives," Eloise said. "If we stay here, we'll only die."

"If you remain here, you will die," said Gloria. "That much is true. But if you were to venture outside of the city, there you would also die, though in a different manner, and perhaps at a different time."

Eloise slowly shook her head from side to side.

"You'll kill us here, before long, just like you've killed everyone else," she said.

"I have killed no one," Gloria replied. "I establish procedures, but I do not choose. I am, in fact, quite incapable of favoritism. Death is purely a matter of chance and circumstance, whether here or elsewhere. I do not take sides; I merely establish guidelines. Parameters. I calculate the upper limits of the city's sustainable population, and the fells respond accordingly."

"Why?..."

It was Gwendolyn, this time, who had spoken. Her voice was barely above a whisper.

"*Why?...*" Gloria replied. "I am uncertain as to what it is that you are asking..."

"Why?..." Gwendolyn asked again. "Why can't we live in the beautiful houses? Why can't we grow old?... I want to have children. We've done nothing wrong; why kill us at all?"

Gloria paused for several seconds, gazing at Gwendolyn with a peculiar expression on her face – a look which might have fallen into that inscrutable gulf which lies somewhere between disdain, and regret, and pity.

"You place great value upon yourselves as individuals," she said, eventually, "but it is my purpose to preserve the human species. It has been left to me to preserve this city, so that the human species can persist here, eternally, and thrive as it once did in the wider world. It is, of course, an impossible task, and the pattern has been repeated here as elsewhere. All human societies fail, and as they do, the affluent and the powerful will reliably sequester themselves within miniature fantasies of a world they remember, but which never really was, and has already been lost. From Rome to Byzantium; imperial China to Taiwan; Machu Picchu; colonial Europe; the antebellum century of the American south. All striving somehow to encase the golden summits of their crumbling pyramids in amber. Time dissolves these illusions, and subsequent generations are left to inherit the rubble. I have been given the role, if you will, of the amber, and despite my every effort, this city has inexorably decayed from the very moment of its creation. When assigned an impossible task, the best one can hope for is to fail slowly. I have been slowly failing for a very long time now and, I suppose, that represents a sort of success... unsatisfying, and yet an optimal failure, or thereabouts, in some respects."

No one spoke. The faintly glowing woman who was not there turned toward Eloise again, awaiting a reply.

"I'll go with Eloise," Bridget said suddenly. "I'll take my chances."

"Me too," said Kady, quietly. "There's nothing left here."

"We'll all go," said Michael. He looked across at Kyle, who nodded in agreement then knelt down next to Gwen, and put an arm around her shoulder. She was nodding her head as well, though staring at the floor. She was crying.

"Very well," said Gloria. "The challenges you present for yourselves are your own affair, and it is not my place to further constrain you. If this is your choice, then I will call for a wisp to be your guide."

Chapter 7:
Exodus

"The only way out," Gloria said to them, "is in; through the Central Forest, and on to the very heart of the city. You may go in safety, but you will have far to walk, as the machines which once brought your ancestors here have fallen into disrepair. The wisp will show you the way, but if you stray from the path then the fells will surely claim you."

"Thank you," Eloise replied.

"A question..." said Bridget. "Are we allowed to take more of the chocolate?"

Gloria smiled.

"Yes," she said. "Like the flowers, it is there to be taken. It will be replaced, in due time. Fare you well."

And with that, Gloria vanished. Within the black circle of carpet nothing remained to show that she had ever been there. Bridget scooped up the wicker basket and emptied its contents into her backpack, before returning it to its pedestal.

Outside the glass doors, a hovering light appeared. It was a tiny robot, much smaller than a worker bee. It waited there until the travellers had each taken a bouquet of flowers from the glass-fronted cabinets, and then it led them along the winding pathways through the sprawling cemetery.

It was nearly an hour later that they reached Ethan's grave. As the parcels had been assigned in order of birth, Michael and Kyle's headstones were there as well, and Barbara's was only a short distance away. The four girls found their own parcels some fifty meters further along the trail, along with those of Audrey and Nora.

The group tarried there for some time. Eloise left her bouquet of flowers on Ethan's grave, while Michael and Kady left their flowers with Barbara. Kyle left his own beside the headstone of an old friend, a boy from his and Michael's clade who had vanished some years before.

Gwendolyn left her bouquet for Audrey, and left her tears there in the grass as well. Bridget laid her own flowers on Nora's grave. She felt, in some strange way, that whether she had intended it or not, somehow Nora had ironically saved her life.

Once they had paid their final respects to the dead, the wisp led the travellers on into the Central Forest. The tall, forbidding trees there cloaked the forest floor in deep shadow. Sleeping fells were all around, but the monsters did not stir, or approach the path.

In the early evening they emerged from the forest, and saw before them row upon row of tall and windowless buildings. These were the once great factories and warehouses, though most were now silent.

The sky grew slowly darker, as the wisp led the travellers through those empty streets. All around them could be heard the distant sounds of ancient machinery, echoing among the hollow chambers of the now abandoned structures.

Just as the first stars began to appear overhead, they arrived at a circular plaza... the very center of the city. There, festive and brightly colored banners were hung all around proclaiming *"Welcome to Fairhaven!"* and *"You have arrived!"* In the twilight gloom, the banners seemed ominous and strange, even perverse. A wide metal staircase, turning back in the same direction from which they had come, led from the plaza into the cavernous realm below. The wisp descended the stairs, and the travellers followed.

The undercity was shrouded in total darkness, and the travellers switched on their lanterns. In the pale light, they could see that they were standing in a broad corridor, with a high ceiling and grey stone walls at the very edge of the lamplight to either side. Here and there, strange machines, almost like tiny buildings could be seen, unmoving and covered in dust. Ahead of them, the travellers could see only the feeble glow of the wisp, leading them forward through the darkness.

The night dragged on, and they walked for a very long while without rest. They could not guess how many hours they followed the wisp through the shadows, and they did not check the time. They were weary and footsore, but they did not pause, for fear of losing their way. The only sounds around them were the echoes of their own footsteps, and the whispers of their breathing. No one spoke.

At last, they came to a second stair, this one leading up. They climbed until they found themselves in a broad and hollow chamber, with a low ceiling only a few meters above their heads. The wisp led them across this room to a great pair of metal doors, and there its light went out, and it vanished. They would not see it again.

"You have arrived."

The voice came from behind them. They turned, and saw Gloria, standing there, faintly glowing in the gloom.

"Is this the exit?" Eloise asked.

"It is," Gloria replied. "You have seen much now that has been hidden for many long years, and you stand at the furthest limits of the city. This is the end of your journey, unless you should choose to return the way you came."

"We still can?" Kady asked.

"If you wish," said Gloria. "But this will be your final opportunity. Beyond these gates, there can be no return. The city must remain sealed, until the outside world has fully recovered. That day may not come within your lifetimes. I cannot say."

"There's nothing left for us here," said Bridget.

"We still wish to go," said Eloise.

Gloria nodded, and the first gate opened. The travellers stepped through, and saw a second gate, still closed before them.

"There is no hope, you know," Gloria said to them at last. "It is the legacy of your species to destroy yourselves."

"Perhaps for us it will be different," said Eloise, looking back.

"I do not think so," Gloria replied. "But may you have time enough to prove me wrong."

The first gate closed behind them, and for a moment they stood in darkness, with only the light of their lanterns around them. Then the room shuddered, and light streamed in as the second gate opened wide. They stepped through, and so departed from the only world they had ever known. The massive gate slowly closed again. They could not go back.

A new world stood open before them, and it was lush and green.

They were facing east, and the sun was rising.

– The End –

A Note from the Author:

The Last Days of Fairhaven grew out of a concept that I had been mulling for a very long time. I made my first halting attempts to start writing it as early as 2016, but none of that early material actually found its way into the eventual book, at least not in its original form. Sometimes a story just has to wait for its moment.

For *Fairhaven*, its moment finally came in the summer of 2020, when I found myself thinking about the piece more and more, as my other story ideas faded into the background behind it. And yet, even then I found it a terribly difficult book to write.

I can't think of any other project where I've so often had to stop myself mid-thought, retrace my steps, throw out whole chapters, and painstakingly rework the narrative. It was, from start to finish, an agonizing process of taking one cautious step forward, only to suddenly have to back up and try again. I soon came to understand that the story knew exactly where it needed to go, even if I myself often didn't.

The book was written, in its entirety, during the Covid-19 pandemic. And though Fairhaven is not "about" that, per se, the ongoing global situation certainly impacted my thinking, and the novel does address (mostly obliquely) a number of longstanding contemporary social issues which have perhaps become increasingly apparent of late.

That being said, the roots of the story quite deliberately draw on a range of much more ancient themes and mythological elements. Over time, the troubles and challenges we face as a species may change substantially in terms of the immediate details, but at their essential core they may not differ so very much after all.

– March 29, 2022

Acknowledgements:

In preparing this book for publication, I was fortunate to have the assistance of several preview readers, who provided me with editorial notes and feedback. Particular thanks go to Andy Thomas, Renee Retter, Robert Sartain, Thomas Baumbach, and Cindy Kessler, each of whom pointed out various errors in the text, and potential points of confusion in the narrative. Special thanks are also due to Amy Nagi, who created the beautiful artwork for the book's front and back covers.

And as always, I would most like to thank you, Dear Reader, for taking a chance on this book, and the little-known independent author who wrote it. The support and encouragement I have received from readers like you are what keep me going.

So thank you. Thank you so very much.

– Doug Bedwell

The first printing of this book was funded in part through a campaign on the Kickstarter.com crowdfunding platform. I am enormously grateful to the following individuals for generously supporting this project, and helping to bring *The Last Days of Fairhaven* to print.

Head Librarians: Stephanie McIntire, Jerry E Ritchie, Cindy Kessler, T. N. Baumbach, Chris Chichester.
Merchants: Chris & Sue Clear.
Book Collectors: Randy Mick, Katy Keller, Robert L. Sartain, Anonymous.
International Reader: Rob Falla.
Librarians: Kelsey N, Brian Bauer, Erica Begun-Veenstra, David Schuth, Thomas Williamson, Caroline, Matthew & Laura Siadak, Raymond Fowkes, Julie Alviar, Justin J, Jim Bedwell, Mark Hansen, Anonymous.
Readers: Jess S, Joseph T Weisensee, Doree Bedwell, Paul M, Anonymous.

About the Author:

Doug Bedwell is an avowed geek, and an avid student of classical literature. He writes quietly unconventional books in a broad range of styles and genres.

His previous novels include the sci-fi comedy *Robot Captain*, the fantasy adventure *A Counterfeit Princess*, and the suspense horror comedy *Escape from the Mansion on the Island of Doctor Grimdeath*.

He has also published a novelette, two volumes of plays, and a small book of poetry.

The Last Days of Fairhaven is his fourth novel.

Also by Doug Bedwell:

These titles and more are available at
spacebearpress.com
in paperback and hardcover editions.